FRAIL AND BRITTLE BONES

D. A. ROBB

This novel is dedicated to Kim for her patience and her encouragement - and to Eleanor, my little girl who doesn't tolerate the mischief of monsters.

And what rough beast, its hour come round at last,
slouches towards Bethlehem to be born?

W. B. Yeats

ACKNOWLEDGMENTS

I would like to start by bowing my head to the writers who have inspired me. The works of Simon Clark, Dean Koontz, Shaun Hutson, Stephen King, Ramsey Campbell, Peter Straub, Clive Barker, and Stephen Laws were what first opened my eyes to the beauty of horror.

Of course, this list would not be complete without due mention to the great Adam Nevill (I can't remember where I first picked up The Ritual, but I remember thinking it was something special).

Special thanks must be given to family and friends (you know who you are) for putting up with me for so long. Long may it continue...

Thanks for the pen Ryan; it's still running, kind of...

Although this novel is set in a fictional world, I have to give recognition to the wilds of the Scottish countryside (particularly when it is at its bleakest) for providing the eye candy that fed my brain in creating the scenery surrounding Agnes.

CHAPTER 1

The first frost of the year had left a residue of pale, milky ice crusted upon the window ledge. The single-glazed pane of glass was smeared from the persistent rainfall that drenched the remote forest for nearly a fortnight, flooding the herbs and laying waste to many of the weaker summer flowers that bloomed wildly in the garden.

Agnes watched the clouds dissipate wearily; the woodland provided her with most of her provisions and the weather had stopped her from leaving the cabin. Her supplies *would* last, but unless she stockpiled dramatically they would likely run out before the snow thawed in the spring. Winter was approaching much earlier than she had expected.

A thick, purple-grey storm cloud rolled over the smear of sky that was the only tell of the sun's presence. The sudden lack of light caused Agnes to see her pallid, weathered reflection in the glass. She shuddered at the sight of the stranger who stared at her with its cold eyes. The lines and furrows on her face had multiplied and grown deeper in the past two years since her Wilson had passed. He had always made her happy; the only wrinkles she had carried back then had been laughter lines around her eyes. Now her cheeks had sagged creating deep vertical lines trailing from the corners of her mouth.

Wilson had died sitting peacefully in his worn, old armchair one chilly October night and had taken her joyfulness with him. She had been sitting sewing by the light of the fire when his gentle snoring had abruptly stopped. She had called his name softly but knew in vain that it was too late. His time had come, and he had gone.

···

The town of Sutter's Mill lay 14 miles away in the foothills of the Great Mountain. Beyond the town, as the Madoes River flowed, civilization spread and grew and flourished into sprawling cities. '*Toxic, violent concrete monstrosities,*' that was what Wilson had always called them.

Together they had shed off the poisonous lifestyle the city folk had called a living, and fled into the forests and mountains to live off-grid as God intended. Living out of an old military tent, they had built their home. Wilson had been a dab-hand at carpentry and had constructed a suitable structure from which their little cabin had grown. 50 something years on, and the pair had settled into a cozy and peaceful existence where they had lived reclusively in one another's embrace living off the rich bounty the forest provided.

They had made a home in this piece of Heaven, it was only right that Wilson be buried here. And so he was, at the foot of the garden. A cozy niche surrounded by hardy alpine flowers from spring through autumn.

···

Wilson never tired of working with wood and had spent one glorious summer fashioning a marvelous bench from the trunk of a single large oak. The backrest was intricately carved with depictions of the Great Valley; bears fished for salmon amongst the rapids, deer watched cautiously from the tree line, eagles took flight overhead in the open sky.

During the warmer seasons Agnes would sit out in the evenings and watch the forest at sundown; the daytime animals of the woods going to bed allowing the nocturnal ones to rule the night. '*The changing of the guards*,' was what Wilson had called the nightly ritual. She would be sat quietly watching the butterflies give way to moths, absent-mindedly tracing her finger tips over the benches complicated designs.

Although it had caused her back to flare up the next morning, she had managed to haul the bench the length of the garden so it sat beside Wilson's grave. When she sat there the loneliness faded to just a dull ache somewhere deep in her chest. It was in the small hours, when the sun still sat patiently waiting for its turn to climb over the mountain and warm the vale - then the heartache hit hard. She would sit up in bed, a strangled lump in her throat. Her hands rigid like claws, raking at the empty void that lay beside her, its unforgivable flatness, the handmade patchwork relentlessly cold and cruel.

By the time the first rays of light shone through the window making motes of dust dance across the room, her tears had dried to leave salty tracks down her cheeks. She would lie listening to the bird calls of finches and thrushes - stony-faced until she could find a reason to get out of bed. Some days she remained bed-bound until nearly midday.

•••

Agnes withdrew from the windowpane, a low sigh exhaling from her withered old lungs. Her slight frame shambled across the worn pine floor to the coat rack at the end of the hall. She pulled down a dark umber scarf and proceeded to wind it around her delicate neck. The valley wind could be vicious, it brought sudden icy blasts that had the ability to chill the very bones and make arthritic fingers curl into gnarled roots.

She slipped Wilsons thick trapper coat over her shoulders, savoring the faint musk of old tobacco and autumn bonfires. She pulled a woolen bonnet down over her ears, her greyed hair hanging either side like she had done ever since she was a little girl.

After making sure her insulated gloves were in the coats pockets she shuffled to the foyer and slid on her fur-lined boots. Prepared for even the harshest weather, she gathered her rucksack and handbasket and tugged open the front door.

Even with all her thick layers on, the cold managed to creep between her clothes and send ice through her veins. She winced, not because of the chill but more the violation caused by its lustful, crawling fingers.

Whereas the warmth of the sun was often like a caress from a lover, the winter freeze molested with the cruel indifference of a malevolent stranger; mercilessly it prodded its way under the skin and raped the gaps between the bones of the frail and brittle. Hoisting the basket up her arm, she hugged the jacket tightly around her and pulled the door shut behind her.

CHAPTER 2

Following a trail that had existed long before she and Wilson had claimed this forest as their own, she weaved a crooked path up the mountain. The original travelers who had tread this way were long dead but a canny eye could sometimes pick up hidden remnants they had left behind. Marks carved into the trunks of ancient trees and charcoal paintings on rock faces lay scattered along the long forgotten paths of the primeval forest. On several occasions Wilson had come to her gleefully with a find of arrowheads he had unearthed; signs of a hunt by a primitive people no longer of this world.

The path lazily meandered through tall oaks and sweet smelling spruces until it abruptly stopped at a clearing where the mountain ridge gave way to a cliff that sprawled high above a lonely valley.

When she was a younger woman '*The Edge*' had been little more than a rush for the two lovers. Each would carefully step out onto one of the large rocks that jutted out from the cliff face and spread their arms wide. She often thought about those times, the wind running its fingertips through her auburn hair, the way her body fluttered with a convulsion of adrenaline as she looked all the way down to where the treetops brushed against the rocks.

Wilson had been much slimmer then, his young body still

developing into the man he would become. His hair had been long and carefree, unshaven and unkempt, and yet handsome. For all his ruggedness, Wilson had the kindest eyes she had ever seen.

She would sneak a glance at him as they stood perched on their individual pedestals, his eyes were often closed and his head tilted skyward as if trying to absorb as many rays of the suns light as he could. Upon his face he would be wearing a smile that went from ear to ear. She never doubted for a minute that her man was truly, truly happy. When they would return to their home, they would usually put some music on the record player. Wilson was heavily into the 60's rock and protest songs, whereas Agnes liked Motown and Sam Cooke, something you could dance to.

Agnes stood at the tree line. It scared the shit out of her. For a moment she was staring glassy-eyed, reminiscing fondly, but also wondering how stupid her younger self had been. She shook her head to break the spell. Her mind couldn't be trusted anymore, sometimes it fogged over and left her in a daze, other times the result was a complete blackout. The latter had been on the increase as of late, and she dreaded to think of the consequences one of these turns could create should she have one so close to such a large drop.

The bitter winter wind seized its moment to howl up the bluff, it billowed over the crest and attacked her with a mournful wail. She gripped her overcoat tightly as the bastard gale tried to have its wicked way once more. Her handbasket fell to the ground as she let out a meagre exclamation. Eventually the wind died down; her feelings of being violated rose.

The time that had passed since Wilson's death had rendered her meek and timid. She sensed that somewhere deep inside she still had the grit and determination that had allowed her to survive out in the wilds for so many decades, but without her companion she felt exposed. It was as if she were a solitary doe, hiding in a forest prowled by wolves that had picked up her scent.

Truth be told 'The Edge' was the one place these feelings escalated, however, there was no better place that she knew of to find the Chanterelle mushrooms she used to stock up her larder.

Agnes set about gathering clusters of the caps, filling her baskets, instinctively knowing the best spots to find the biggest ones. She always made a point of leaving a handful so that the spores could spread and grow into the next year's harvest.

Half a baskets worth was her limit. Her back would bend no more. She knew from hard-earned experience that to continue would keel her over and she would be strung out for days. Standing upright and rubbing the small of her back, she rolled her shoulders and assessed the pain. It was only a dull ache, fine for now, but one badly calculated move and an ache could swiftly become agony. No sense in tempting fate.

The last time she had allowed herself to get carried away on a foraging trip something in her spine had jerked out and her hip had paid the price. For 3 days she had lain in bed barely able to move, her only painkiller a weak tea made from ginger and willow bark.

'No, not worth it,' she thought to herself. Besides, she still had a reasonable bounty of the mushrooms at home. It would be enough to make ends meet.

She slowly crept on tender joints to the nearest tree, a massive Alder, and rested her hand on its thick trunk. Steading herself and slowing her breathing which had become strained due to the little exertion, she cast her eyes out over the drop-off to the rolling valley beyond.

Her view was not of the picturesque landscape she had expected, but instead obscured by a thick, dirty fog that had quietly unfurled while her attention had been elsewhere. Visibility only extended to just shy of a stone's throw away. A low-lying, muddy white cloud reared up before her like the walls of a sinister fortress she had no intention of entering.

Uneasy about the dramatic change in her surroundings, Agnes

trembled slightly. She was about to scurry quickly away to the relative safety of the tree line when something on the ground caught her eye. It was an animal track, left behind in a section of waterlogged mud. Cautiously, she hunkered down for a better look.

The creature had left a sporadic pattern in its wake; large patches of topsoil had been dug up as the beast searched the undergrowth, presumably, for something to eat.

Agnes furrowed her brow trying to decipher the prints owner. The paws or hoofs had four toes, two longer middle ones with a shorter one on each side. She knew deer had a similar shape but did not think they were the culprit. The spread between each toe showed there to be a slight dexterity to them that deer did not have.

Something else...

The size. No deer was that big. The marks in the sodden earth were easily 7-8 inches from front to back. Whatever the animal was, it was a giant. A monster.

The great forest provided; creatures of all shapes and sizes thrived under its leafy canopy. There were predators such as bears and wolves but their numbers were few enough that the herbivores of the woodland were left to grow old and fat generally with little fear of the food chain.

Wilson had been a natural hunter. He'd had a flair for tracking and was always genuinely humble of the kill. *'Their lives so we may have ours. Not that ours have more worth.'* He had often said. Agnes never doubted he truly believed it.

On several occasions Wilson had taken up a track that had pulled him deep into the heart of the valley. He would kiss Agnes goodbye and leave with nothing more than a backpack stocked with enough provisions for a two day hike and his rifle. Agnes had never ventured with him. The thought had crossed her mind when youth was still on her side but as the years passed she had learned to read his signs and knew, although he would never say it, that he enjoyed, or maybe needed, these solitary trips.

She would patiently wait for his return; gazing out of the kitchen window while she scrubbed the dishes, her anxiety never quite reaching the surface. He would appear over the rise more often than not with some magnificent beast hoisted over his shoulder. She would become ecstatic and rush out to greet him, leaving the screen door swinging on its hinges. The joy was never for the bounty he carried but for his safe return. There had been too many times, especially when the weather had changed and storm waters had turned many of his hunting grounds to quagmires, when she had allowed the dark voice to be heard, heralding its solemn mantra: *'Maybe he's dead... Maybe he's dead...'*

She would leap right up into his arms, her eyes swelling on the brink of tears. The animal's carcass quickly tossed out of the way so he could catch her. Once they had embraced in silence for a moment, Wilson would flash her a smile and caress her cheek, the animal would be stored in the outbuilding and Wilson would take a load off by the fire, always with a large whisky as his pay-off.

'Something else...' Agnes pondered, absentmindedly thumbing a button on her coat. Her self-awareness kicked in and she realized how foolish she would look to a passer-by, a befuddled old woman standing in a trance in the middle of the woods. Then she thought about how long it had been since a passer-by had passed her by. Vaguely, she recalled seeing a group of hikers on one of the lower trails, but that had been years ago, and even then they had been so far away they would have gone unseen had it not been for their brightly colored, water-proof jackets.

Christ, no wonder she was lonely!

With eyes verging on cataracts, she stared hard at the darkening sky. The white fog bank was turning dirty; sickly patches of yellow speckled its edges making it appear other-worldly.

It was time to go.

Swiftly, she made her way back along the beaten path. Many of the deciduous trees had already lost their leaves, leaving behind bare, jagged limbs that stuck out at odd angles like bones from a creature long dead. Although these branches clawed and raked at her as she pushed past, they were far more welcoming than the despicable conifers that lay just off the trail. Closely packed together, they allowed no light from the sun to breach them. An eternal darkness dwelt within them, not even brave Wilson had ever found reason to venture too deeply in there.

Often the call of some shadowy beast cried out from beyond the pines. A shriek in the night. A howl in the dark. No, man was not meant to go to those dark places.

The first drops of rain broke through the canopy of bark. Agnes hurried herself along, night would descend abruptly and she didn't like being away from the cabin when the *'Big Black'* arrived.

Clumps of mud clung to the soles of her boots as she trudged on. She tried to stick to the edge of the path, to where the leaf litter was decaying, becoming mulch.

CHAPTER 3

The temperature was sinking, the rain like ice water running down her face. Her handbasket was growing heavy, her arm strained under its weight. She had reached the grassy patch of flat land where they kept their pick-up truck. Agnes had never learnt to drive, so now it sat pointlessly gathering dust and sinking into the dirt. She still turned its engine over to make sure it could rock and roll if needs be, but as far as she was concerned, it had found its final resting place.

Not far now, ten, maybe fifteen minutes and she would be able to see her dwelling. Any minute now she should be able to spy the tower of smoke rising from its chimney through the trees. How she craved to be warm by the fire!

A scream tore through the twilight. It sent birds flying from the treetops. Crows cawed in angry shock as its shrill tone owned the forest. Startled to a degree she had never matched, Agnes cried out a reply of her own and lost her footing. Her basket spilled its contents as she tumbled roughly down the embankment. Her frail body collided with rock and root until she came to a hard stop amongst a copse of hawthorn trees.

She lay on her back trying hard to draw a breath, the fall had winded her and pain shot through her body like an electrical current. The sky above hung low, black thunderheads rolled and folded upon each other as like breakers on a distant shore.

Groaning, she tried to sit up. A violent spasm of fresh pain jolted up her forearm from her wrist. Collapsing onto her side she flipped onto her belly and managed to pull her knees up under her. Here she waited with her head pressed to the dirt for the worst of the pain to pass. Once she felt like she could move, she shakily got onto a knee and managed to get upright. Her head thumped relentlessly and through blurred vision and tears she could she her wrist was in a bad way.

'Please don't be broken.'

She remembered the blood-curdling scream and hastily bent down to gather up her basket and its scattered contents. Blood caked the earth all around her. Fallen leaves and broken branches lay in a circle of gore. At first her heart raced as she thought it was her own life juice that pooled in the dirt, then she realized her petite frame could not hold as much viscera. A smear of red disappeared from sight into a deer run between two hawthorns.

Limping and cradling her defunct arm she moved towards the shadowy opening. The air around her became cloying with the metallic scent of death.

'Like old pennies…' she thought.

As if in a dream-like state, she slowly lowered to her knees and peered into the blackness of the undergrowth. The buzz of fat blue bottles hit her moments before they swarmed her face. Frantically waving her good hand to swat them away, she laid eyes on their source.

It stared out at her with one large, dark eye, unblinking and unseeing. Its tongue lolled foolishly from its gaping mouth. Its antlers were misshapen and one looked to have been broken roughly off. Entrails hung from its exposed stomach and disappeared into the undergrowth where some small creature had dragged them to gnaw on in relative safety.

Agnes balked and staggered back from the vision of brutality. In a blind panic, she climbed up the incline and was soon running along the path as fast as her arthritis would allow. She nearly lost her sanity when the first billow of chimney smoke came into view. Her eyes bugged out of her head and when she finally set eyes upon the cabin she screamed in triumph. Her boots pounded the mud and only stopped when she had thrown open the front door and slammed it behind her. She slid the deadbolt into its holster and pulled a small cabinet in front of the door.

Going from room to room she made sure every entry point was locked and all the curtains were drawn. That night she glugged down a half liter of scotch and passed out in Wilsons favorite chair. She knew sleep would not come naturally; no way to sleep knowing a beast roamed her forest capable of slaughtering the biggest stag she had ever seen!

...

She woke slowly. The neat spirits she had gulped down throughout the night attacked her kidneys, making them ache with the pain of a long-term illness. Her brain drummed a rhythmic beat against her skull and the rays of dull sunlight that reached through the threadbare curtains burned her retinas.

With a shake in her arm that had not previously been there, she reached down the side of the over-sized chair and frantically searched for the bottle. Her hand found it lying side down and she curled her fingers around it. As she tried to raise it upright a sharp jolt of pain raced up her forearm.

"Please, don't let it be broken," she pleaded to a higher power. Carefully, she hooked her whole hand under the bottle and pulled it up onto the arm of the chair. She eyed it distastefully. The amber liquid sloshed gently below the label line. She had drunk far more than intended, something she was rarely guilty of.

Unscrewing the cap and tossing it to the side, she shrugged and told herself that after yesterday's ordeal no one could blame her. She tipped her head back and polished of the remaining whiskey.

'Hair of the Dog' had often proved to be a working remedy in the past, but never before had the Dog sent her back to the Land of Nod.

Hours had passed when Agnes next roused, she could tell by the daylight having moved to the other side of the house. The light of the sun defiantly broke through the murk, sending its beams streaming down either side of her chair.

The huge patchwork quilt - which Wilson used to wrap around them when they would sit out under the stars - now lay in a heap at her feet, as if disgusted at having only one half of the pair to embrace. Sorrowfully, she leaned to pick it up. Holding it to her face she could feel its soft fabric, smell its memories. A single tear spilled over her eyelid and slid silently down her cheek. With a profound heaviness in her heart, she gently folded it into a neat square and cradled it in her arms like a new-born.

Outside, the late afternoon sky was on fire. Still, the dark clouds rolled across the winds, but they were broken and far-spread, upon a backdrop of a fiery inferno. From the kitchen window she could just make out the horizon through the tree tops, there, the sky was so dense with vibrant color it could easily have been made from lava.

Admiring the awe-inspiring display, Agnes poured herself a glass of water and swallowed it down until the pain in her head subsided. The setting sun, for all its beauty and spectacle, heralded the coming of another cold, wintry night. Even now, droplets of water were turning to frost in the deeper, darker patches of the forest. Out of the window, Agnes could see a thin layer of ice forming over the outside basin and bird bath.

She had awoken too late in the day to forage in the woods. A part of her wondered if maybe she had deliberately slept so long to avoid having to venture beyond the garden fence. Even after a decent rest she still found herself rattled by the previous day's events.

Being rational, she could admit to herself that maybe she had not been of completely sound mind, a trip to *'The Edge'* often left her with feelings of vulnerability, especially when it brought back vivid memories that she was not prepared for.

And yet...

And yet, no emotional trauma could claim responsibility for the carcass in the undergrowth. Whatever beast, be it bear or wolves, had taken down such a stag, likely still skulked within the area. Of course, it could simply be the perpetrators were only passing through, but decades of studying and sharing the forest with all of its inhabitants had left Agnes with a fair amount of collected knowledge. Most predators were territorial.

If a rogue bear...

Or a wolf pack...

The possibility made her skin crawl and her bones cold. Her mind had no problem conjuring up fleeting shapes and shadows along the tree line around the cabin.

In an effort to ground herself, she threw a tatty old shawl over her shoulders and pulled it up to cover the back of her head. The hallway mirror reflected her and she nearly wept. The shawl had been a gift for her 40th birthday from Wilson. Although time had taken its wicked toll with it, the fabric still maintained a flicker of its former grandeur. Crimson red, but slightly stained and faded in parts, minor moth holes, a bit frayed at the edges, yet it still had an appearance about it that Agnes could not explain. In a way it made her look younger; not by much, but it somehow gave her color, it washed away some of the greyness that had become her.

"Like little Red, through the woods to Grandmas..."

She shuddered, clenched her teeth, and went to visit Wilson.

...

Poor Wilson's grave was the final part of the garden to succumb to the coming season. Elsewhere the flowers were either dead or quickly dying but Wilson's final resting place was putting up an admirable fight. Wildflowers and hardy alpines still speckled the quiet nook with pastel shades of blue and pink. Sometimes, Agnes would sit under the stars and cry to the heavens, but even the infinity of space was too small to carry her grief.

Softly, she wiped a gloved hand across the bench to clear it off fallen leaves. Being mindful of the pain in her hips, she sat down with her hands folded in her lap. She sat lost in silence. Still, except for the gentle rise and fall of her chest.

'Wilson,' she said, quietly. 'Something bad is coming.' She paused, trying to decide if she was being foolish. 'I've felt it, Wilson,' she continued. 'I've felt it for a while, in the cold wind, in every drop of rain. I think the animals and trees feel it too.'

Her long, slender fingers kneaded her swollen wrist. The pressure made the pain rise, slowly, as it steadily gained heat like a fire was being stoked between the bones. She barely noticed as she looked with glassy eyes at the molten horizon.

'It lingers in the forest, like a scent, Wilson,' her thin lips trembled. 'I think it might be death...' she trailed off. 'Wilson, I think Death is near.' She slipped back into silence's void. The sun lost its battle and fell beyond the reach of day. Agnes did not doubt it would rise to fight again in the morning, of that she was sure. But concerning herself? Of that, the jury was still out.

Chapter 4

Time had passed. How long she could not say, but night had spread its blanket and Agnes sure as hell did not feel comforted by its embrace.

Swiftly, she shuffled inside and locked the door. She made as if to go to bed *(an act she performed regularly but never saw through)* but upon seeing the tangle of sheets and clutter piled over it, decided she would be happier in Wilson's chair. Making a point of grabbing a fresh whisky bottle from the sideboard she furled the large patchwork quilt around herself and settled down for the night.

...

She awoke with a start and a shiver. The room was icy cold and her breath fogged the air in front of her. The sky was clear apart from the white of moon illuminating patches of the room in a monotonous blue tone. The smell of the fireplace told her that its embers had died a good while ago.

With haste, she tossed the blanket to the side and dropped down to ignite a new flame. Beyond the walls of her home the woods looked dark and no sounds called out. In all her years living in the shadow of the Great Mountain, Agnes had never once heard the forest be so meek and still.

The stone fireplace was the centerpiece of the room. Although it lacked ornate detailing, its craftsmanship was of a high standard and when lit exuded a welcoming, homely appeal. Nestled into its stonework were four little pigeon holes where various knick-knacks had been placed and inevitably lost over time.

The top left one was always kept clear though, and in it sat a stack of matchboxes for nights exactly like this one. Instinctively, Agnes carefully palmed the little shelf until her hand closed around the closest box. She slid the carton open and pulled out a matchstick, pressed it to the striker and...

Wait...

Something awoke her senses, something familiar, yet new. The room had a faint musky smell that she had not picked up on before, old cloth and an earthy aroma that was tainted with copper.

The hair on her arms tingled as the very air in the house was displaced like when someone opens a window in another room. Frozen with fear she tensed, bracing herself for something to reveal itself.

'Hello, Aggie.'

Even with all her foresight, the quiet voice in the dark still made her leap out of her skin. The voice was whispered and dry, as if wheezed through weathered lungs and threadbare lips. The last time she had heard the voice was two winters ago and she had expected to never hear it again.

The shock had shot through her like she had treaded on a livewire, matchsticks sprayed through the air in an arc before falling to the dark floor below. Agnes turned slowly to the direction the voice had come from, one hand trembling against her thudding heart. Eyes wide and starting to brim with tears she peered in the corner of the room.

Although tucked away from the moon's glare, the corner was unfeasibly dark, too dark to be naturally occurring; it was as if the very air had been painted black. Her eyes adjusted only enough for her to make out a faint outline of a figure huddled where the two walls met.

'Aggie, don't be afraid,' the voice croaked, 'It's me... It's Wilson.

Chapter 5

Agnes didn't believe in fairies, Santa, or Bigfoot, she had never even considered the possible existence of the Loch Ness monster, goblins, or God, but at that very moment she fully changed her beliefs about ghosts. If you had asked her she would have told you with the conviction of a Southern preacher that ghosts were as real as fish in the sea and birds in the sky. She tried to speak but no reply came out. Her brain was awash with so many mumbled questions the voices droned in her head like white noise.

'I know you must have a million questions' said the voice, 'but we don't have much time.'

'But you're dead...'

'Yes.'

'So... how..?' She swallowed down a bubble in her throat. The shadow shifted just enough so Agnes could see it was even more disheveled than she had first thought. It seemed to be falling apart.

'Never mind the *'how'*, Aggie,' it said in its brittle, dry wheeze, 'It's the *'why'* you should be concerned with.' The shape motioned for her to sit in the armchair with gesture from an arm so emaciated it appeared skeletal.

Agnes nodded and did as she had been asked. Tears flowed freely down her wrinkled cheeks. Her Wilson reduced to so little.

So far beyond gone. He leaned back so the wall was holding him upright. Unseen parts of him cracked and popped like winters twigs under foot.

'Does it hurt?' She wanted to know. She remembered how badly he had suffered with the arthritis those last few years. A hoarse yet loving, laughter erupted with rattle from Wilson's chest.

'Oh Aggie, always worrying about everyone else. No it doesn't hurt, not anymore.' The room dimmed briefly as a wisp of cloud crossed the moon, distorting its light and disfiguring its face. Neither of them spoke until it had passed, as if they were mourners paying their final respects. 'Aggie' do you know what I'd fair enjoy?' Wilson asked, his tone hopeful. 'My old pipe. Do you still have it?'

'Of course I do,' said Agnes with a faint smile curling the corners of her mouth, 'I sometimes use it too. The smell helps remind me of you.'

'Would you bring it to me, please?' Agnes rose up from the chair and reached into the cubby-hole below where the matches were kept. From the alcove she pulled a small tin box. 'Slowly. Please,' said Wilson, as she crossed the floor to his dark hollow, 'I'd rather you didn't see me. It isn't pretty.'

Agnes caught a lump in her throat. Wilson's hand emerged from the shadows. Agnes gasped and put her hand to her mouth, more from shame than shock. 'I'm sorry,' she uttered from between her fingers in response to his withdrawal of his gnarled, decaying appendage.

'Don't be sorry, darling,' he said, solemnly. 'It is inevitable. As sure as the sun sets and the tide comes in.'

A flame came into existence with a 'hiss' as Wilson struck a match. Agnes lowered her eyes when she caught a glance of his face in the dim orange light. His once plump cheeks now sallow and papery, lips curled back displaying the teeth of a long dead corpse.

Wilson drew on the pipe to stoke the embers and exhaled a plume of blue-tinted smoke. His silhouette slumped with satisfaction. They sat together in a silence that was both comfortable and, at the same time, tense. Agnes resisted an urge to gather her knitting needles and wool. As much as she longed to return to those days, she knew it would be nothing more than a fabrication, an ill-fitting mask to hide behind.

'Wilson, why have you come back?' Her voice was small and timid. She suspected whatever answer he replied with was going to be one that shattered her little world like glass. The figure shrouded in darkness held his silence. Agnes believed he was likely trying to choose the right words. His reluctance to divulge the purpose of his midnight visitation did nothing to soothe her fragile nerves.

'Something is coming, Aggie,' he said, softly. 'But I reckon you knew that already?' Agnes nodded, she knew. 'Something foul and ancient, coming from somewhere yonder but that calls this mountain home. It's too primal to be called evil but that don't mean it ain't wicked, Aggie'

Agnes bit her lip; she stopped when she tasted blood.

'What does it want?' She asked meekly.

'Who knows? A creature as basic as this just simply exists. It has no rhyme or reason for its actions. It may dwell on the astral plain, but it's still an animal, as we all are, nutrition and shelter may be all it seeks.'

'I don't understand, Wilson. What has any of this got to do with me? Do you expect me to cook it a meal and tuck it in for the night?'

Wilson tried to stifle a guttural laugh and failed. 'Oh Aggie, I've missed you so damn much. You always knew how to get me grinning.' He took a long, slow draw on his pipe. Agnes heard a disturbing rattle coming from his chest. 'No lass, I hope it passes through here and you never encounter it. But you should know - its mere presence will have an effect on the mountain. The skies will darken; the winter will be the worst you've witnessed. The fauna will rot, the crops in the garden will be soured so make sure and stock the larder full. You'll need to watch yourself around the animals in the woods; they will sense 'It' and will be easily spooked. Some might see you as a threat and scatter but the bigger ones, the ones with pointed teeth...'

Agnes held a hand up to silence Wilson. Some sentences need not be finished.

'Is old Bess still in the case under the bed?' Agnes shut her eyes and nodded. 'Give her a clean. I don't think you should leave the house without her.'

The old woman's heart sunk. 'Wilson, you know I'm useless with that thing. Hell, the kick-back alone would knock me off my feet.'

'Aggie,' Wilson interrupted her. 'Enough. Don't fight me on this. You get close enough and you pull the trigger. You blow 'em to Hell. You must.' Agnes fretfully knotted her fingers. What horror to face in her state of age and frailty! She would do as he asked, she submitted to his will with a bow of her head, her eyes brimming with tears. The moon slipped behind a curtain of cloud and the world darkened. 'Goodbye Aggie.' The shadows grew and merged around her, thick and with substance. 'Until next time.'

Wilson was gone, her eyelids grew heavy and then she was gone too.

Chapter 6

She wakened to the growl of thunder. The patchwork swaddled around her as she sat curled up in Wilson's old chair. The carriage clock on the mantle said it was a little past 5. Even if the sun could penetrate the coming storm clouds it would still be a few hours until daylight crossed the mountain ridge. Lightning cracked the sky followed by another, louder, rumble. The sky forge was open.

Agnes rubbed the sleep from her eyes, milky residue smeared across the back of her hand. She cursed at it under her breath, her eyes were getting worse. She tossed the heavy blanket off of her torso, immediately feeling the drop in temperature, she shivered as the chill crept through her bones. Blast this season!

She tried to look out the window but her breath was too warm and steamed up the glass. The woods around the cottage were steeped in a low, hazy mist that made her feel unwelcome. The gnarled trees and hanging lichen showed the forest in its primitive glory, beautiful, but lurking with danger.

She wanted to open the front door and have a better look at this primordial display but dared not interfere in the solitude with her presence. The forest was not hers, it never had been. It would not tolerate a spectator.

A hand went to her temple. She closed her eyes and tried to conjure a memory. A dream...

'Wilson...'

It was as though he sat on the edge of her vision: A blur that never quite came into focus. She dreamt of her deceased consort often; usually in dreams that were reflections of her memories with him, but this one had been different.

She kneaded her painful fingers as she tried to recall what it had been that had unsettled her so. He had spoken to her, but of what? A message perhaps? She bit her lip but could not get her brain to reveal the secrets it kept. She pulled herself away from the window and scuffed a path to the bedroom.

The small room had become a dumping ground for forgotten things. Agnes was, like most hoarders, unaware of the piles of clothes, books and tat that littered the oak floor. With rehearsed grace she trod around the debris until she stood before the wardrobe.

Inside, the wooden cabinet was a mirror of the rooms disarray; scraps of material draped over heirlooms and various items that had lost their purpose. From the depths she pulled a large fur-lined wrap and tied it around herself using a coil of cord.

Wilson had made them one each in case of a particularly bad winter from some deer pelts he'd had in his workshop. The fur was coarse from age and itchy, but the warmth it provided was second to none.

On the wall opposite hung a long mirror Wilson had bought from a jumble sale at Sutter's Mill many, many moons ago. She peered past the socks and scarfs draped over the mirror and tittered at her reflection. Wilson would have said she looked as if she had 'gone native'. No matter how silly she thought she looked (and out here, who was to judge?) She had to admit, Wilson had done one hell of a job.

A raven somewhere close by broke the eerie silence of the wood. The bedroom window started to pitter-patter as the first of the large raindrops fell from the heavens. As if sensing its cue, a shot of lightning lit up the dull room as it raced across the grey expanse. The subsequent rumble of thunder was much louder than the rest. And drawing closer.

Old men used to say they could *'feel'* a change in the weather in their bones - recent years had made Agnes think there might be some truth to their tales.

Using the timber bed frame to lower herself, she heard the familiar rusty creak of her hip joint. She gritted her teeth, trying to ignore the hot flames spreading down her leg. She kept her hand on the bed for support while the other cleared space on the floor. She resisted the urge to take a moment in time when she came across some old instant photographs from Wilson's younger years. Satisfied there was ample enough space, she hunkered down and peered under the bed.

Agnes released a sigh of defeat. The worn, red-painted box with the copper clasps was there.

The monster under the bed.

Using her elbows to hold herself up, she leaned forward and heaved the box into the clearing. It was heavier than she remembered. Or *(and probably more likely)*, she had grown weaker since the two had last encountered one another. The 'thing' in the box carried a different kind of weight entirely.

Her fingers flexed nervously as she flicked the two rusted claps open. The monster lay dormant. Wilson had always taken great care of the Springfield 1903. Any given evening, especially during the Summer months when the deer took their refuge in the safety of the meadows long grasses, he could be found sitting on the porch stripping and cleaning 'Old Bess'.

There was no arguing that the rifle had provided plentifully. Meat and pelts were instrumental to their continuing survival and for over half a century, Bess had been the breadwinner. Agnes just didn't like the damn thing.

Her hands hovered over the walnut finish. No. She would clean and assemble it later. She wasn't quite ready to touch it yet. She shut the lid and carried the box through to the kitchen. The dining table was covered in battle scars from decades of craft projects but had not been used for its main purpose since Wilson's death.

She placed the kettle on the stove and watched it come to boil. Coffee would clear her head. Agnes sipped the brew, savoring the bittersweet aroma. She held the mug in both hands and shuffled back through to the living room. A frown creased her forehead. The room had been tainted with a scent other than the old widow's coffee. Curiously, she scanned the room for the source until her eyes settled on Wilson's pipe sitting on the windowsill. Thin wisp of blue smoke still trailed gently upwards. Agnes stared at it, eyes unblinking; lips thin and taut.

Not a dream then..?

Not a conventional one anyway. Agnes could not explain the presence of the pipe and therefore left it alone. It was what it was.

...

Outside the gathering storm is still many wheels beyond the mountain. Later, it will arrive and bring with it a slow, but heavy snowfall that will be the first whiteout of the season, the first of the true storms.

The inhabitants of the Great Forest watch the horizon with grim black eyes. Many hide deep in their burrows or dens and try to slumber. There is a certain refuge in sleep, should sleep grace them.

The larger beasts, whether antlered or fanged, stand still and silent, their ancient feud on hold in the face of a shared adversary. Each creature touched by a sense deep in their genetics attuned to read the changes in the air and shift in temperature, to feel and understand what is coming and how to survive it.

Chapter 7
(Interlude)

*T*he Lord of the Forest lies weary in his den. He has had reasonable success during his hunts of late and built up substantial fat reserves to sustain him during the coming months when food will be scarce. His powerful bulk is heavy and he knows his body is preparing for 'the long sleep'. His movements are slow and sluggish; soon he will be in a state of torpor, the closest a bear gets to hibernation. Looking up the slope to the mouth of his cave he can see the first of the large flakes heralding the arrival of the snowfall.

Across the furthest tree line, mayhap in the flatlands where the two-legs dwell, he sees the dark, bruised purple thunderheads clash against one another. Their collision marked by sky fire that chases the roar of warring Gods. He is no stranger to the sky battles; he has trod the grounds of these woods for enough seasons to have grey in his fur. So what unsettles him so, and keeps his rest at bay?

A new scent wafts in from the cold. It is not the smell of ozone, nor the earthy stink of rotten leaf litter. It is the musk of an animal. Leathery nostrils flare as he takes in this unfamiliar aroma. His tongue slaps his lips at the smell of meat. Even though this meat smells old and foul.

Curiously, the King of the Mountain lumbers his stocky frame up the slope to the caves entrance. His massive paws crush tiny bones that litter his home like scree.

Before he is even halfway up the gradient, he is casting his big, brown eyes back towards his nest of moss and soft twigs, reluctant to leave its warmth. He grumbles a mournful growl and proceeds to finish the ascent.

His home is situated high up on the Great Mountain where the last of the hardy trees struggle to endure the microclimate of the peak. Water runs down from above and forms a consistent stream dropping from the mouth of the cave. Even with his dense fur it is ice cold and makes him shiver.

The majestic giant surveys his Kingdom; from here he can see the trail that leads down into the wild woodland below. In the distance he spies a thin plume of smoke clearing the treetops before being dissipated by the growing winds. He knows that place well and makes sure to avoid it, a couple of two-legs live there and the male one has a stick that makes the same loud noise as the sky Gods.

At the furthest point in his vast view, where the carpet of treetops stretch up to touch the Big Blue, lies the Western Ridge, a spine of rocky hills that cross the land like the raised remnants of a scar. Were it not for this formation he would be able to see the lights of thousands of two-legs twinkling far away where the land gives way to ocean. But that is a sight he has never seen, and never will. He was born upon the mountain and as far as he is concerned, the world stops at the Western Ridge.

The boulders that lie around the entrance to his home are sodden and slippery with moss and lichen. The huge stones fell during a landslide thousands of years before his birth, so to him they have always been there.

Except one is not in its usual position.

It has been dislodged, shifted by an immense weight. Its indentation still marks the ground in a large crater that is steadily filling with murky water. The stone lies down the trail, the foliage between spread flat from its descent.

The elder bear puts his giant head to the crater and sniffs, inspecting the puzzle with curious snorts. Even with his fantastic bulk and incredible strength he knows that with all his might, he could never have moved a rock that size. Whatever has pushed against the stone and sent it southward must be far stronger than he.

Its scent fills his nostrils. It is a sickly smell, rife with decay and disease. His huge maw opens wide and he gags, chunks of his last meal decorate the muddy floor. He steps back towards the cave still retching, desperate to expel the foul taste from his throat.

His eyes pool with salty tears and thick mucus hangs from his nose. Never has a creature smelled so vile. Not even the skunks he has had the unfortunate luck to encounter.

A flash illuminates the valley. The late afternoon sun cannot penetrate the thick soup of black clouds. Day and night have blended, time has frozen; along with everything else the winter chill has touched.

Although his vision is skewed by his tears, he sees movement to his side. Using the fur on his shoulder, he wipes his eyes until they are clear. The majestic Lord has never felt true fear. In this land he has reigned unopposed as the biggest and strongest. With the exception of the two-leg and his thunder-stick, he has never shrunk away from a confrontation. What stands before him now makes him cower like a new-born cub.

A lull in the wind that feels as unnatural as the monstrous beast standing on the rocks, settles eerily upon the mountain. The fat drops of rain and sleet spatter heavily upon the mud and rocks, drumming a tattoo of uneasiness.

The creature is a silhouette against the blackened sky, if it were not for the rain running dirty from its matted, bristly hair you would be forgiven for thinking it just a nightmarish hallucination.

It stands solid on all fours, its enormous mass focused on its front end. A flash sparks the sky and the terrified bear catches a glimpse of a face so wicked and repulsive his bladder relieves itself on the ground. With the lightning past, the things head once more becomes shrouded in darkness. The red burning in its eyes remains.

Desperate to flee, the great bear nervously takes a step towards the trail. If he can make it into the trees there is a chance he can escape. He will leave the valley. Abdicate his throne.

The beast snorts; thick, white breath expels from its snout. It moves quickly - too fast for the bear. In four rapid bounds it has positioned itself between the bear and safety. It lowers its enormous head, daring the King to try and flee, challenging him to fight. This would not be the first territorial dispute the Lord of the forest has been involved in. Many have tried to take his crown, but most had been younglings with less experience and less meat on their bones.

All he wants to do is crawl back into his cave, curl up and hide until spring in the hope that the monster will have moved on to somewhere far, far away. One look at the sinister determination in the things eyes tell him it will wait.

The bear studies its adversary. Under its thick, fatty hide it is all sinewy muscle, tight knots ripple beneath its bristly skin. This will be a fight to the death; of this the bear is certain. The beast tilts its head low to the sodden earth, two long tusks aim at the King. Its eyes, wicked and brimming with malevolence.

It charges.

The ground shakes as its heavy feet stomp the dirt. Clumps of sod fly up behind it as it closes in on its victim. The bear rises up on his hind legs, an instinct embedded from centuries of evolution. Defiant to uphold his reputation, the King fights back a betraying tremble and roars as loudly and ferociously as he can.

The creature bearing down on him seems to be pleased with this reaction, it wants a challenge. It too, roars. The sound is like nothing a creature of this forest has ever made. It freezes the blood. The bear recoils, wishing he had never left the relative safety of his homestead.

The beast thrusts its twin lances at the bear. The King brings his huge paws down on the monsters head, but only as a defensive move to avoid being impaled. The creatures head is thrown to the side but the blow has not deterred it. Viciously, it swings its bulky head so that its spears jab at the air, herding the bear towards the cliff edge. The King has no choice, no way past, no exit.

He skirts the drop-off; the trees below are so far away. He rallies himself, now he must fight. His fear becomes anger, his anger widens to rage. This is his Kingdom, to hell with this invader!

He clubs the beast over and over; his long claws score the creature's thick skin but can't get deep enough to do any real damage. He bares his teeth and makes a move towards his opponent's fat neck. It clocks his tactic quickly and steps back, his teeth close on empty air.

All too late he realizes he has made a fatal mistake. The world slows down. The snowdrops seem to linger as they fall. The bear's eyes soften in the knowledge of his defeat. The monster seems to grin as it stabs forward and upwards with its mighty tusks. The bear feels the pressure on the underside of its jaw. A moment of blinding pain is followed by nothing but darkness.

The beast grunts and tosses the bear over the cliff edge. His lifeless body tumbles down the face and is swallowed by the white below. The wind gathers to a gale once more. The beast stands triumphant. The King is dead. The mountain is under a new reign.

Chapter 8

Agnes had awoken from a rough night of broken sleep in a frightful disposition. Insignificant things, like spilling coffee grinds across the kitchen counter, were chaffing her mood and making her irritable. More than once, she had caught herself drifting aimlessly from room to room, aware that she was doing so, but unable to intervene. These spells where her brain switched to auto pilot were getting worse. It wouldn't be the first time she found herself standing outside holding the kettle with no recollection of how she had got there.

A few days had passed since the first great storm had ravaged the valley and assaulted the mountain with powerful blows of wind and ice. Agnes had spent much of her time buried beneath the patchwork reading paperbacks and nursing whiskey. The windows rattled in their frames, as if trembling in fear of the thunder rolling by. Spring seemed like an impossible dream, a period in time that would never come. The white banks of winter were eternal; a dystopian future of ice and snow.

The storm had travelled further inland; beyond the ridge, beyond Sutter's Mill, beyond the far away city of lights. By now it would be raging over the Great Plains, a vast expanse of land, wild and untamed, where only the hardiest laid their roots and whose children dreamt of a life far from the flatlands.

Drifts of snow blanketed the forest around the cottage in deep clumps so that it looked like the picturesque scene in a snow globe. The branches of the conifers slumped as they fought to hold the weight of the storms payload, while the other trees stood bare and frigid as if in shock at the violence unleashed upon them. Some stragglers still fell from the sky, as large as down feathers and just as delicate.

The winter wonderland may have looked pretty but Agnes eyed it with a bone of contention. She had burned through much of her firewood supply over the last few nights and would have to stock up on logs from the woodshed if she wished to continue. Scornfully, she slipped on her boots and Wilson's coat. The energy spent getting herself geared up didn't feel worth it. She felt light-headed and breathless; and don't think she hadn't noticed the black-bruised skin of her wrist peering out from beneath her sleeve.

By now she was convinced that the bone was not broken, but the muscle and tissue damage would take a long time to heal. A small mercy really, a broken bone out here alone could lead to no end of trouble and misery.

Agnes pulled the front door open and recoiled from the chill. The snow had piled up in a drift against the door a foot deep. Agnes kicked it out of the way and grumbled when it spilled over her boot-cuff; her leggings and sock instantly felt wet.

She stood in the doorway, taking in the changes to the scenery and observing the strong scent of pine. The old woman had witnessed hundreds of mornings like this in her lifetime, but could never deny the slight flicker of joy she experienced at the sight of fresh, untouched snow. In her younger days, when her love was still alive, she and Wilson would often run out and play in the blanket of white like children. Merrily, they would laugh as they built snowmen, created angels, or initiated snowball fights.

A sad smile creased the corner of her mouth as she reminisced. Now, old and alone, frail and injured, the sight of such a heavy snowfall made her nervous. How cruel of life to give such precious, wonderful moments, only to confine them to the past as memories. What future happiness could she possibly expect when she had been robbed of the one thing that had put joy in her heart?

A solitary tear ran down her weathered cheek as she stepped outside, her feelings as bitter as the winter air around her.

A robin was battling a small flock of waxwings over the rights to the berries growing on a cotoneaster. The garden had already had a few early morning visitors judging by the little paw prints left by rabbits and other foragers.

Agnes went to Wilson's corner. From her coat pocket she fished out her mittens and put them on. The beautiful bench had been buried by the blizzard and that seemed unfair – it was one thing to have had to bury the man, his craftsmanship needed not suffer the same fate.

She shaved the snow clear of the wood so that it formed a mound to the side. She was about to speak some affectionate words towards Wilson before resuming collecting the firewood, when she noticed something rather strange. The benches backrest had been damaged. The mural that Wilson had spent so many hours dedicated to had split and cracked in several places, Agnes assumed due to the frost seeping in to the wood.

What made this peculiar and unsettling was where these cracks had developed; the largest bear fishing in the stream, a stag standing proud amongst the pines. The worst split of all ran horizontally through a pack of wolves playing in a meadow; here the damage had rendered some of the carvings unrecognizable and beyond repair.

Overcome with sadness, Agnes fell to her knees and wept. Was nothing sacred?

'Oh Wilson,' she spoke, solemnly. '*I'm so sorry.*'

She wiped her eyes with the back of her mitts; the coarse fabric was rough against her paper-thin skin. It was only when she tried to imagine what Wilson would say that she found comfort. He would have rested a warm hand on her shoulder and told her, *'It was just a block of wood...'* and that *'The forest was just trying to take it back. Where it belongs...'* She leaned on the bench, her wrist flared up with a jolt of pain. She barely noticed.

Agnes dusted the snow from her knees and grit her teeth. She accepted her place in the forest, she knew that the wild merely tolerated her presence, but the damage to the bench felt cruel and personal. Not for the first time, Agnes felt as though she had worn out her welcome.

The woodshed was round the side of the property. For many moons Wilson had used it as a workshop then, when his years had caught up with him and he had downsized his projects, it had been converted to a dumping ground for the odds and ends that never found a place in the home.

It had been a somewhat cathartic moment the day the couple had decided to empty the shed and build a bonfire from the tat inside. Agnes had wept as the flames licked and devoured items that held no real meaning to her other than the fact they had been shared in her life with Wilson. It is funny how we attach such sentiments.

The following day the pair awoke in one another's arms under the patchwork quilt. The morning sun was warm on their faces. Dragonflies chased each other, their bodies shone like emeralds and topaz. The pile still smoldered, wisps of smoke curled lazily in the gentle breeze. They had spent the night watching their unnecessary junk turn to ash until they had fallen asleep under a sky full of diamonds. That morning they had been in higher spirits than they had experienced in years; it was as though they were lighter, younger.

For over 30 years they had piled their firewood in a low shelter connected to the cabins outer wall. It had been Wilson who had suggested using the workshop to store a surplus of logs, citing: '*We are getting too old to risk running out of dry stick.*' Before adding, prophetically, '*I ain't gonna be around forever and I'd hate to imagine you traipsing around the woods neck-deep in the white.*'

From then on they had managed to maintain a fully stocked supply by gathering branches throughout the year. Even after Wilson's passing, Agnes had no problem collecting small bundles every few weeks to get her through the colder seasons.

...

Agnes followed the path that led around the cabin. Underfoot the snow compacted with a satisfying crunch. She flinched slightly at a sudden rustling noise behind and turned to see the waxwings take flight. A sly smile spread across her mouth as she shot the robin a wink '*Good for you, girl.*' The bird tilted its head to study her with one eye then disappeared into the shrubbery.

The old woman stepped over a fallen rake and started to whistle to herself. Robins always made her think of Christmas.

A mournful howl interrupted her. Her blood turned to ice water. She crouched low using the corner of the cabin to steady herself. She slowed her breathing, like Wilson had taught her to do while on a hunt and cocked her head, listening.

The air felt too thin, too exposed. She was considering running back inside, closing the door and ignoring the outside world when the howling started again. This time it ended in a pitiful whimper. Whatever it was, it was close.

This side of the house faced North so did not receive as much sunlight as the rest, because of this it had been used for practicality over prettiness. The garden here was overgrown and strewn with discarded relics from engineering projects and art sculptures the pair had tinkered with over time.

Wilson had once wanted to try and divert the stream that ran further up the mountain by the side of the cabin. He had built himself a mill wheel and mounted it at the edge of the property, but digging a channel across the rocky terrain had proven difficult and time consuming. After throwing his back out for the umpteenth time, Wilson - a man who never left a job unfinished, threw down his shovel and gave up.

When he hobbled through the garden gate he was met by his concerned wife. Agnes helped him inside but could see by his expression that it was not the pain in his back that was bothering him. His eyes would not meet her own as she questioned him. Eventually, he relented and told her he was sorry, he had failed her; the labor was just too intense for him. She had cradled his weather-beaten face and kissed his red nose.

'You could never fail me, my love.'

She led him to the small window at the rear of the living room and together they looked at the wheel. Wilson had started to mumble something about taking it down for scrap but Agnes had shushed him.

'Leave it be,' she had said. *'It's too pretty to destroy. We will make it into a water feature or something.'* Wilson had thrown his strong arm around her shoulder and the two quietly envisioned what a beautiful scene they would create.

The scene was no longer beautiful; it wasn't even vaguely pleasant. The millwheel was rotten, abandoned and neglected it stood decrepit and strewn with threads of hanging weeds. The pond itself had been reduced to nothing more than a stagnant swamp. The water had been left to become a thick soup of algae and pond scum. Below the layer of dirty ice that rested on top was a cesspit of murky filth 3 foot deep. Reeds and waterlilies, that provided a sort of glamour during the summer months, now appeared straggly and brown and dead.

Agnes wondered why, living in such close quarters, she had never noticed how repulsive it all was. She vowed there and then that if, god-willing, she survived the winter she would do her best to spruce up this side of the property. She couldn't stand swamps.

The workshop door was not visible from where she crouched but she could hear the soft '*thud*' as the wind caught it. She wouldn't have been surprised if it was open; the lock had been stripped off years ago when Wilson had lost the key. Staying low, she edged closer.

Once she was level with the living room window she could see the door, but only at an obscure angle. She was more concerned with what lay outside the shed. The snow had been turned over. It was piled either side of a furrow where something had been dragged down the slope that led into the woods behind the cabin. Scarlet smears tainted the glossy white snow like a geisha's lipstick. A traitorous voice crept into her mind like a serpent, '*Go back. This does not concern you. You don't belong here...*'

Agnes banished the voice, knowing it may have been silenced but still lingered in her head like a cancer. The dread weighed heavily upon her as she moved closer and closer to the shed.

On the way she stopped to collect an axe from a stump. The blade was dull and rusted but its presence made her feel a whole lot better. Although no longer in its prime, it could still bring a whole lotta hurt.

CHAPTER 9

She was close enough to the shed now to smell the copper scent of blood. She approached from the side; no sense in exposing herself to whatever lay within, especially if the door *was* open.

Agnes leant around the corner, axe held before her ready to swing if needs be. The door was *partially* closed; the wind appeared to have shut it most of the way, but the latch was undone. In truth, Agnes was not sure if she had set the latch the last time she had visited; no matter how hard she tried to remember.

A faint rustle, accompanied by a whimper sounded out from inside the wooden structure. Something was alive in her wood shed. Judging by the amount of blood, it was hurt, badly.

Agnes cast her eyes to the crimson path leading into the forest, how quickly the darkness swallowed the trail. A robin (*the same?*) peered at her from the jagged tangle of a blackthorn tree. Its black eye watched her. The old woman read its expression as, '*Don't! Turn back!*' Together, they shared a moment of understanding. Agnes gave the bird a subtle nod to show appreciation for its concern. Biting her lip until it frayed and bled, Agnes moved in.

The vertical boards that made up the door had become soft and rotten. From the side of the shed Agnes could see that the bottom of them had all but disintegrated. A gap of 4-5 inches could have allowed some small beasts' entrance to the shelter, but nothing containing as much blood as spilt outside.

Agnes thought back to the stag; the blood, the carnage.

Fists clenched, she prayed whatever lay beyond the door would not be as brutal a vision.

A mitted hand reached out and tentatively pulled on the moldy wood.

The door creaked and squealed quietly, although the calmness of the forest seemed to amplify the sound and made Agnes wince. She held her breath. The door was open wide enough to have a peep inside. So she did.

A deep, vicious snarl, a flash of snapping teeth and amber eyes.

Agnes shoved herself backwards, grateful for the cushion of snow she landed on. Still too close, she scooted backwards on her hands and buttocks. A wolf.

She had seen them many times in her years in the valley, but always deeper in the woods or higher up the mountain. None in her memory had ever ventured so close to her property. She braced herself for the assault. The door would swing open any moment now, her death would be dealt by the savage jaws around her throat.

Her mittens, soaked through, dug deep into the snow down to the dirt below. Nothing moved; the door remained shut. From behind the veneer of wood that stood between Agnes and predator there lay a void of silence. The beast, like the woman, was waiting.

The tension swelled, expanding to a size that made her feel as though her mind would snap and her world would descend into a well of impenetrable darkness and madness. Her eyes were so wide the chilly air dried them out, turning them red and sore. She didn't blink.

Her teeth hurt from the pressure clenching in her jaw and she struggled to swallow the lump in her throat. She found herself willing the wolf to attack, to end the anticipation, to bring her balance and peace even if it meant blood and pain.

A wave of panic struck her like an open palm. The axe, where was the axe?

She had dropped it in the fall. Her hand only grasped clumps of fresh white powder. Keeping her eyes firmly on the small, dark gap between door and frame, she fumbled desperately for its reassuring steel. Her shaking fingers brushed against its long handle and she clasped hold tightly. With its solid weight back in her hand an air of confidence touched her. One good swing would be all she needed.

Time lost all meaning. Agnes felt as if she were stuck in a moment. The old woman and the wolf: two players entwined in a game of chequers; neither willing to make the first move. Agnes broke down the situation in her head. The wolf was hurt, that she knew. The real question was, how badly?

Running was something she doubted her body could do much of anymore, but if she could just make it to the cabin door…

The decision was made. She would break for it. Push her body as hard as it could go. Once behind the security of the locked door she could collapse in a heap if necessary. But not before she had retrieved the rifle.

The workshop door burst open, bouncing on its rotten hinges. Agnes screamed; curling into a tight ball she waited for the wolf to rip her to pieces. The strike never came. The huge beast collapsed in the doorway. A plume of sawdust and powdered snow whooshed out from under it accompanied by a sickly wet '*slosh*'.

Agnes peeped at it from between her mittens. The wolf looked back with beautiful, pained eyes. *'Help me',* they pleaded.

Cautiously, Agnes rose to her knees. She clenched the axe so tightly the skin on her knuckles whitened and stretched thinly. An old woman and a wolf sitting alone in a forest, all that was missing were a woodsman and a girl in a red cloak.

Agnes crept closer to the wolf, no longer afraid but not stupid either, dropping her guard now would be foolish. It was still a wild animal. As if to remind her of such, the wolf issued a quiet, throaty growl.

'Easy, easy you,' Agnes said, her voice quivered. 'I'm not here for a fight. It's you who's come wandering into my home; the least you can do is let me be a good host.'

The wolf, whether from submission or loss of blood, collapsed onto its side; its large head thudded softly on the floorboards. Agnes was within touching distance, but chose not to. Not yet.

From here she could see its belly fur was stained red. A nasty gash lay under its front armpit and what looked like a puncture mark had caught it in the abdomen just below its ribcage.

Agnes flinched at the gore. 'Been in the wars, have you?' The wolf's eyes fixed on hers; they seemed to say, *'You don't know the half of it, lady.'*

Agnes needed to think. She had performed minor first aid on Wilson every now and then; they had even joked about how accident prone he was, but never on wounds as serious as the ones before her.

'Stay here,' she whispered, fully aware the beast wasn't going anywhere. 'I'll be back shortly.' Keeping low so not to spook the animal, she moved backwards until she was confident she could safely stand up.

Making sure not to turn her back to the wolf, she retreated around the cabin wall and went inside. As soon as she heard the *snick* of the latch she dropped to the floor and started to cry. It had all been too much. It *was* all too much.

...

The bathroom cabinet contained an array of medical supplies and out-of-date pills. As much as the cabins occupants had shunned the modern world they were not as ignorant to deny themselves a few luxuries. On the odd occasion when Wilson visited Sutter's Mill to restock supplies he often popped in to Laymon's Tobacco and Pharmacy for a few packets of painkillers and anti-inflammatories. *'Nowt better for a headache than 2 aspirins washed down with 3 fingers.'*

Agnes traced her fingers over the various labels and wondered if the residents of Sutter's Mill spoke amongst themselves of the old man on the mountain and his absence these last few years. Wilson had spoken fondly of his conversations with Shep down at the Bait N' Tackle Shack and of Mr. Brautigan at the greengrocers. She wondered if anyone had considered checking up on the old hermits.

From the shelf she gathered a blister pack of paracetamol and a bottle of peroxide. From under the sink she pulled a first aid kit and selected some gauze and dressings. It would be impossible to know the extent of the wolf's injuries until she had cleaned it up a bit but she would try and do right by it and help it on its way; wherever the destination be.

Carrying the supplies in her arms she took them to the kitchen and dumped them on the table. Her eyes kept drifting towards the disassembled rifle. *'Not at that stage yet...'* she told herself.

Although she had adopted an almost exclusively vegetarian diet since Wilson's passing, there was still meat from his final hunt stored in the large, generator run, freezer box. At some point, possibly while she was inebriated during the storm, she had taken out a haunch of rabbit to defrost in the sink. Its sinewy flesh did not appeal to her in the slightest now but the wolf was unlikely to be as picky.

From the drying rack she took a paring knife and made an incision in the meat into which she pushed one, then two, paracetamol.

Agnes considered herself well-read; she had thumbed through many books sitting on Wilson's bench, a good number of them about animals and fauna. Somewhere, there was a veterinarian book that may have been some use to her, but finding it now would take time, and time was not something the wolf could spare.

A voice in her head was uttering something about ibuprofen...*bad for dogs*...

Agnes threw her hands up in exasperation. Tough. Tough luck! She had paracetamol, if it relieved the beast of some of its pain then good. If not... well, at least she had tried.

She bundled all the gear into her handbasket and boiled some water that she poured into a bowl. Grabbing some clean towels, she gathered up her things and went outside to play nurse.

...

The sky was a blend of navy and pink; the low sun still caught the feathery edges of the remaining clouds as they chased the storm over the horizon. Forgotten and abandoned, their pilgrimage to the distant North would end no further than the Great Plains, where they would become stretched-thin wisps and then nothing.

Agnes looked upon the quiet forest; it seemed sharper, more *defined*. She reasoned it was down to her renewed vigilance. The bedlam she had experienced as of late had awoken her senses and left her permanently *on edge*.

Carefully scanning the tree line for anything foul, she made her way around the path to where the wolf silently waited.

It was asleep - or dead. She knew not which. She would not have been surprised if it had succumbed to its injuries. She knelt down beside it, but kept it at arm's reach. If it was playing possum then it was doing a damn good job of it; but it was still not a risk worth taking.

Agnes laid one of the towels down and arranged the various items from the house on it neatly. The wolf's ears twitched and turned to follow the small sounds she made. It was still alive but the puddle of blood it lay in had nearly doubled in size. Agnes cooed and tutted at it to try and wake it from its slumber. One eye, gunky with sleep, opened slowly; the eyeball rolled back. The wolf was barely holding on.

Agnes always carried a penknife when she left the cabin. Wilson had insisted until it had become second nature. *'The one time you'll wish you had it, is the one time you'll need it.'* She pulled the tiny blade from her pocket and cut a ribbon from one of the towels. She gave it a tug and was satisfied it would be strong enough. She formed a loop and slid it over the wolf's snout. The beast rocked its head slightly but did not appear to panic. *'A good sign,'* Agnes thought. *'But the worst is yet to come.'*

Agnes stroked the fur of its cheek. Her hand trembled but it was more from excitement than fear. The fur was thick and warm, coarser than she had imagined. 'I'm going to clean you up now,' she said, gently.

The water had cooled a little from the outside air; it would not burn the creature. Using a sponge she started to wipe the grime around the wounded areas. When the wolf showed no reaction she proceeded to clean the wounds themselves.

The animal flinched as she swabbed its injuries, but evidently did not have the strength to fully acknowledge the pain, for which Agnes was grateful. Next up was the peroxide. Agnes unscrewed the cap and poured some of the solution onto the sponge, the pungent smell burned her nostrils.

The wolf raised its head at the new scent, a comical moan grumbled from its mouth. Whatever this stuff did, it wasn't going to be pleasant. Agnes gave him a reassuring rub behind the ears and told him he was doing fine.

She dabbed the cut below its armpit, when the wolf didn't try and bite her face off she continued until the area was coated in disinfectant. Not wanting to drag out the poor creature's discomfort, she moved straight onto the puncture wound.

This one was a bit trickier; the wound kept weeping. The old woman was going to have to switch from nurse to surgeon.

'You're doing so well, but I'm going to have to sew you up. I'm just going to pop back inside for a moment...' she trailed off. Got up on her feet. Her patient seemed to have nodded off again.

Inside the cabin she got busy raiding her sewing bag. She selected two fine needles and boiled them in the kettle to sterilize them. A further rummage and she found some fishing line buried near the bottom of the bag. She was sure it would work. What an eventful day she was having!

...

Agnes did a fine job; especially considering the difficult circumstances and location. Her needlework was neat and tight. The largest problem she faced was trying to wrap the bandages around the heavy animal *(her damaged wrist didn't help any)*, but through sheer determination she had managed to find a way.

Only once did the wolf react to the needle penetrating its skin; a low, mournful howl that sounded to Agnes like the loneliest sound in the world. But the wolf was not alone, it had her. A bond was forming in her mind, she found she liked that the creature needed her. She had meaning in her life again.

As she tidied up and admired her handiwork, she noticed that the rabbit haunch was missing. A warm smile spread across her face, the wolf had clearly mustered enough strength to gobble it down when she had gone inside - Paracetamol and all.

She gently clapped its ruff as it let out a deep snore. How nice to have found a friend with character. Agnes reached past the sleeping beast and gathered an armload of firewood.

Night had fallen and she was exhausted from the day. She retired to the comfort of the living room and fell asleep beside the warm fire. But not before coming outside once more to give her patient an armload of stones she had heated by the fire, and an old blanket.

CHAPTER 10

He came to her again that night. Her personal ghost of Christmas past. She had been unaware that she had woken up; sitting in the chair with her eyes still shut she had been listening to the soothing crackle of the fire.

The sweet aroma of tobacco wafted around her yet still she kept her eyes closed, savoring the memories, living in them, afraid they would disappear if she tried to look upon them.

'Are you here?' She asked the silence.

She heard the '*putputput*' of his pipe followed by the long, slow, wheezy '*whoosh*' of the exhale. A short bark of a cough, then 'Aye, lass, I'm here.'

Her fingernails bit into the arms of the chair.

'Be true to me, Wilson,' she said. 'Have I snapped? Is this insanity? Because if my mind is broken then I should have the right to know.'

Wilson cackled a hoarse laugh. 'Will you not open your eyes, dear? I'm still in the shadows; you won't need to see me.' Agnes trembled, her teeth worrying her lip skin again until the metallic taste of blood laced her tongue.

'I can't,' she murmured. 'What if you disappear? If I open my eyes and you're not there then I'll just be a mad, old woman talking to herself in the middle of the night.'

Wilson laughed, heartily. 'Fine. Fine keep them closed.' She heard movement. Her heart thudded against her ribs as she felt his presence disturb the air as he drew closer to her. The next time she heard his voice it came from right in front of her. 'Now, keep them shut tight...'

A hand, unlike any other, gently held her own. She shivered at its touch; a gasp of shocked surprise betrayed her mouth.

'Oww!'

Wilson pulled back. 'Sorry...'

She clenched her eyes and reached out to him. She held his gnarled hand tightly. The skin was loose, like he was wearing a glove.

'It's alright, I was just a little taken aback. Your hand, it's so cold.'

'Let me warm them by the fire while we talk,' he said, pulling away from her gently.

She let him go. She allowed herself to peep through narrowed eyes; her eyelashes hid most of the horror but she could still see enough to know that the creature that rounded the coffee table was no longer wholly human. She watched as the 'Wilson thing' hunkered down before the flames; its knees cracking in rhythm with the burning logs.

He sat watching the flames quietly. When he spoke, it was the voice of a man not completely in the here and now. 'I forgot how beautiful fire is; the way it dances, it's so wonderful. Incredible how something so magnificent can be so devastating. One day the entire mountain will be engulfed in flames. Pillars of smoke and ash will block out the sun.' The fire reflected in his eyes a vision of dystopia. 'Not just here either. This world will burn. I think we always knew that, don't you?' Agnes did not answer. 'It is part of what brought us here; we wanted no part in humanity's decline. We tried to separate ourselves from the rest of the herd.'

Agnes felt uncomfortable; the secrets of the dead should not be shared with the living. The universe could spill its guts to her all it wanted, but not before she punched out.

'Wilson,' she whispered. 'Enough. Please.'

Her words pulled him from his reverie. He looked around as if he had been taken from somewhere far away. 'Yes, you're right. Sorry, not my tale to tell. Anyway, we have more pressing matters to discuss.'

Agnes interrupted him. 'There's a wolf in the wood shed. It's hurt.'

Wilson's reply to her outburst was short. 'I know.'

Agnes pushed, 'It was this… *Thing*, wasn't it?'

Wilson stood up, his body made some unsettling noises. He coughed, it sounded rusty and painful. 'It was. I had hoped it would pass you by, but it appears to have landed right on your doorstep.' He paused as if holding back some vital but unpleasant information.

'What is it?' she asked. 'There's more, isn't there?'

Wilson sighed, sadly. He had always hated being the bearer of bad news, especially when it came to Agnes. He rested with his hands on the mantle as if it would support him during the delivery of his latest bombshell.

'It has begun attacking many of the creatures of the forest.' He rubbed his brow, the same way he had done in life when a migraine was settling in for a long haul. 'It appears to be deliberately singling out the biggest and the strongest. I doubt it feels threatened by them, no, that's not it, its attacks are methodical; it is showing its dominance as an apex predator. I believe it has developed a taste for the bloodshed.'

His voice trailed off towards the end of his last sentence. Through her eyelashes Agnes watched his withering body slump. He was little more than bone and cartilage.

'Wilson,' she said, tenderly. 'Why don't you slip back to the corner and I'll fix you a drink?' he nodded slowly and retreated to the comfort of the shadows.

'Ready,' he said when he was concealed by the dark.

Agnes rose up from her seat and crossed the room to the drinks cabinet. From the shelf she picked the glass with the least amount of dust on it and poured him a generous nip of brandy. She watched the golden liquid as she went to hand him the glass. She dared not look upon him, even if the darkness hid the worst of his condition. Wilson took the drink and thanked her. Before she could return to her seat he said, 'Wait, just a minute.' He put the glass on the sideboard and held her hand.

'Wilson, please,' she protested. 'I can't.'

'Trust me, Aggie. Just close your eyes.'

She did as she was asked. Trusting him had been the one safe bet in her life. His fingers traced over her palms and the backs of her hands. Their fingers intertwined like those of young lovers. At first his touch was unpleasant; although the fire had warmed his flesh there was no masking that brittle, papery texture. Agnes sobbed openly and freely, under her breath she muttered the mantra, *'I can't...I can't...I can't...'*

She wanted to pull away, was going to, not repulsed by Wilson but the cruelty inflicted upon his earthly vessel. And then...

And then it was *different*. His skin felt plumper, his callouses softened and the warmth within his hands was that of something living. She went to open her eyes, to gaze upon the man she had devoted her life to, the man she had loved unconditionally. Wilson stopped her.

'No Aggie,' he said, regretfully. 'It don't work like that, I'm afraid. Take it for what it is; a veneer, a type of glamour, call it what you will, it's not real though.'

Agnes pouted like a child denied her favorite toy. 'But Wilson, I want it to be real. I want you back.' Wilson rubbed her hands, how she had missed such a simple thing!

'I know, dear. But it's a one way street. Consider this a gift. It may not be much but it's better than most get.' She agreed but said nothing. Instead she guided his hand to her face and enjoyed his caress.

...

After a while, Wilson asked her to take her seat. Whatever power had allowed her such wonder was wearing off. He sounded tired, maintaining the façade had evidently taken its toll. For a brief period she had found comfort in hands she had thought lost to her forever. Sitting in the old chair she felt content.

Wilson sipped at the brandy; the old familiar burn was divine. 'I have to go soon, Aggie,' he said putting down the empty glass. 'Before I do though, let me say this – be vigilant, be aware. Try to read the forest for signs the beast is near. The animals will show you.'

Agnes felt her eyelids grow too heavy to keep open. Before she fell into the deepest sleep she had had in years, she heard his voice say, 'And never go outside without the gun…'

CHAPTER 11

Murky light spilled in from the grimy window. The fire had burned itself down to the last few embers which glowed bright and defiantly. Agnes awoke to a chill blowing across her cheek. The cabin may have cooled but wrapped up inside the quilt she was uncomfortably warm and sweaty. She kicked it off and yawned.

For the first time in a long time she felt well rested and refreshed. She looked upon the fallen blanket distastefully. When had she allowed herself to become such a slob? Grabbing it by the corners she flapped it out and folded it neatly. Perhaps tonight she could bring herself to sleep in the bed she had shared with Wilson. Perhaps not.

Dust motes pirouetted in the air, disturbed by the wafting of the quilt. Agnes made a mental note to at least attempt a spot of housework.

On the sideboard, still lined with the residue of brandy, sat the glass she had fixed for Wilson. She picked it up and examined it in the morning light. A set of lips had left an imprint around the rim, Wilson's visits, no matter how improbable, must have been real. Unless she *had* lost her mind and was drinking his brandy and smoking his pipe in her sleep. Either way she had found comfort, and if this was madness then she was going to embrace it with open arms.

Agnes rinsed the tumbler and placed it on the drying rack. Her attention turned to the rifle parts scattered over the dining room table. She would make cleaning and reassembling it her main priority this morning, but first she had a guest to attend to.

She filled a bowl with fresh water and ground up some painkillers, hoping the animal would not be put off by the chalky taste. Cursing herself she realized she had forgotten to take out anymore meat from the freezer. The wolf would need feeding, and that meant only one thing – Agnes would have to go hunting.

It was as cold as hell. Never in memory could Agnes recall a winter so vicious. She grasped her fur coat tightly across her chest, pulling the edges so her neck was covered. More snow had fallen during the night, covering most of her tracks from the previous day with a layer of fresh powder.

Although it would certainly have made things a hell of a lot easier for her, Agnes hoped the wolf had not died in the night. She had warmed to its company and was not ready to say goodbye yet. Luckily, her prayers had been answered. She rounded the wall to the woodshed and was greeted by a welcoming wag of its bushy tail. Agnes thought it looked pleased to see her. She felt a flutter in her chest as the wolf's reaction to her arrival warmed her heart.

'Well boy, don't you look chipper today?' she said, placing the bowl of water on the ground and sliding it towards the wolf's thirsty tongue. It responded by slurping wildly at the water; nearly toppling the bowl in the process. Agnes laughed, 'Woah, take it easy! It ain't gonna make you better if you spill it everywhere.'

She stroked its ruff while it drank. When the bowl was empty the great beast looked up at her with a forlorn look in its eyes. Its stomach growled. It was hungry. Any fear Agnes had had towards the creature was gone, she did not know when it had happened, but she found herself looking at it as if it were a beloved family pet; rather than a highly dangerous wild animal.

'I know you must be starving. I'm going to see what I can do about that, but first I need to check your wounds, so be a good boy and don't maul me, ok?' The wolf gazed up at her, its quizzical expression saying that it had no idea what she was saying. Agnes laughed to herself. 'I must be crazy!'

The wolf rubbed its snout and face against her thigh

affectionately. A gesture that said, 'I don't know what you said, but I liked the way you said it.'

...

Back inside the cabin, Agnes sat at the dining table sipping a cup of hot cocoa. The wolf's wounds looked fine, no sign of infection, and the bleeding had stopped, but they would take a long time to heal; Agnes accepted that she would likely have a guest for the winter.

The gun parts that lay strewn across the table before her were a constant reminder of how lazy she had become. No more wallowing in self-pity, no more day-drinking, there were things that needed doing. The rifle would have to wait, the wolf needed meat soon otherwise it would become weak, perhaps too weak to come back from.

Agnes thrust her seat backwards, the wood-on-wood scraped loudly. She'd had an idea. She moved between rooms like a lady with a purpose. At the end of the hall was an insignificant wooden panel. Agnes pressed her weight against it and it popped open revealing a small storage cupboard. Like the rest of her home, it was cluttered with broken and forgotten things; however Agnes immediately spotted the item she wanted.

Hanging on the wall (and covered in cobwebs) was her bow and quiver. Wilson had been the craftsman of the pair, but that didn't mean Agnes had not dabbled in her younger days. One long summer she had painstakingly carved her own bow from the branch of a walnut tree. Wilson had left her to it for nearly a week before his curiosity had gotten the better of him and he had asked her what reason was driving her. She had rubbed the sawdust off her calloused hands onto her overalls and told him, while wiping the sweat from her brow, that she wanted to participate, to be a part of the lifestyle they had chosen. She had smiled and said with a coy look in her eye, that he might not always be around, and she should learn to hunt and provide for herself. Back then she had never really believed such a future could exist.

Agnes pulled it off the hook and turned it over in her hands. It had been years since she had taken it out on a hunt but, surprisingly, the bow string was still taut and free from any faults in its line. The weight felt good. Agnes slung the quiver over her shoulder. She suddenly felt much younger. As she shut the cabin door behind her she realized she was grinning. The thrill of the hunt had awoken inside her.

...

The sky was a low ceiling of deep purple; even though it was still early Agnes didn't imagine the day would get much brighter. Thick flakes drifted lazily down from the heavens, their descent hampered by the gentlest of breezes. Agnes retraced her steps back to where the wolf rested. His huge head slumped on his fore paws, eyelids heavy but open. She gave him a clap on the ruff.

'Okay, boy. Wish me luck,' she said, her eyes firmly focused on the trail the wolf had come crawling from. Even though it had snowed since his arrival his blood still seeped up to the surface like an unwashable stain. Agnes stood up, still staring at the crimson smear. If she had turned to look down at the wolf she would have seen it raise its head with eyes that pleaded, '*Not that way. Anyway but that way. That way only leads to death.*'

Without another word, she set off.

Into the woods, where she would find death waiting.

...

Gnarled limbs curled overhead like arthritic fingers. The trees in this part of the forest were beyond ancient, their bark, like most things, had greyed with the passage of time. Agnes felt uneasy, here was too wild, too primordial, a pocket of the world devoid of the presence of Man. The wind picked up briefly, as it spiraled along the bloody trail it pulled and twisted the branches so that it looked as though they were reaching towards her, willing to sweep her up into their secretive canopy where they could hide her until her bones were as grey as their own.

Each step was hard-going, the snow drifts were deep and hid treacherous rabbit holes and raised tree roots. She scanned the snowfall for the tell-tale paw prints of her prey but saw none.

A half hour of slow progress later she was further from her home than she would have liked. She was still following the scarlet smears left by her new companion. She hadn't meant to retrace his route but her subconscious harbored a curiosity that would not be sated until she found the source of this red river.

She had been steadily moving higher into the mountains; the terrain was rockier and the majority of trees around her were hardy pines. She came to a sudden steep incline and had to scramble on her hands and knees. The blood was darker at the base of the stony out-crop and spread out in all directions. The poor beast must have fallen from the top in a desperate bid to distance itself from its attacker.

When she reached the top Agnes took in her surroundings and tried to get a bearing of her location. Towering high in the distance, obscured by the low hanging clouds, loomed the peak known as Vernon's Watch, by Agnes account that meant she was somewhere on the Calston Plateau. In the spring it would bloom into a wonderful high meadow, peppered with vibrant mountain flowers; an ideal picnic spot and one of Wilson's favorite hunting grounds. Although oppressed by the cold hand of winter, Agnes had to admit that it was still a beautiful place. Albeit, a dangerous, ominous beauty.

Because of the higher altitude, the snow was deeper here. The wind chill stung her cheeks, she could feel the instantaneous drop in temperature the moment she crested the ridge.

Almost immediately, Agnes spied a large hare grazing on a handful of long grass stocks that had broken through the fresh powder. Instinct took over and she loosed an arrow before she even knew what she was doing. The hare went down, even after years of no practice and deteriorating eyesight the old woman could still nail a bullseye.

It had been a long time since she had made a kill, and although it had been a natural part of the day-to-day life she and Wilson had made for themselves, she found herself somewhat morose on this occasion. Walking towards her prey she quietly told herself off, long ago she had reasoned that just because you take its life to sustain your own doesn't mean you can't show it your gratitude. She picked up the hare by the hind legs and looked at her reflection in its dead, black eye.

'I thank you,' she said. 'For the life you give. I thank you.'

She felt better. It was only when she strung the carcass over her shoulder that she realized she had tears streaming down her cheeks.

She could turn back.

She could.

She had found what she had come for.

But an itch like curiosity can grow to become a burning fever; and Agnes was on fire.

The blood trail was harder to keep track of due to the amount of snowfall gathered on the plateau. Agnes followed it as well as she could but lost sight of it when it skirted off under the bottom branches of a wall of conifers. There was no way a woman of her age was going to go crawling beneath the pine needles.

Ready to admit defeat, Agnes holstered her bow and prepared herself for the long traipse back home. Going downhill meant she could be back at the cabin with enough hours of daylight left to have a quick nap then a decent cleaning spree. The thought made her smile, it felt good to be getting back on track; now that she had recognized and addressed the way her life was going.

A burst of excitement ahead drafted her attention. Crows took to the air cawing wildly, their cackle echoing off the distant mountain walls. Agnes went to investigate the commotion. Her bow unslung, an arrow notched. No matter how hard she tried she could not steady her trembling hand. The crows carried on their chaotic chorus. Far up in the sky overhead much larger carrion birds were circling, that explained why the crows had retreated to the surrounding trees. Agnes chewed nervously on her lip, but what had attracted so many birds?

She found a break in the trees that she could push through, the disrupted branches rained clumps of snow down upon her. She brushed off the worst of it from her hat and shoulders and shivered as some flakes managed to sneak down the back of her collar.

Agnes looked up and gasped. Then, she fought back a scream.

CHAPTER 12

She had entered a clearing. In the center of the ground here was a mass of rock protruding from the earth; the trees had formed a large circle around it. Everywhere she looked she saw carnage.

Blood and viscera covered every surface. To her left, half buried, was a hind leg of a wolf; a pile of guts nearby appeared to be all that was left of the animal. Agnes walked further into the clearing with her hand over her mouth in shock. One wolf had been torn in half; it had evidently tried to escape into the undergrowth. Only its hind quarters had been dragged back. The entire pack had been destroyed.

Agnes rounded a rock formation that concealed a small niche, she cried out at the cruelty she witnessed there. The pups, five in total, had been hauled out and slaughtered. Each had been methodically decapitated. The heads were nowhere to be found. Backing away from the horrific sight, Agnes called out to God.

'*Oh God...oh God...Oh God...*'

But out here, where the air was thin and the land was shrouded in a white veil, God could not hear her cries.

The dense branches of the tree wall pushed against her back, she could go no further. Frozen in fear she was forced to look, to see the savagery and take it in, to absorb the inhumanity.

A patter sounded on her shoulder then spread to her lapel. Her weight had disturbed something in the upper branches. Agnes ran her finger tips across her coat and was not surprised when they came back slick with blood. You couldn't walk through such brutality and emerge clean on the other side.

Another sound; heavier, *growing…*

Agnes looked up just in time to throw herself out of the way as the canopy tried to rain down a mass of guts down upon her. She scrambled away from the tree line as the entrails splattered a revolting soup where she had just stood. She looked up to the source and saw a wolf, the largest by far, impaled upon broken branches. A tear ran the length of its abdomen with an almost surgical precision. Finally, Agnes vomited. Her eyes stung with the acrid taste that choked her throat and nostrils. She ran with no destination in mind except: AWAY!

Downhill. Downhill and away…

She wiped her eyes, eyes filled with tears, stung by the icy cold air, betrayed by age. Her decent was a blur of branch and rock and snow. Her legs burned with a fire long forgotten; one extinguished in most people her age. Her lungs, fit to burst, screamed for mercy.

Then falling…

Like the wolf before her, she had not seen the drop. Her stomach reacted to the queer sensation of weightlessness. Something cold and sharp caught the skin of her brow, instantaneous warmth cascaded down her face. Her tender wrist collided with stone in a fresh firework of pain. She lay at the foot of the rocky outcrop, a victim of the elements and natures combined forces. The back of her legs and her coat soaked up run-off that had formed a dirty, cold puddle that seemed to find its way into her joints and grab hold of her very soul.

She screamed. A scream of anger and of pain, of frustration and of grief. A murder of crows, unsettled by her cacophony, took to the skies and joined her in her angst. The scream dwindled off and became a sob. Something else cried out. Not a scream but a roar. The crows fell silent. Every hate filled sentiment in the world united in that one terrible, ferocious voice. The mountains themselves seemed to tremble in fear at the bellow of a thousand enraged baritones.

Agnes held her breath, her fingers clawed into the dirt. Never before had she heard such a dreadful sound. She forced herself to get up, she had to keep moving! Her entire body ached. The laceration above her eye had swollen into an egg that pushed the flesh down; this, coupled with the steady stream of blood, had rendered the eye blind and useless.

Onwards she ran, half blind, half delirious. She had lost her way, drifted from the trail that had led her to the killing ground. A mess of scree and twigs added to her perilous route down slope. Twice she stumbled, the second of which twisted her ankle.

Then...

Then a hauntingly familiar sound tinkered through the trees ahead. It signaled a feature in the vast landscape that gave Agnes the strength to carry on. She grunted and shoved her way through a barrier of young blackthorns; the spiny needles jabbed and scraped her.

She misjudged how far the river was and ended up knee-deep in it - A tributary stream that would, eventually, flow into the raging waters of the Madoes. Instead of trying to climb back onto the side she had emerged from; she trudged onward through the frigid water. From the far side she would be able to follow the stream downhill to more familiar territory – and having the fast-moving river between herself and the source of that hellish sound also provided a little comfort.

Agnes wanted nothing more than to be home and warm, but the stream had stolen the last of her energy. If she was to try and go on now she would likely collapse and die, lost and alone. She sat on the riverbank and hugged her knees to her chest. Two minutes, just to catch her breath.

She watched the river flow. Ice formed on the surfaces where the water was pooled and still. Something in the water caught her eye, a piece of debris bobbing along from upstream. Agnes watched it drift by where she sat but could not tell what it was; it was followed by more of the same, coming down the river.

Puzzled, Agnes rose to standing for a better look. The objects were around a foot long and shiny. The water around them seemed tainted with rust. It was fish. Dead fish. Twenty, at first, then fifty. A hundred. They had been torn to shreds, their blood colored the water like iron silt.

Agnes knew their corpses were a warning, a threat. Some malevolent being had sent them to her, to taunt her, to say, *'I know exactly where you are, you cannot escape.'*

But damn it all if she wasn't going to try!

Not wanting to wait and see what the river would deliver next, Agnes grit her teeth and ran. On the way she passed a beaver dam. Instead of being tucked away in the cozy confines of their lodge, each member of the colony had been brutally impaled on the branches that stuck upwards from their home. Agnes sped past the abhorrent pin cushion. She got the message; this horrific act was just the exclamation point.

CHAPTER 13

It had been the hardest physical challenge she had ever endured, but she had survived. Following the stream, she had finally come to a familiar fishing spot. Agnes was shocked to realize how far off course she had been.

Once on a known path, Agnes had been able to judge the distance to the cabin and how hard to push herself. She broke through the bushes; the wolf raised its head, alerted by her sudden arrival. She was too cold and sore to sit with him so she just tossed him the hare, which he was very grateful for.

Inside the cabin Agnes immediately began stacking a fire. Getting a heat in her was priority number one. Soon the fire was roaring, its warm glow thawing her fingers and toes.

She changed into a clean set of clothes, put her swollen brow on ice, and settled down with a glass of whisky. The amber liquid burned delightfully down her insides. Another glass and Agnes fell asleep; when she woke she sat at the dining table and cleaned the rifle. That night she slept with it on her lap.

...

'You looked cold,' croaked Wilson's voice, drier and raspier than before. 'So I moved you.'

Agnes eyelids still shut, sensed by the warmth on her face that she was laying on the rug in front of the fireplace. The soft fur cradled her cheek and gave her a sensation of safety and comfort not unlike that of a mother's womb. Reluctant to leave the safe haven, but pleased to hear his voice, she raised herself up so she was leaning on one arm. Vision had returned to her beaten eye; the swelling had reduced nicely.

'What time is it?' she asked, yawning wildly.

Wilson chuckled, hoarsely, 'Between midnight and 'morn.'

The events of the day leapt from her memory, spiraling through her brain as a kaleidoscope of terror and chaos. She sat up rubbing her temples. 'Oh Wilson, the things I saw today. It was so... so grim.' She fought back tears as the image of the decapitated wolf pups swam across her mind. Wilson, shrouded by the darkness he seemed to emit in his far corner, remained silent. 'Didn't you hear what I said? It was horrible!' She saw a portion of the darkness break off and shuffle forward. Wilson's silhouette was just visible against the matte-black.

'I told you to get the gun cleaned and assembled. I said to you Aggie, I said don't leave the cabin without it.'

Agnes felt like a child being reprimanded. Without meaning to she went on the defensive. 'It wasn't my fault, the wolf needed to eat!'

Wilson's face leapt out of the shadows. Agnes bore witness to its grotesqueness in all its abominable glory. The skin was as dry and cracked as ancient leather; the eyes, formerly as blue as the Aegean Sea, now shriveled and sunken, yellowed and blind. A hole in his cheek allowed a glimpse at the maggoty world inside.

'I told you!'

Wilson's anger dissipated when he saw the shock and revulsion spread like wildfire across Agnes aghast face. His decaying features softened as he retreated back into the dark. 'I'm sorry,' he whispered. 'I didn't mean to shout. I just want you to be safe.'

Agnes could not push the image of her beloved's rotten face from her mind. She was glad she was of old age, as that picture would stick with her until the day she died. 'Don't apologize, Wilson. We both know I was a fool. I should've listened to you.'

'It's pretty bad, huh? He replied, breaking into a wheezy laugh. 'My face..?'

Agnes erupted in a fit of hysteria. What else could she do but laugh?

...

They sat in a comfortable silence for a short while. Agnes sipped at a brandy while Wilson puffed softly on his pipe, the blue tinted smoke drifted lazily towards the chimney. He had to be patient, allow her time to come to terms with his new appearance.

He watched her and wondered if behind her glassy stare she was aware of the disease infesting her mind. It was still in the early stages but the first tell-tale signs occasionally manifested themselves; subtle moments of forgetfulness, the confusion, the day drinking and depression.

One quick glance around the living room told Wilson she was struggling with the everyday chores she had - until his death, breezed through. Discarded coffee mugs sat forgotten and festering; precariously balanced upon stacks of paper and books that never found their way back to the shelves they had previously called home. A veil of dust coated every surface. He wondered if she was eating enough.

Her face was stoic, a carving of unreadable marble. Her unblinking eyes gazed beyond the slowly dancing flames of the fireplace. Wilson would have to pull her back from whichever distant shore she had drifted to.

'Aggie…' he said softly, letting sound flow into the near

vacuous room. 'Agnes?'

Her eyes swam left, right, left, as if searching for someone who had called her voice from very far away.

'Do you remember the doe..?'

CHAPTER 14

It was late September, two days before Agnes' 40th birthday. An Indian summer had stretched the warm period into the beginning of autumn and would continue to do so for three more weeks. Only the leaves on the furthest reaching branches had given up their green for the gold and russet tones befitting the season, making the vast woodland appear to be rusting along spidery veins.

The forest was still beautiful, fat berries hung from sprawling vines, their lush fruit catching the low sun like precious gems. The grasslands and meadows were peppered with an abundance of rabbits, while higher up the slopes large herds of deer roamed and rutted.

Sky, earth, and stream - all teemed with life in its perfectly balanced chaos.

The mornings smelled of ozone and dew, while from late afternoon until sundown the air carried the sweet scent of cyclamen and honeysuckle.

Even though she was right in the middle of this awe-inspiring Garden of Eden, Agnes felt miserable. For weeks she had moped about under her own personnel black cloud. Wilson had tried and failed on so many occasions to cheer her up that he was now at his wits end. Any attempt on his behalf to enquire about what was 'wrong' was met with a snippy retort, eventually leading him to stay for long periods at a time in his work shed. He figured whatever was bothering her was something she had decided to take on alone, he could only wait and be there for her when she emerged on the other side.

Agnes could not quite put a finger on what was making her feel this way, she simply felt devoid of joy. The things she favored; the smell of the pines, fox cubs playing just beyond the garden fence, the chirrup of birds saluting the rising sun, all these things she loved seemed to irritate her.

Frequently, she had caught herself spacing out while Wilson spoke, her thoughts as blank as her expression. Repeatedly, she chastised Wilson for showing concern and then scorned herself when he left the room, which made her feel worse. It was only after an extensive self-examination (soul-searching, Wilson would have called it), that she came to the conclusion that the source of her despondency was the encroaching landmark birthday.

40.

It didn't seem possible. She had been duped, all this time she had thought herself still young, so how could she be turning the big 4-0?

It wasn't about reflection either; Agnes had no qualms about not bearing children, nor did she look back on the life she had lived excluded from society with regret, hell, up until recently she had wandered the woods and mountains in a state of bliss and satisfaction. It was pure and simply the fact that she was approaching that dreaded bend in the road, youth was falling behind her, abandoning her to walk the path alone in worn out shoes.

Further to her frustration, Wilson, who had already turned that corner in the spring, had remained utterly indifferent to the approach of 'old age', truth be told, middle-age seemed to have given him a second wind, an extra bounce in his step. It was this reason she had aimed her temperament in his direction. It wasn't fair that he should carry on as if time held no affliction over him. Why could he not feel that invisible force - *that weight?*

...

Agnes sat alone on the porch swing. Wilson had awoken before dawn to forage a basket of blackberries from a grove near the drop-off. She had pretended to be asleep while he had quietly dressed and slipped out.

She didn't blame him, she had practically goaded him into a fight the previous night and, in his typical gentlemanly way, he had taken the blame *(for what, Agnes could not remember)* and excused himself. She knew how much he resented confrontation and had still antagonized him by conjuring a situation out of nothing at all.

She played with the tips of her hair, running her fingers through in the search for greys (of which there turned out to be many) and chided herself. How could she be so selfish? She wanted nothing more than to make amends and explain to him the reasons behind her attitude, but try as she might she found herself unable to pull free of this quagmire.

It was then, when dismay threatened to drag her under again, that she saw movement in front of her at the edge of the thicket. She had to squint to try and bring it in to focus; her eyesight was another item on the checklist of 'Things-that-were-going-to-crap'.

Keeping her eyes forward, she slowly crept a hand down the back of the seat. Wilson had reported seeing a large bear not too far from the cabin around a week ago so the pair had been extra vigilante when outside. Her fingers found the bow and she gently pulled it up to rest on her lap. She notched an arrow, just in case.

A shape was moving cautiously in to the open, its elegant

movements barely displaced the long stalks of grass it waded through.

The young doe entered the open, head swiveling left and right on the lookout for danger. She clocked Agnes sitting by the cabin and froze. Agnes held her breath, worried the slightest movement would scare the deer and send it fleeing back into the woods.

It studied her, assessing what sort of threat this new animal posed. It's deep, brown eyes slowly blinking behind long, dark lashes.

Agnes watched as the doe, after what felt like an age, finally decided the two-leg meant her no harm, and began casually grazing on the juicy, green grass. The woman, who was at this time too young to be considered old at all, sat in peaceful silence watching the deer go about its business.

A half hour later when the sun had arced across the sky to sit behind the treetops in front of her so that she had to squint and raise a palm to block the shades of golden light piercing through the leaves, the deer left. Possibly a sound or scent, unheard or undetected by Agnes, had spooked it, but in an instant it had raised its head, neck extended upright, and bolted away behind the shrubbery. Agnes sat for a while longer, her spirits lifted a little by the encounter.

An hour after the deer's departure, Wilson came traipsing along the path. Bars of sunlight ran over his face as he approached his partner sitting on the swing. His expression was that of a man preparing for an inevitable brow-beating. Beads of sweat formed on his forehead and nestled on his beard, he didn't imagine they were caused by a hard day's work under a blistering sun either.

'Everything…alright?' he inquired, warily. Something had changed, she didn't look so weighed upon; she was even smiling a little. When she spoke it was as though the previous few weeks had never happened.

'Let me give you a hand with the basket. Wow, there are

enough berries here to keep us going for months! Shall I make us a pie? There are still plenty of apples in the larder. Might even be some pears left, although they…'

'Woah, whoa!' said Wilson, his hands up like he was trying to calm a wild horse. 'Aggie, slow down. What's gotten into you? You're practically radiant!'

'Come on inside and I'll tell you.'

And she did. She spoke of the deer and of her true feelings. Wilson listened without interruption until she had finished laying herself bare. He assured her that, of course, he had felt the weight of turning 40 but decided not to dwell on it. What could be done anyway?

He said to her, 'Time is like a river, try as hard as you want you'll never get it to flow uphill, but sometimes it forms pools and those are moments for rest and reflection before you hit the next set of rapids.'

She raised an eyebrow as he spoke his words like a sage. 'Why didn't you just say *'go with the flow?'*

They both burst into fits of laughter. Later that night they feasted on the generous harvest the forest provided and made love with the exuberant passion usually reserved for teenagers and newly-weds.

...

A few days later, Agnes was busy in the kitchen baking when Wilson burst in from outside. 'Agnes, guess what I've just seen? I was out on the Northern trail when…' he paused when he saw the mess. Flour seemed to be coating every surface, including Agnes face. 'You've been…um…busy.'

Agnes wiped the back of her hand across her cheek, which only seemed to spread the powder further towards her hairline. She looked at him sheepishly. 'I may have gotten a little carried away.' She used her forefinger and thumb to emphasize the '*little*'.

Wilson laughed heartily. 'Never mind, never mind. As I was saying, I was out on the Northern trail, you know, just past Fawcett's Walk? Anyway, I was stalking a stag, big one too, but I lost the trail, so I was just about to give up and head on home when I spotted some smaller tracks pointing towards the cabin. I followed them and, sure enough, they led me right back here! I set up behind that timber pile - I know, I know, I said I'd move it into the shed, and I will - and scanned the garden for our visitor.' Agnes grinned; she'd never doubted the deer would come back. 'Aggie, you never mentioned she was pregnant!'

She clapped her hands excitedly. 'I never noticed! How can you be sure?'

Wilson shook his head. 'I've stalked enough herds to know which ones not to hunt; that and the slightly swollen belly hanging from her. I'm amazed you didn't clock it.'

'Oh, what wonderful news, I do hope she keeps coming back. Is she still out there now?'

'No, sorry,' said Wilson. 'She scampered when I tried to get closer. I could have a look tomorrow if you'd like, see if I can pick up her trail?'

Agnes thought about it. 'No, let it be on her terms. If she wants to come back then she is more than welcome.'

...

It was nearly a full month before the doe appeared again. It was a particularly frigid October morning when it was just cold enough to see the thin mist of your breath. Wilson had come down with a cold three days previous and was (although he wouldn't admit it) severely weakened by it.

Agnes, who had been in high spirits on and off since her birthday, was beginning to slip back into that pool of despair. She had kept herself busy fussing over Wilson, much to his chagrin, but occasionally caught herself wading into negative waters. At times, when she had finished working around the cabin and was sat alone with nothing to do but relax, it was if a shadow moved across her mind; a blanket of gloomy thoughts.

Wilson was asleep in his chair. He had spent the night there because he was worried his sputtering and shivering would keep Agnes awake. Agnes had panicked when she had woke up in the bed alone, it was only when she found him wrapped up to the nines in the living room that she relaxed and felt her heart burst with love at the sight of her poorly woodsman.

She had let him sleep and set about making a big batch of vegetable soup quietly in the kitchen. Once the pot was full and simmering she slipped outside to fetch some firewood.

It was still too early for the sun to have warmed the earth and Agnes shivered, wishing she had at least thrown on a scarf. She clapped her hands and breathed on them, rubbing them together to get the blood flowing.

The dirt under foot was slippery and boggy due to heavy rainfall from showers that seemed to be getting more and more frequent. Agnes neared the wood shed, grumbling under her breath as the mud caked her shoes.

A rustle, followed by the cracking of delicate twigs, caused her to pause and look towards the tree line. The deer stepped into the open; it was staring right at her. For a moment the pair stood transfixed on each other; an air of tension was swiftly brushed aside by recognition and acceptance. Agnes had been positive the short distance between them would not be far enough for the deer to feel safe, so she was pleasantly surprised when it bowed its head to graze. She watched it for a while. Wilson had been correct, the doe was certainly pregnant. Not wanting to intrude, Agnes slowly edged towards the shed, retrieved an armload of firewood, and retreated quietly back to the cabin.

Wilson recovered through a diet of hot baths and hot toddies, (although Agnes had put some serious consideration into getting him into the pick-up and hauling his ass to the hospital in Elliedale when his barking cough became a chesty rattle).

Winter came and went with little fanfare. Spring, sprung, and was glorious. It brought warmth, and color, and life - and through it all was the regular presence of the doe. Each sighting she grew bigger; the swell of her stomach hung lower and fatter.

Agnes had found something to focus on; she could not pass a window without systematically scouting for her acquaintance. Once or twice a week the deer would emerge from the woods and Agnes would watch, she could not explain the profound effect the animal had on her *(it wasn't as if she had not seen hundreds of deer cross the mountain in the decades she had lived there)*, it was as if something inside her had *reset*.

Then, a week in mid-April, the doe never showed. Agnes became irate; the way a worried parent feels when a teenager misses curfew. Wilson did a few calculations in his head (and on his fingers) and sat her down.

He was beaming at her which only fueled her irritation. 'God dammit, Wilson, what're you smiling like an idiot about? She could be hurt; it's not like her to stay away so long!'

Wilson held her shoulders. 'Aggie, do the math, will ya?'

She was bewildered; they should be out there, tracking her, seeing if she was alright. They had...

The penny dropped.

'She's birthing!' Agnes leapt to her feet. 'Oh Wilson, she's having her baby!'

Wilson could not help reacting to her exuberance, his smile broadened as he embraced her. He couldn't fathom what was so significant about this particular doe *(and he had spent many hours pondering over it)*, but it had helped Agnes deal with a difficult time when he had been unable to do so; for this he was eternally grateful to it.

The next three weeks were hard on Agnes. She had started biting her nails again and seemed permanently on edge. Wilson insisted on plying her with relaxing cups of tea and reassuring her that all was fine and well.

'Give her a chance. She'll show up fine and dandy. I'm positive.'

Agnes sat rigidly on the swing, often for hours at a time. It was there she was perched one Friday evening when her wistful prayers were answered. She was preparing herself to go inside for the night when a wonderfully familiar sound broke the calm twilight air. Fireflies buzzed around in disturbed spirals as the foliage around them parted. The doe had returned.

She moved prudently into the grove, majestic and elegant as a queen should be. Agnes clasped her hands in a state of bliss. The shrubbery rustled again and wide-eyed, Agnes watched as the doe was joined by a nervous looking fawn on jittery, bandy legs.

A gentle tap on the window behind her broke the spell; she turned her head to see Wilson standing on the other side of the glass. His wide grin said, *'I told you so.'*

She was about to reply to his unspoken remark when his expression changed and he began jabbing a finger in the direction of the deer.

A smaller, more timid, fawn had joined them. The doe had been carrying twins. Taking their mothers ease as a sign, the two fawns played and grazed in the long grass until the setting sun became a rising moon. When the time came for them to vanish, as only deer can do, Agnes went inside. Wilson had fixed her a brandy, which she savored by the glow of the fireplace. Her return to joyfulness had been reaffirmed.

...

Nearly a year passed since the first visit. The family of deer came and went as regular as clockwork, and all the while Agnes would be sat there waiting patiently.

Late one evening, Agnes had been sat at the dining table, her knitting needles click-clacking an up-tempo rhythm. When Agnes knitted it was like she became a machine, she would become very still, only her fingers would move with an incredible dexterity.

That night, like so many others, she had lost herself to the mesmerizing noise and motion, so that when Wilson burst through the door bringing with him a whirlwind of chaos and disarray, it gave her the sensation of being pulled from under water.

'Aggie!' he hollered as he shunted the door open with his back. 'Clear the table, Agnes!' Still surfacing, Agnes took a moment to comprehend what was unfolding around her. Her mouth hung dumbly open, eyes wide but not really seeing. 'Aggie, now!'

She swept her arm in a wide arc across the dining table, her sewing kit clattered to the floor in a jumbled heap of spools and yarn.

Wilson was lugging something heavy through the doorway draped over both his arms. Grunting with the strain, he shuffled forward and, carefully as he could, placed it on the table. The mother deer had been hurt. An oozing, bubbling wound over its right eye looked like a bullet hole.

'Oh god, Wilson…What did you do?'

He shook his head vehemently. 'No, Aggie. Not me. I heard the shot and found her like this. I'd bet my bottom dollar it was some drunken city boys. They always show up this time of year. Trying to prove to their buddies how 'manly' they are. Been hearing them all day, whooping n' hollering to each other, every now and then a shot fired. No respect. From the sound of things they're heading down into the low valley. Hope they get lost.'

Wilson, who was all in all a good natured soul, bore an intense dislike towards the 'sport' hunters that passed through the forest every year killing anything in sight without remorse. Often he would come back from a trip into the woods with his backpack full of their discarded beer cans and other rubbish.

Frantically he started pulling open the kitchen drawers until he found a length of cord that he cut with his buck knife. 'Aggie, she's in shock, but I don't want her suddenly freaking out in a panic. You stroke her and keep her calm while I bind her legs. I don't want either of us getting mule-kick dental surgery.' Agnes did as she was asked, cooing softly to the injured animal.

It suddenly dawned on her. 'Wilson, her babies!'

Wilson waved her off as he struggled to wind the cord around the doe's hind legs. 'Not to worry,' he said. 'They followed behind me. They are hanging around the bottom of the garden. It was the big one those bastards wanted.'

'Should I go check on them, give them something to eat?'

'Aggie, they'll be fine. I need you here-' Wilson was cut off mid-sentence as the deer tried to rise up from the table, its instincts telling it to flee. Wilson spread his weight across the length of its body. 'You've got to keep her calm while I work.'

...

It was many hours later when Wilson declared that he had done all that he could do, and was retiring to bed. The animal had been cleaned and patched up to the best of his abilities but had unfortunately lost the use of her eye when he had removed the bullet.

The spent shot had settled in the bone behind her eye socket, essentially severing the optic nerve. When Wilson had tweezered the shrapnel out of the bullet hole it had freed the lose eyeball to roll uselessly in its cavity. Wilson had made the call. He looked at Agnes, then at the bloody, puss-oozing wound: the eye would have to come out.

Agnes tried to watch as Wilson fished out the poor creatures eyeball but even with the knowledge that it was no longer connected to the animal, it was still too ghastly a scene for her to process. She excused herself and quickly made her way to the bathroom to be sick.

Wilson had carried the creature outside in a blanket and put her down for a night in the woodshed Ritz *(a fact Agnes did not dismiss as an ironic twist decades later when the out-building would house a second tenant)*.

Back inside he found Agnes peering out the window from behind the net curtains. 'The little ones are curious,' she said without looking at him. 'They're coming to investigate.'

Wilson gave her a gentle pat on the shoulder, too weary to reply further. 'Don't stay up all night watching them. It's already well past midnight. She might need us in the morning.' He ambled towards the door, grateful she hadn't turned to see him. The weight of the animal had put enough strain on his back to make him tender and sore, a niggling pain that would remain persistent until the end of his life decades later.

'You're right,' mumbled Agnes, still focused on the intimate theatre beyond the windowpane. 'I'll be just a minute.'

Wilson lay in bed counting the knots of wood in the timber trusses overhead until exhaustion cast its spell of slumber and he was pulled down into a deep black pool of sleep. Agnes joined him over an hour later, but the waters of her sleep were choppy, and filled with macabre creatures waiting below the inky surface.

...

The following morning Wilson woke to an empty bed. He found Agnes in the kitchen, two cups of coffee steaming on the counter. He picked one up and supped carefully at the milky contents. He felt as if he were nursing a hangover.

Agnes looked pale, dark purple bags puffed below her eyes, her lips were drained of all color so they matched the chalkiness of her cheeks. He was about to ask her how she slept, but one look at how she fidgeted and jittered around the kitchen, aimlessly moving things from one spot to another was all the answer he needed, so instead he cut to the chase. 'Well, how are our distinguished guests?'

Agnes pushed her hair behind her ears as she often did when anxious. 'They're gone. Must've taken off at first light. That must mean she's alright, right?'

Wilson drummed his fingers on his chin as he thought. 'Well, I guess if she felt well enough to leave… it's probably a good sign. Let me sort my head out - I don't feel great right now - then I'll go see if I can find their tracks.'

Wilson followed their trail up the mountain until he came to a river where he lost them. Downtrodden, he trudged home, knowing his report would give Agnes little piece of mind. She saw how physically exhausted he was and, for his sake, put on a brave face. 'Don't worry about me, dear,' she smiled. They'll be back.' She took his calloused hands in her on. 'What you did for her was amazing. You're my hero.'

...

The summer that year was one of the wettest on record for the region. The sky seemed to have a permanent grey filter to it that tarnished the mood of all under it. Wilson had taken the truck down to Sutter's Mill on several occasions, and on his return he would tell Agnes of how miserable the town's children looked as they forced play on the sports fields and streets.

The lack of sunshine coupled with the endless cycle of showers played havoc with the vitality of the forest. Where carpets of vibrant flowers blossomed most years, larger, hardier shrubs sprouted; their delicate contemporaries swept away and drowned by a cruel hand of fate. The burrows of small mammals that would normally have been teeming with life consisted of far too many empty chambers and tunnels.

Agnes had developed a chest infection that, by the middle of August, had prompted Wilson to drive her down to Sutter's Mill's only doctor. As she peered nervously out the trucks window at the people, the houses, the tarmac and cement, she realized that this was the first time she had laid eyes on civilization since they had properly established their home in the mountains. The doctor's would be the first face she had seen besides Wilson's in decades. Anxiety clawed at her throat, she wanted nothing more than to go home now; far away from the cars and the brick buildings. She wanted to scream.

Wilson took her trembling hand. He reassured her as he pulled the truck into the vacant lot that served as the doctor's car park that she would be alright. 'We'll be home before you know it. Let me do the talking.'

The doctor was a kind, professional man with over sixty years servicing the town under his portly belt. He created a picture of the pair from the information Wilson had provided him, and was nothing but courteous and respectful to Agnes' stand-offish inclination. He handed a prescription for Wilson to pick up at the pharmacy on his way out of town and waved them off without judgement. As much as Agnes would later admit to quite liking the doctor and his gentle demeanor, she would never again set foot on the concrete walkways of a human town if it could be avoided.

On her 42nd birthday, under a sky as grey as slate, Agnes sat by the kitchen window picking at a breakfast of bacon and eggs (that Wilson had lovingly provided), and watched the rain beat an anthem on the tin roof of the wood shed. She had given up all hope of seeing the deer again. She had accepted that the creature that had had such a profound effect on her emotions, an effect she could not rationalize or put into words, had succumbed to its injuries and passed on.

Wilson had presented her with a necklace he had been secretly fashioning in his workshop for weeks. He had come across a gemstone protruding from a fresh rockslide several months ago and kept it hidden; sneaking out to work on it while Agnes pottered around the house. He couldn't be certain, but he believed it to be garnet. It had been mounted using some wire that he had formed into an elaborate depiction of petals and leaves, elegant trails of fern fronds hung from its centerpiece; it was truly beautiful.

She traced her fingertips over the delicate spirals as it lay upon her chest. She prayed that her reaction to Wilson's gift had been close enough to the response that he had been hoping for. In truth, she had been amazed by the thought and craftsmanship that he had put into it, especially considering his usual projects involved large slabs of wood, his big hands were usually quite clumsy when it came to such delicate work.

Even though her appetite was close to non-existent, she forced down the last few bites of her breakfast and washed it down with a cup of coffee she had forgotten about. Its bitterness left a foul taste in her mouth.

Wilson had gone out to see if he could catch a rabbit for dinner, Agnes crossed her fingers in hope she would be hungry come suppertime. She slipped on a pair of boots and gathered up her washing basket and clothes pegs. With an apathetic sigh she went outside to do her monotonous chores.

A solitary crow cried a tuneless din from somewhere unseen.

Agnes crossed the sodden ground to the washing line being careful not to skid on the wet grass. An earthy, stagnant odor assaulted her nostrils and she gagged. The pond, which Wilson still tended to regularly, had become the final resting place for some unfortunate animal several weeks ago and its remains were now putrefying and causing a stink. Agnes grumbled to herself about how the clothes would now capture that rancid stench in their fabric.

A pillow case escaped her grasp, she swore as she fumbled after it and swore again when it settled in the dirt and immediately became soiled. She bent down to gather it up, gingerly pinching the corners to avoid getting it into a worse state than it already was.

A shadow cast down upon the white linen, assuming Wilson had returned with supper, Agnes began nattering about how fed up she was with the wet weather.

'I tell you, Wilson. I am so done with these constant showers. The whole summer's been a washout. And the sky! Would it hurt to be blue for just one day? I'm so sick of grey, grey, grey…Wilson?'

Agnes looked up. The pillowcase billowed down to the ground and became saturated in filth as she let it go in shock. She made a small sound in her throat and stumbled backwards.

The mother deer had returned and was standing close enough for Agnes to smell her breath. The unexpectedness of the encounter would have been enough to warrant such a reaction on Agnes' part, but was made worse by the poor doe's grotesque appearance.

Her wound had, at some point, become infected. The tissue around the eye socket and along the side of her muzzle was slick with dried puss and shiny with sores. A putrid miasma emanated from her once beautiful face and Agnes drew away from it for fear of contamination.

It was only when she took in that terrible face as a whole, that she was able to shake off her apprehension and allow the tension in her neck and shoulders to release and relax. The other eye, with its deep, black well, ringed with an iris of hazel and gold, and crowed with long, dark lashes, looked at her with an untold gentleness and kindness.

'It's still you in there, isn't it?' Agnes clapped a palm to her chest. 'You poor thing, they couldn't take your life so they robbed you of your beauty.' The deer turned her neck so she was looking behind her, back towards the tree line.

As if an unspoken permission had been granted, the shrubbery shook and then parted and two healthy, young bucks entered onto the open ground. Their antsy demeanor showed they were uncertain but trusted their mother's lead. Agnes felt as though she was in the presence of a higher force as all three sets of eyes looked upon her. She felt a need to break eye contact, to bow her head as is expected when addressing royalty or a spiritual leader.

'Aggie? Aggie, you here?'

Wilson was calling from the other side of the house, by his joyous tone he had secured dinner. Agnes found herself unable to use her voice in reply.

The doe dipped her head slowly, a long blink with her one remaining eye. One last thankful look, and she and her brood about turned and glided gracefully to be lost amongst the greenery.

Wilson plodded around the corner of the cabin, a huge rabbit swinging from a length of rope. His salt and pepper beard doing little to hide his ecstatic grin. 'Everything alright?' he queried, his smile changing to a face of concern brought on by the sight of the woman he loved standing rigid with soiled linen at her feet. He hoped she wasn't in the middle of one of her '*moments*'. She had that glassy look in her eyes, the one where she seemed to be lost in a mind fog: the one that kept him up at night.

Then surfacing...

'That's it, Aggie, come back to me.'

She blinked several times in quick succession; she smiled as if noticing his presence for the first time. 'Wilson...the deer...'

'Aggie, are you alright?'

Agnes grabbed the fallen linen and crammed it into the washing basket. She laughed heartedly at Wilson's worried look, how soft and child-like it made his face appear. 'I'm fine, you worry too much!' she said playfully, bumping her hip against his. 'Come inside and I'll catch you up on the amazing scene you just missed.'

...

It was several months before the family of deer were seen again and even longer the next time. The time after that only the two siblings showed. Wilson tried to assure Agnes that the mother was okay, but they both knew that time and fate had finally caught up with the old girl. Agnes hoped she had gone painlessly in her sleep.

Eventually, the younglings stopped visiting the cabin grounds all together, likely having joined one of the roaming herds that speckled the mountain sides. Agnes never forgot them, or the comfort they had provided when she had needed it the most.

CHAPTER 15

'I remember…' Agnes said in a faint whisper. 'I remember her, she had been beautiful but some cruel monster had stolen her beauty away…Her face…'

Wilson coughed and finished the sentence that she could not. 'Her face looked an awful lot like mine does now.' Agnes stared at her fingers, unaware that she was picking at the hacks and cuticles. Wilson, careful to keep his head in the shadows, reached a hand out and placed it gently on her thigh after motioning her to come sit by him. 'Aggie, I need to tell you something, something I suspect you already know.' She would not look into the dark to meet his eyes. 'It's your brain, Agnes. Something in there.' He tapped his papery temple, it sounded hollow and soft. 'Something just ain't right. You're slowing down, losing your edge - forgetting things. You keep drifting away in your mind.'

Even though his heart had stopped beating years ago, he still felt a pang of pain at the sight of her in tears. She sniffed and dabbed her nose with a tissue and blotted her eyes and cheeks.

'I know,' she sobbed. 'I've known for a long time. But when you… left, I couldn't control it. It got worse. With you around I had something to focus on; you helped me keep it in check. Now I can't even keep tabs on what day of the week it is. When you went away time became insignificant.'

Her chest felt tight as her words escaped in short breaths over her quivering lips. It should have been cathartic to finally have it out in the open; instead Agnes felt nothing but shame and guilt. This '*condition*', this burden she carried, weighed on her as if she had conjured it upon herself.

'I'm still here, Agnes,' Wilson said. 'I might not look the same but, like your deer, I am still me, no matter what I look like on the outside.' He squeezed her leg; the strength in his fingers was weak. 'If my being here was what kept you functioning then you need to know, I'm still with you, always. I'm still here.'

A generous, but necessary, glass of brandy later, Wilson prepared himself to give Agnes yet more unpleasant news. The alcohol stung her tattered lips, he got the impression she didn't wipe her mouth because she was savoring the pain, at least she knew the sensation was *real*. He tried to clear his throat but only managed to dislodge some unseen rot which resulted in an arduous coughing fit. Agnes slipped quietly out of the room, unable to stand by and watch the unpalatable spectacle. She returned when he had composed himself and handed him a glass of water which he accepted graciously.

'This *Thing*,' he started, 'is getting stronger. It isn't mindless like it was. I think when it broke through from wherever the hell it came from it began *evolving*. Before it was more of an entity, like a dark cloud, a sinister vapor, aye that's it, its powers were limited to disrupting its surroundings, spreading unease, casting a foreboding shadow over the mountain.' He paused to gulp a mouthful of the water, aware some it was escaping through the hole in his cheek. 'When it started killing the animals I should have realized how it was changing, not just physically but objectively, it seems to have found a purpose, a motive.' Agnes listened attentively, her chewed fingernails cutting little crescent moons into her palms. 'This mountain, the forest around it, it's special, Aggie, always has been. You remember the stories we heard growing up?' Agnes shook her head.

'I can't remember them. I know there were legends though, every kid knew at least a couple from sleepovers and camp.'

'I believe those stories, every one of them,' he said, stifling a tickle in his throat, 'because whatever ancient magic allowed this thing to come here is the same magic governing my visits.'

Agnes creased her forehead into a frown. Wilson cut her off before she could protest.

'Aggie, think about it. I died - I'm dead. I shouldn't be here. Hell, I should be out there,' a withered arm swept out of his shadow and pointed to the window, 'in my plot, fertilizing the soil and feeding the worms. Maybe some part of me still is, I don't know.' He calmed himself before he got her upset again. 'It's no accident that I'm back,' he said solemnly. 'Nature requires balance, maybe that's why I've been granted these moments with you. To give you some insight, prepare you, give you a fighting chance.'

She slumped, burying her head in her hands, knitting her silver hair between her fingers. 'But I told you, I want no part of it. I don't want to fight it. I just want to be left alone!'

Wilson's response was not forthcoming so she pushed him. 'Why won't you speak?'

He spoke; softly yet fastidiously, 'I don't think you have a choice.'

CHAPTER 16

A gnes sat on her bed. Motivation was steadily coming back to her. She had already cleaned up the kitchen and tidied some of the clutter in the living room. After Wilson had said his piece (and delivered to her a mission that filled her full of dread) she had felt the darkness consume her like a deep sleep; only this time it had happened quickly, urgently.

Agnes believed that the power that maintained Wilson during his appearances was depleting. Pretty soon it would become exhausted.

During cleaning up the bedroom she had come across Wilson's bug-out bag, most of his essentials were still present, tucked away in their individual compartments.

How Wilson came by his information she did not know, if he tried to explain it to her she doubted she would be able to comprehend the logistics. The two worlds they occupied were separated by a void of scientific understanding and a wall of mysticism.

Reluctantly, he had informed her about a group of hikers making their way along one of the abandoned trails in the Logan's Pass region. Judging by their route they were looking to make camp at a ruined settlement, a collection of run-down log buildings that didn't appear on any map.

Decades ago Wilson had stumbled upon the site by accident. He had poked around in the moldering ruins for a half hour before getting spooked and high-tailing it out of the forsaken hamlet. When he had arrived home he had told Agnes all about the forgotten dwelling; the artefacts left behind by the original occupants, the strange and unnerving sounds that echoed in the dark and ominous water well at the center of town.

Wilson was not a superstitious man, nor was he easily scared, but that night he sat in his chair with a bottle of whiskey and his rifle in his lap; eyes fixed on the moonlit branches dancing outside the cabin. He never went back to that neck of the woods, but every now and then, when his mood would become solemn and uncharacteristically quiet, Agnes knew his mind was back amongst the dying trees and rotten timber. *'I don't know, Aggie. That place just ain't right. Bad vibes all over. The air, it sort of sticks to you, you know?'*

Agnes didn't know, but she suspected she would find out soon enough. As she prepped the bag she replayed Wilson's request over and over in her head.

'You've got to warn them, Aggie. Tell them; tell them what they are up against. You've got to save them.'

...

After stopping briefly in the kitchen to grab some provisions (and the freshly assembled rifle), Agnes wrapped herself in her hide garb and fur-lined boots. She stood with her forehead pressed against the door and asked whatever higher power was listening for the strength to accomplish the dubious task ahead. With a steely, determined glint in her pale eyes she pulled the door open and took the first step on a journey she was already regretting.

The wolf was asleep. Better that way. Agnes resisted the urge to seek comfort in its thick fur; instead she quietly stepped past with only a quick look back over her shoulder.

'See you soon...' she hoped.

She headed in the direction of the Pass, glad that Wilson had mapped out as much of the mountain range as he could over the years. The map was drawn roughly, but if it was anywhere near accurate she estimated she could be at the settlement within a couple of hours.

Wilson had insisted she take the one-man tent with her, but she had zero intention of being out after dark - never mind spending the night.

...

An hour into her trek and a quick look at her map made her aware she was now in unknown territory, with each step she was breaking ground on a trail that had alluded her all her life. The excitement and uncertainty boosted her adrenaline and she felt energized in a way she had not experienced since the early days when they had not yet thought of the forest as home. The crisp mountain air filled her lungs, cleared them of the clogging misery that had settled in like dust since Wilson's death.

The trail itself was treacherous. Jagged rocks jutted out from beneath the snowdrifts as evidence of the frequent landslides. Long furrows cut grooves into the dirt where once wagons would have risked the difficult passage in a bid to cut days or even weeks off their journeys.

Agnes started to remember stories from when she was a little girl about highwaymen and cannibals residing in the area. Looking at her surroundings it was easy to see why. To the right flowed a slow-moving stream, frozen solid in some parts, beyond it the cliff wall rose almost vertically and was dotted with small caves and rocky protuberances that would have provided ample shelter or hiding spots for those with sinister intentions. On her left young juniper bushes blocked any access to an already dense and unwelcoming grove of Douglas firs and Blue spruces. Back when civilization was not so civilized, this path would have been ideal for an ambush. Agnes cast a nervous glance towards the top of the ridge, half expecting to see some Indian braves lining its crest, sharp spears pointed skyward.

Whether it was a result of her over-worked imagination or the change in altitude, she suddenly felt dizzy and somewhat sick. Her vision became speckled with dark spots and her legs felt weak.

She spied a flat topped boulder that looked to have rolled from high up on the cliff and settled on the trailside recently. From her shoulders she unslung the rucksack and placed it on the rock. Steading herself using the huge stone, she raided the bag for some nuts and strips of cured meat. She savored the salty taste and took a moment to recover.

The nausea past.

Refueled, she allowed herself a few minutes rest and thought about the hikers she was (hopefully) pursuing. It was easy to see the appeal of their expedition, thrill-seekers often sought out adventure in the sprawling woodland and hillsides of this vast landscape; but not normally at this time of year. It would not be the first time she had looked to the skies as the distant sound of a helicopter searched for missing campers. She crossed her fingers and hoped they were experienced backpackers.

If Wilson's map was correct then the trail would curve to the right up ahead and take her between two sheer rock faces. Agnes, who held a strong aversion towards small or enclosed spaces, grimaced at the thin line on the make-shift map. There was no other way around.

She slid off the boulder and threw the rucksack over her shoulder. The air was very still in the Pass and although she could still see vibrant sunlight reflecting off the snow-capped peaks above, none made it down into the rocky gorge. This was very disconcerting as it made Agnes feel as though she were standing behind a veil, looking at the world beyond the crevasse from the other side of a mirror, a side forever in shadow and gloom.

A wispy, low-lying haze was settling into the gully, seeking out the deepest parts and forming strange pools of fog that further accentuated the unnatural and alien allusion of the region. Agnes, although grateful for the respite in snow storms, found the developing mist vexatious, if it continued to roll in at the rate it was currently moving at she could easy become turned about. The very thought of being lost in the unknown sent shivers down the length of her spine.

Far up above, against a blue and gold backdrop, were the faint shimmers of birds on the wing. They were too high up to identify but Agnes thought they could be eagles; the way they circled in rings put vultures to mind.

'Just you keep your distance. You ain't picking at these bones yet, you feathered bastards,' she thought.

Wilson had called it. The crumbling path did indeed turn right, and quite sharply too. She stood disheartened at the entrance to a vision from her nightmares. It seemed at some point in its immense history this particular mountain had split in two. The two rock walls formed a narrow 'V' where the earth had torn itself apart.

CHAPTER 17

The trail ran like scar tissue along the base of the 'V' until it disappeared behind a turn up ahead. Because of this slight bend, Agnes could not tell how long the chasm ran for, or how long she would be trapped inside it.

She knew the longer she procrastinated about crossing the threshold the more time was wasted; time she didn't have. She bit down, cursed loudly, and entered the corridor of rugged stone.

Her only saving grace was the lack of snow underfoot, because of the depth and narrow width of the fissure, the wind had blown the flakes across rather than down into it. Looking up at the sliver of sky above made Agnes feel off-balance, she felt as though she were sinking down and down, deeper into the earth's crust, away from the light. Trickles of run-off water found their way amongst the grooves and ledges, cutting thin veins through the rocky surfaces. Disorientated, with a cyclone in her head and eyes unable to remain focused, Agnes thought the walls of the canyon beat with the cardiac rhythm of a living being.

She strode on past solitary bushes and withered trees that clung to their residencies by desperate and exposed roots. When she finally came to the bend in the path she was dismayed to find another similar bend lay ahead. So much had she willed to see daylight and sanctuary before her that she felt betrayed; as if she had been lured by the promise of salvation, then left abandoned in a labyrinth of towering walls.

Panic rose in her chest, the air, there wasn't enough air!

She lost her footing and went down hard. Instinctively, she threw her injured arm behind her to save it from the inevitable collision with the compacted ice and stone. Looking to see what had caught her foot she saw the groove of a wagon track. People had come this way with horses and all their possessions?

'*Madness,*' she thought.

She picked herself up and forced herself to keep moving, to stop now would certainly bring about the end of her.

The world was spinning; no more could she differentiate between up and down, left and right. Her calves burned as she ran, pounding the ground with every step. A sound caught her attention for a moment, then passed when she realized it was her own beating heart thumping between her ears. Her mind in its state of delirium conjured beasts from the dark cracks that ran throughout the chasm walls. Through the distortion of tears, from the corner of her eyes, she saw them scurrying like spiders, all clamoring behind her forming a mass of teeth and claws.

Just when she could sense their foul breath warming the nape of her neck, just when her mind was ready to admit that all hope was gone and shut down as a defensive measurement; fate cast a lifeline.

A narrow column of blinding light split the gorge like a lightning bolt thrown down by some enraged, forgotten god. Agnes heaved in hysterical laughter; an exit was within her reach. She erupted from the belly of the mountain into an ocean of heavenly light. Even through the skin of her eyelids it was dazzling and radiant. If she had not collapsed in exhaustion she believed she could have swam in the golden rays as though treading water. She lay basking in the sweet relief until the fire in her lungs calmed from an inferno to a burning ember, then sat up to see whereabouts she had emerged.

Agnes was somewhat taken aback by the new location, gone were the tall pines and clear water springs of the valley she had spent the majority of her life in, instead she found herself surrounded by a much older and gnarled woodland situated in a boggy swamp.

Most of the trees were bare and twisted into hideously contorted sculptures, their thick branches knotted and intertwined like a tribute to the Gorgons of ancient Greece. From their warped trunks sprouted creeping limbs that stretched horizontally like blind and desperate feelers. From her elevated position she could see that the marshy forest was completely enclosed by the surrounding mountain range, cut off from the rest of the world by a cage of stone and ice.

To brave the inhospitable peaks and treacherous weather systems only to come across such an unwelcoming place didn't strike Agnes as a fair reward, this should have been Shangri-La, not a putrescent quagmire.

Beside her ran a crumbling, make-shift dyke wall, likely fashioned from fallen rocks and boulders by some long forgotten trailblazer trying to make this path more homely. If this was the unknown builder's objective then he had failed. Agnes scoffed at it dismissively and was about to move on when something glistening amongst the stones caught her eye. A plastic bottle had been forced into a gap between the rocks in a half-assed attempt at what Wilson called '*tidy littering*'. Without thinking, Agnes pulled it out and shoved it into her backpack. The bottle looked new; she was closing in on the hikers.

The snow had not fallen as heavily here but she could still make out fresh footprints leading down the path into the eerie forest. Agnes followed and thought about what she was going to say to the first humans she was going to encounter in a very long time.

CHAPTER 18

The path wove through the abominable trees like a prehistoric snake, many times Agnes found herself coiling back on a previous section and the temptation to attempt a short cut would become overwhelming; a quick glance at the surrounding mire put those thoughts out of mind.

Evidently, Agnes was not the only one to be enticed by the promise of a shorter route, bleached bones stuck out of the boggy ground, the remains of a goat lay partially submerged; a single eye stared lifelessly at her as she passed.

'Don't be like me...Ignore the siren's song...'

Every inch of the forest seemed to be covered in thick, ropey lichen that interlaced between the trees and bound them together in strangling braids. Even though the trees had no foliage of their own, the mass of lichen and the severe spread of their long, winding limbs created a canopy that was dense enough to block out the majority of the daylight. Agnes absolutely despised this place and cursed Wilson for not warning her just how vile this excursion would be.

Strange animal noises occasionally broke the unsettling silence, each time some unseen mystery creature blurted out an obscene call Agnes flinched and braced herself for an attack. The primeval labyrinth seemed to go on forever, more than once Agnes felt terror rise in her when she thought an area looked familiar: if she was moving in circles then she was already doomed.

Her ray of hope appeared in the dismal form of an ancient wagon cart. Although the marsh had claimed it long ago, its pitiful appearance was the first sign of humanity she had glimpsed since crossing the threshold of the loathsome forest. Not that the sight of its rotting, decrepit husk, its wooden spars jutting from the filth like an exposed ribcage, gave her much to rejoice about. If anything it was just another exhibition of how unwelcome mankind was in this corner of the wild.

A short trek further along the path and Agnes found herself standing in a small clearing. Through the breach in the treetops she could see she was close to the other side of the strange flat-floored valley. A snow-capped peak composed most of the scene, its steep walls, purple and unforgiving tried to hide the dark clouds rolling behind it. At its base, where it disappeared into the woods, Agnes could make out what looked to be a handful of shadowy buildings obscured by the trees: the ruined settlement lay yonder. Her terrifying incident in the narrow canyon must have been in the area known as Logan's Pass. She was nearing her objective.

...

Grudgingly, Agnes adjusted the rifle strap and trudged on. As soon as she was back under the gnarled canopy she felt a cloying weight on her chest, as though the clearing were an air hole, and she was trapped under a body of ice with no inclination as to when she would catch her next breath.

She rounded a bend and came to a fork in the road. The trail weaving off to her left looked to have come straight out of an Irving novel, complete with a lowly mist and the ominous silhouettes of crows perching on the sinuous branches. She checked the ground for boot prints but her rheumy eyes lacked the required sharpness, and her tracking skills had never been on the same par as Wilson's. She chose the path on her right, based purely on the principal that it was the one that she would have opted for, had she been a member of the hiking party. This passage was wider, more likely to lead to the encampment. Agnes could not help but steal a glance over her shoulder, thankful no headless horseman was creeping up behind her.

A wave of anxiety washed over her when she pulled out Wilson's pocket watch. Both hands pointed to twelve. She hadn't checked to see if it was still running before she left and was far from home with only a dead clock to tell the time. Flustered *(and bordering on hysterical),* she began emptying the contents of the backpack onto the dirt, maybe Wilson carried a spare battery or a second timepiece? A small brass object bounced and started to roll away from her, greedily she snatched it up; certain she had found what she sought. Her face fell in dismay. It was only Wilson's compass. Upon opening its face, she discovered the needle spinning randomly on its pin. Agnes was not naïve enough to put the two separate devices malfunctioning down to mere coincidence.

Through the twisted canopy Agnes could see she was nearing the mountain range. She was confident she had chosen the correct path. As if to clarify her thoughts, she began to detect a new scent in the air, something rather appealing compared to the stagnant odor of the bog; a campfire. With each step she took forward the smell of charred wood and smoke grew stronger. The fragrance conjured images of warmth and safety in her mind. Maybe even the possibility of hot food. Her stomach grumbled at the prospect.

Her trepidation of encountering 'others' still held a strong stranglehold around her throat, but the potentiality of resting beside a fire outweighed her anxiety. Besides, why else had she come this far? Safety in numbers was also a factor she had not neglected to consider. Agnes unwittingly picked up the pace, the promise of sanctuary providing her muscles with the adrenaline needed for one last big push.

Soon enough, the disheveled remains of a long forgotten settlement spread out before her. A crumbly, stone bridge over a particularly putrid and deep portion of the swampland separated her from its unreceptive, shadowy structures. Agnes had hoped the town would be a step towards amicable in comparison with the hellish terrain she had just ventured through. It was not.

Maybe it was the vertical mountainside that fortified the opposite end of the village, maybe it was the sinister impression the gloomy and decaying buildings emanated, either way, it was darker here and not just in terms of 'light'.

Agnes counted six structures in total, two of which were little more than piles of moldy wood. The largest building sat to her right, it appeared to be the town hall or church, it sat at an angle, its back end sinking into the swamp. From its crooked spire protruded a long iron spike with a peculiar crescent shape depicted where a cross would normally have been. Window slats covered a little room where a bell was once likely housed. The other buildings looked to have been used as houses for the residents of the pitiful village. Agnes tried to picture how the scene would have looked in its prime, fresh and clean, bustling with frontiersmen. Even on a beautiful, sunny day Agnes thought the location would have projected a foreboding and even hostile aura on any traveler unfortunate enough to have wandered in from the swamp. Why anyone would migrate to such an unpleasant place and decide to call it home was beyond her understanding.

A stone well sat in the town square. Agnes was unaware that she was steadily navigating towards it while studying the surrounding attractions. An object, hidden from her line of sight by the well's circular wall, slowly came in to view. She rounded the stone barrier and set eyes on two nylon tents. Their vibrant neon colors stood out in defiant contrast to the bleakness of the dying forest and long dead town. A small campfire was situated in front of them; it had been left unattended and was burning out, its weak flames only producing a faint orange halo on the dirt around it. Agnes sighed in relief; she had caught up with the hiking party.

CHAPTER 19

A ny apprehension she had about the company of strangers had flown south; she found she craved companionship; to look upon the face of another living being would make her ecstatic.

'Hello, hello in there..?' she called, unable to mask the urgency in her voice. 'Can you hear me? I didn't mean to wake you if you were asleep. I'm afraid I have no idea what time it is. My name is Agnes, I've come to find you because…because…'

The tents remained still and lifeless. Something was wrong. Agnes slowly approached the camp, her face tensed into a hard grimace. One of the tents - the closest to the forest's edge - was semi-collapsed. Several of the guy ropes had either been cut or wrenched from the ground. A tent pole that ran through the fly sheet to support the apex had snapped and the frame had folded in on itself.

Down the length of one side was a jagged tear where the tent had been torn open. Various items scattered the earth leading away from the tent, debris from whatever chaotic event had occurred here. The tents door was still zippered half shut. Whoever had been inside must've been in an awful hurry. Agnes felt a heavy leaden weight swell in her stomach when she spotted the dark crimson stain that led to the town hall's main doors.

The other tents occupants may have had more luck, judging by the flap that billowed gently in the soft breeze, they had heard the attack and sped off. Agnes checked the sodden mush of slush and soil for tracks and, sure enough, there were two sets of prints that left the tent before taking off in separate directions. She was too late.

A noise, wet and sloshy, rang out to her left and she lost a little control over her bladder. Agnes turned to the source and was embarrassed and relieved to see it was just a chunk of loose snowfall sliding from the eaves of one of the residences. If she was to survive this situation she was going to have to be in complete control and of stable mind.

Instead of over-analyzing her predicament, Agnes let the primitive part of her brain guide her in her next move. She had two choices – the first option was to investigate the town hall, the sight of the carnage that led to the building immediately put her off; anything would be better than going in there. Her other option was to try and follow the tracks left by those who fled and hope that they had better luck than whoever had painted the ground red.

The two sets of foot prints were notably different than each other. One pair were made from large clunky hiking boots with a wide stride, their placing looked panicked, as though the wearer was unsure of his route. The other, smaller pair, headed directly towards one of the neighboring residences. Agnes, although not certain, thought they looked to be made from a woman's footwear.

If the woman had made it into the shack there was a chance she had found somewhere to hide, the other runner might need her help more. She ran her eyes over the scattered prints, found the pattern, and followed them into the swampy undergrowth.

...

Agnes grunted as thorny branches and gnarled, exposed roots

clawed at her. Whoever had fled this way had done so in a desperate blind charge. Rough-cut stones occasionally broke through the thick mud but whatever path had once existed here had long been repossessed by the quagmire. Agnes took her time, careful to remember every twist and turn. There would be no point rescuing the poor soul if she couldn't find her way back. The meandering path had already taken her out of sight of the forsaken settlement and, although she didn't want to return, it sure beat dying in this hideous bog.

Some smaller twigs and branches had been broken; the runner had done whatever was necessary to distance himself from the attack zone. Agnes spied droplets of blood on a splintered branch. What could make a man flee in such absolute terror?

The ground fell away from below her. She screamed as her legs disappeared, swallowed by the marsh. She had miss-stepped, distracted by the fresh blood. The sludge came up to her thighs and still she was sinking. Every terror-stricken moment caused her to drop further into jeopardy. She saw it happen as though she floated above, a witness to her own demise. She would be lost. Forgotten; submerged and consumed by the swamp and the creatures it housed.

CHAPTER 20

'**N**o.' The thought came to her with clarity.
'No, not now. Not like this.'

She thought of Wilson and the knowledge he had imparted on her over the decades of wild living. Hell, she had lived with him. The knowledge was her truth as well. She was a survivor. She had out-lived Wilson, for god-sake, if anything she was THE survivor!

Agnes stopped panicking. Slowed her breathing.

Wait.

Wait.

Think…

In predicaments like this, one of two things got you killed – fear, or irrationality. A level head could pull her through, she just needed to remain calm and verify her situation.

Think…

She spread her weight. Her chest went under but that was alright, just by doing this she felt the drag on her feet loosen slightly. She was somewhat dismayed to see no branches or vines close enough to provide leverage but the peat had a thick crust and was littered with debris. She clawed at it. As wild as any beast that roamed the harsh mountains. She fought tooth and nail until she could feel herself pulling against the dense grip of mud, then she pulled some more.

A primal holler formed in her compressed lungs and when it hit her throat it broke through her gritted teeth as a deep and ferocious growl. She used every ounce of energy her muscles could give. She tore at the clumps of sod, tearing them from the ground by the fistful. Her hand brushed a tree root and it was over. She pulled herself out of the mire and was free. Lying on the bank she began to sob as a rush of too many emotions overwhelmed her.

To Agnes surprise, the person she was tracking had not succumbed to the same pit fall she had. A set of prints ran precariously along the rim of the boggy bank. 'Lucky sod,' Agnes thought as she wiped vile smelling crud from her legs. With added caution, she picked up the trail and resumed the chase, treading much more carefully now.

Deeper and deeper she went into a part of the swamp where no man should have a reason to go. The plant life here was denser; the trees wound together like ropey, sinewy muscles. The weave of their limbs created a blanket that blocked out what little day light still remained. The absence of light and warmth here made everything appear hostile. The trail came to an abrupt halt. A wide expanse of shiny water lay ahead. Lily pads rested upon it while cattails grew around its edges. Agnes could see that the opposite bank was lined with a thick, impenetrable briar patch.

Staring at her from the center of the stagnant water, submerged from just below the cheekbones, was the upper part of a man's head.

Too overcome with shock at the grotesque and frightful image to scream, Agnes threw up her hands to shield her sight. The pallor of the bald head was a sickly albino white against the stark blackness of the stale water. His eyes, inky dark pits – the whites of which were pink with exposure, were wide, as though locked in an expression of surprise. They seemed to stare right at her and yet, at the same time, through her.

Agnes slumped wearily. The poor man must have ploughed headlong into the murky cesspit and became tangled in the vines and roots hidden below the surface. Agnes could vividly imagine the terror he must have felt; isolated on all sides from a shore far beyond reach, the irrepressible struggle as unknown forces pulled and constricted. The desperation as his lungs expelled what would have been his last breath.

The longer Agnes looked the more she thought there was a sadness to the man's gaze; his eyes seemed to plead to her for answers to why he had to die, and why like this?

'It's not fair... It's not fair...'

She was too late. Again. Something that was becoming an unwelcome habit. The runner's luck had run out and Agnes couldn't help but feel partly responsible. If she wasn't so damn hesitant, if she wasn't so weak and old!

Alas.

There was nothing she could do for him now. If the cards that fell permitted her to survive this debacle she would do everything in her power to alert the authorities. She felt sure she could point out a search area on a map but one thing was for certain, she would not join them in the search. She would not, could not, return to this horrible place.

Readjusting her pack and rifle, Agnes tipped her head to show her respects to the dead man and turned to try and find her way back to the abandoned village. Two steps in and she stopped. From behind her, from the center of the slop, a faint gurgling sound was rising. The sinister circumstances made her resistant to turn and face the noise. Besides, it was probably just swamp gas disturbed by the intrusion of the foreign body occupying its space.

The sound escalated as air bubbles rose in rapid succession from below. Agnes slowly pivoted on her heels. The man's cold, black eyes still held her in their vacant, yet accusing, gaze. She watched with horrified fascination as swamp juice bubbles formed and popped in front of his face. The man's head rose and started to lean back until the lower half was exposed. Muck and slime ran down his cheeks and dripped from his chin. Slowly, his mouth began to open. It looked as if he were about to scream.

'Good Lord,' Agnes thought, her feet felt rooted to the spot. *'He's still alive!'*

The mouth opened fully - and then to her horror - continued to open. The skin pulled taut and started to split at the commissures. The tearing of the flesh forced any other sounds of the swamp into the background. Agnes could do nothing to block out the hideous display. Against her will, her eyes and ears were already storing the details to memory, no doubt to wake her up in the small hours with exquisite nightmares.

The pageantry stooped to even lower dark levels when the man's head shook unnaturally and the snout of a fat, black swamp rat emerged from his torn orifice. Agnes vomited. The rat dropped into the water with a plop and skittered along the bog's surface, up the bank and into the briar. When the man's head rolled back even further to reveal a mess of gore at the end of its neck where a body should have connected, Agnes vomited again.

Black water pooled into the decimated mouth and filled the sockets of the still-open eyes. The severed head sunk into the obsidian darkness and Agnes prayed that such a violent death had at least been a quick one. She traced her steps back to the settlement; a shiver ran through her that was not to be solely blamed on the cold.

CHAPTER 21

Agnes sat on her haunches between the two tents, her back pressed against the cold, slimy stone of the village well. If danger still lingered in the area then there was a small chance she would be hidden from it. The swamp gases were making her nauseous; they seemed to drift in yellow/green clouds no more than a foot above the putrid ground. Dizzy spells continuously rolled over her like little drunken waves.

She had already made the mistake of going into a situation blindly, before she moved again she intended to gather the facts. Facts, she believed lay strewn in the campers' belongings in and around the tents.

Using the barrel of her rifle, she cautiously pushed back the entrance flap to the tent with the least damage; the gun swung left, right, left as she fully expected something to be lurking within. Two sleeping bags lay side by side, the tops open, evidence of a hasty exit. Down one side was the usual camping gear; flashlights, a portable stove, two water bottles. Only one backpack remained present meaning one of the runners was likely to have the other in their possession. Agnes crossed her fingers it wasn't the one at the bottom of the swamp.

The rucksack she had available didn't shine much light on the reason the hikers had traipsed out into the inhospitable wildlands. Amongst the expected camping bric-a-brac of clothes, tarps, and first aid supplies were various electronic items Agnes was unfamiliar with. She picked up something that resembled a cassette player (Wilson had traded some furs in town for one when they had first come out. He had played with it constantly for months listening to the same three tapes over and over. Agnes personally preferred the record player, in her opinion it just sounded better). She pressed the rewind button and the machine '*whirred*'. She hit play and listened, a man's voice was mid-sentence:

'*...missing from records, but evidence suggests a search party was sent out from Fort Condor. McCarthy and his group were not the only ones to disappear in the area. Documentation is sketchy but we have reason to believe many prospectors and fur traders were also among the missing. Simon even found some papers that claimed an entire cavalry unit vanished up here when they tried to take a shortcut to Fort Eustace...*'

A papery rustling sound muffled what the man was saying for a moment. Agnes could hear an excited exchange between the man and someone further away. In the background a woman cheered. The man must have been making the recording whilst on the move.

'*Alright, so Tony has just informed me that he thinks he has found Logan's Pass, if he is right then we should be at our base camp in less than an hour.*'

A yelp followed by laughter.

'*Hahaha... you alright, Michelle?*' asked the man on the recorder.

The woman grunted, '*Screw you, Gavin. I nearly twisted my ankle... Look at my ass, it's covered in muck.*'

'*Here, let me wipe it for you,*' said the laughing man. The tape cut off as the woman apparently started whaling on him playfully.

Agnes left the tape quietly rolling to see if the man had recorded anything else. The small tent cackled with static as Agnes searched through the rest of the bag. She found some potato chips and a jar of peanut butter tucked away at the bottom which she began feasting on greedily. When the man's voice spoke again Agnes nearly choked, so lost in her feeding frenzy was she, she had all but forgotten about the cassette.

'*Ok, ok,*' said the man, the one called Gavin, sounding flustered. '*So we've made it through Logan's Pass. Didn't expect this… Simon, hey Simon! Can you climb up those rocks and get some footage of this fucked up forest?*'

'*Yeah, Gav. I'm on it!*'

'*Alright, ok… so Simon's gone up the slope to get some shots of this… this weird forest. We came out the Pass intending to set up camp for the night, but when we saw this strange woodland sprawling in every direction…*'

'*Gavin, come over here and look at this!*' Agnes didn't recognize the shouter but assumed it was the one called Tony. Gavin must have left the diction machine running as it picked up his heavy breathing as he ran.

'*What is it, Tony?*'

'*Sign of civilization. It's a wall. Looks real old too.*'

'*Well, it would make sense. I haven't found any information that indicated any other group trying to establish a colony out here. I'm sure this means that not only are we on the right track, but probably close to finding the town too.*'

When the woman spoke, Agnes detected a significant pitch-change in her voice.

'*No Gavin. Nuh-uh. We all agreed we camp here. The village, if it is even here, has stood for hundreds of years, it will still be there in the morning.*'

'*Michelle…*'

'*I don't want to hear it, Gavin! You did the same thing down in Westford and look how that ended!*'

There was an uncomfortable silence, Agnes felt as though she were eavesdropping. From the sounds of it the group had been on previous adventures and, although they quarreled, were well acquainted and tight-knit.

'Tony,' muttered Gavin. 'You're our resident wild man, what do you say?'

Tony spoke in a gruff voice and seemed to be a man of few words. 'You see that ridge? That'll be the sites location. I guarantee it. We move now, keep our speed up, be there well before dark.'

Michelle sounded pissed. 'Tony, it's a fucking swamp. Look at it. We have no idea what to expect in there!'

Gavin tried to calm her with reason. 'Alright, settle down. Look, we will put it to a vote; we will... what are you doing?'

'Getting my gear. We better get moving.'

'But I said we...'

'Oh, fuck off, Gavin. We all know Simon does whatever you tell him too.'

The tape returned to static. Agnes let it run while she checked the other tent. There was a form of comfort to be found in the disembodied chatter. The contents of the second tent had not fared as well the first. Whatever had occurred inside had devastated the hikers' equipment, leaving what Agnes believed to be cameras and audio gear in fragments of broken plastic.

Notes and photographs littered the canvas groundsheet like a mosaic depicting their journey. Agnes picked up a photo that showed the group posing in front of a van. They all wore smiles as well as their camping equipment; those smiles would be long gone now. Their leader, Gavin had his arm affectionately thrown over the shoulders of the pretty, young girl, Michelle. Their relationship may have been more than a professional one. He had his hair cropped very short and dark eyes, if Agnes only memory of him was not of terror and repulsion, she would have called him handsome. She shuddered at the thought of those eyes staring at her from just above the swamp's surface.

There were other pictures that showed the same group in various different locations and terrains. Many of the documents were of faded black and white photographs or photocopies of handwritten letters and diary pages. All the clues led Agnes to believe they were researchers or a documentary crew. They had come looking for a story, following a trail that history had tried to hide. Now they were part of that story.

CHAPTER 22

There was little left to salvage from the remains of the second tent, even in mint condition Agnes would have struggled to figure out the individual purposes of the electrical devices. She did, however, pick up a head torch that she found tucked away at the toe of a hiking boot.

A full moon sat fat and heavy overhead. The stars speckled the dark sky in their thousands. Night had crept in while she had been occupied under a thin layer of canvas. Agnes removed her wool hat and ran her fingers through her hair. Shit. The one damn scenario she had wanted to avoid was being out after dark.

Shit.

Moon-glow illuminated the village in a pale, milky sheen. The brilliant highlights did nothing to warm the settlements appearance, if anything they deepened the contrast of the shadows giving those that dwell in darkness more places to hide.

Agnes was procrastinating.

She could read every note and document in the tents, study every photo until the information formed enough of a story to provide her a vital clue about her adversary, but there were still three of the four group members unaccounted for. She had to try and find them.

She unshouldered the rifle, strapped on the head torch (which blinked several times before lighting the way) and pocketed the diction machine. The girl had run off to a log building that appeared to be in reasonable condition compared to those that lay in ruins around it. Agnes followed her tracks.

As the cabin drew closer, so did the stench of vegetation. The door had all but decomposed from over a century of neglect, the few remaining boards hung pointlessly from a single corroded hinge. Agnes let the gun barrel lead the way inside. The light shining from her forehead showed decade's worth of leaf litter piled up in the corners of the musty room that had been carried in on the winds. That, at least, explained the smell.

The room appeared to be the main living quarters and was far bigger than she had expected. Silken threads of cobwebs covered everything from the eaves to the floorboards. A dining table and chairs, fragile from the termites and woodlouse that feasted upon it, sat pressed up against the far wall. A cabinet, that had once possibly been considered a prize possession, lined the interior wall to her left, a mirror rendered useless by time and grime hung over it. Opposite the mirror was a large brick fireplace, not dissimilar to the one in her own home. Various artefacts decorated the walls; faded pictures in rotten frames, strange iron tools rusted beyond repair, rags caked in mildew and funk that the pioneers would have worn.

Agnes gingerly crossed the room, sweeping the torch over every shadowy nook, the floorboards felt soft and precarious under foot. The temptation to call out was great, but something in the pit of her stomach warned her to resist announcing her whereabouts.

The next room was much smaller, probably a washroom or used as storage. Heaps of pigeon excrement buried any clues to the actual function of the space. Arcing to her left and left again, she found the construction of the building to be in a 'U' shape. The last room lay behind a hardwood door that was in remarkable condition considering how long it had been in existence. A steel ring acted as a handle, when Agnes tugged on it the door pulled open with only slight resistance from the rusted hinges. If the girl had made her escape this way then maybe she had loosened the binding?

Beyond the doorway was the bedroom. Two pine bedframes occupied the space along with shards of wood that had once been miscellaneous items of furniture. Agnes had always considered the lifestyle that she and Wilson had led to be one of necessity over frivolousity, but the way these people had lived made her rethink this. They had little in the way of comfort, their possessions sparse. Even in their hay-day, Agnes couldn't imagine getting a decent night's sleep on their hard, unforgiving beds.

Besides the fragments of furnishings, the room was empty. Crouching down low Agnes shone the torch under the bedframes; nothing but inches of dust and spiders fleeing from the light. Where was the girl? The old woman was puzzled. The tracks had definitely led into the cabin, the bedroom door would certainly have put up more of a fight had it not recently been opened. So what was she missing?

She tested the bed closest to her, making sure it would take her weight. Not that her weight amounted to much. Her shins were on fire and her left hip was up to its old tricks. She rubbed it, kneading the muscle to relieve some of the pain. Her body may have been rebelling against her unwanted expedition but her mind seemed to be savoring it, she felt more alert and focused than she had in years.

'Focus then...' she thought. 'Focus and find a solution.'

Using the rifle as a crutch she got back on her feet. She regretted stopping and sitting down, it always made it so much harder to get moving again. Through the house she went, back to the front door to start over and see if she could find any trace of the missing girl.

CHAPTER 23

Her back to the exposed campsite, Agnes nearly died of fright when an owl hooted from somewhere behind. She turned just in time to catch an unseen creature screech in alarm and bolt from a pile of purulent timber to the swampy depths here it disappeared into the murk leaving a trail of collapsing loose planks and chaos.

Her teeth were already chewing on her fingernails before she was aware she was doing so. '*Jesus H. Christ*,' she thought. '*Anymore frights like that and my tickers gonna conk out!*' her teeth chattered as she stood in the chill, icy air. She would have loved to have pulled shut what was left of the door, but she needed to pick up any prints the girl had left, and the sour light of the moon allowed just enough detail on the grime-caked floorboards to be picked out. And deep down she didn't want to close her only exit if '*bad shit*' went down.

Wilson had told her tales of his youth - the years *before* she had come into his life. Wrong crowds, wrong places. She had never pushed him on the subject, not once, but whiskey has a tendency to loosen lips. He was a firm believer, a first-hand testimonial, that if 'bad shit' could happen, then 'bad shit' would happen.

She turned off the head torch and closed her eyes, allowing them to readjust to the ambience and natural lighting of the environment. Behind the veil of her eyelids she listened to the sound of her own breathing, the gentle creak of old timber, it sounded like the groans of a ghost ship on a calm sea.

Breathe in. breathe out.

Calm.

When she opened her eyes, it was like looking at the scene from a fresh perspective. Details became clearer, sharper. Grains of dust and dirt floated aimlessly, unsettled by the intrusion of the living. Warm bodies disrupting a cold crypt.

Not only could Agnes see better, she could also detect the faint aroma of lavender and vanilla, the girls perfume? Crouching down, Agnes studied the dust patterns on the floor. Firstly, she eliminated the marks she believed to have been her own boot prints. With them dismissed, she was able to focus her attention on two indistinct scuff marks that led in a bee-line towards the smaller room.

Other tracks pocked the layers of dust; Agnes reasoned that the group, excited by their find, had explored the ruins before setting up their campsite. The scuff marks looked fresher, and hurried. When Agnes came to the entrance to the small utility room she could see that, in her haste, the female runner had not maneuvered the turn well and careened off the opposing wall. An impact mark scored the grime. She had fled like the devil himself had been snapping at her heels.

Entering the bedroom for a second time, Agnes spotted something that had somehow eluded her on her first walk-through. One of the beds had been moved fairly recently, a long arc cut through the dirt and bird scat at a 45 degree angle. The bed had concealed a secret for well over a century; a trapdoor had been cut into the floorboards: There was a cellar.

Agnes knelt beside the hatch. Her left knee locked up and knocked her off balance. She shot her hands out behind her to steady herself which resulted in her wrist sending out a fresh jolt of electric pain. She was aware of the constant flow of tears staining her cheeks, not from the physical pain (well, not solely), but the exhaustion - the persistent mental endurance she was being forced to endure repeatedly. Her instincts cried out for her to go, go home and forget the cursed vale beyond Logan's Pass. Every fiber of her being craved sleep. But she felt there was something more at play, something that, given due contemplation, would have the power to shatter her tired mind like glass. Agnes was not convinced she had a choice.

Without delving head first down the rabbit hole, she had the perception to consider the possibility that she was being led, that the darkness that had swept over the valley was playing some drawn-out game with her.

With these thoughts niggling at her subconscious, Agnes slowly clasped her hand around the iron ring attached to the trapdoor. A rickety wooden ladder descended into a pool of infinite shadow. Anxiety coiled like a viper around her chest. Claustrophobia only counted for a fraction of the fears being brought to the forefront of her imagination. The head torch on, she placed her foot on the first rung. Each step felt inevitable.

Down into the cold earth.

Down following the path of fates

CHAPTER 24

So thick was the air with dust, Agnes immediately felt choked. Her lungs burned with the dry residue. She had to stifle the urgent need to cough. The subterranean level below the cabin was dense with the aura of privacy, never, in all her years, had she felt like such an intruder. Her trespass carried the promise of dire consequences.

Tucked away from the surface world, all exterior sounds were blocked by the layers of dirt and sod above, the only noise Agnes could hear was a wet drip resonating from somewhere in the cavernous dark.

She pulled her scarf up high enough to cover her mouth and nose, this created a barrier against the worst of the air-carried particles, but her eyes still stung with the grit. Worse still was the earthy, fungal stench that made her imagine she was inhaling thousands of toxic spores and molds.

The beam of light from the torch was dimming, the batteries running low, what little light the device could muster was swiftly consumed by the Cimmerian shade of the unfathomable cellar. Even without the grey screen of dust filtering the torches weakening radiance, the walls of the basement were still beyond the reach of the light. Agnes had wrongfully assumed that the cellar would not extend out with the cabin's foundations. Instead, she found herself in an area that evoked the sensation of standing in an amphitheater.

A stone wall lay behind the ladder she had dismounted. She paced backwards to it until the cold rock bumped against her coat pelts. Marks on the dirt floor showed the girl had hit the ground running, and taken off straight into the vast darkness. 'Not a chance in hell,' Agnes mumbled, one foot sliding to the other she edged along the wall. This time she would survey the play area and navigate with caution.

Surface water trickled down the slick stones when she reached the corner of the huge room. A dirty green smear of moss draped the smooth rocks like mucus. Scattered over the moist ground were a number of large iron rings, corroded and fragile. Tangled amongst them were some rotten, bowed planks of wood. Barrels used to store provisions no doubt. Closer inspection showed a few remaining husks of grain. Agnes struggled to imagine, despite the evidence present, that the people who had settled here had, even for a short period, thrived in the swampland.

The blue-tinged light from the trapdoor looked further away than Agnes would have liked. Following the corner round, she stuck to the wall like glue - and frequently gazed towards her escape route woefully, as it drifted further and further away. The texture of the walls changed; the stones that had been shaped and smoothed-off became rougher, jumbled. Only a dozen steps later and Agnes noticed that they were no longer rocks slotted into space, but carved out of the bedrock itself. She wasn't in the cellar anymore. She was in a tunnel leading towards the mountain base. She was in the mines.

CHAPTER 25

The opposite wall slowly materialized out of the darkness with each passing step. The shaft must have been cut away from the cellar in a bottle-neck shape. A thin line of silver was all that remained of her exit point. From this distance all she could see was a shimmer as the dust swirled like a mirage. As the tunnel narrowed, her visibility improved. She could see the walls were made up of huge boulders and compacted clay, they stank where the swamp water had seeped down into them. Running down the middle of the shaft were recently plodded footprints.

Back on the trail.

The wide spacing between them showed the girl had not slowed down. Agnes walked parallel with them, careful not to disrupt them in case she needed to back-track. Underfoot, the earth started to slope down at a steady angle. Agnes felt sick at the prospect of straying even further from the topside.

Deep ruts ran in tandem down either side of the girls boot prints, track marks from a small wagon. They must have used a small cart to haul the rocks and ore up to the cellar where it was disposed of. The torch picked up the glimmer of minerals speckled throughout the stone cavern walls, thousands of tiny stars trapped underneath a mountain, hidden from their place in the sky.

Agnes stopped moving. She had heard something. She strained to listen, and yes, there was definitely a noise coming from up ahead, a peculiar monotonous note - the gentle rasp of static. As she drew nearer the sounds origin, she became aware of a light source other than her own. A dim white oblong bleached the soil ahead. Agnes spotted a large clump of dirt that had been kicked out of one of the wheel tracks; the ground was marked from where a body had collided with it forcefully. The girl had tripped in her haste to get away and dropped a video-recorder.

Agnes picked up the device and turned it over, it looked fancy; she couldn't help but wonder what other marvels she had missed out on during her hiatus from society. The camcorder had a built-in torch on the front, this being the cause of the halo she had spied. Its brightness was more powerful than the head torch and, although she couldn't be sure, its battery seemed to have more juice. This alone was a good enough reason to take it with her, but she was also curious about any footage on the tape. If (and it was a big 'if') she made it home, she might be able to figure out how to watch it.

For now it would make a good replacement for when the head torch failed her. She thumbed the power button and the screen blinked off, the torch followed a second later. Agnes shoved it into her pack; there was just enough space on top of her own supplies for her to securely fasten the drawstring dongle.

The tunnel gradually began levelling out. Agnes could not estimate how far down she had travelled, nor did she want to. The excavation appeared to have broken into a natural vent in the mountain. The shaft split into a 'Y' junction, to the left the ground sloped quite severely down into the earth. The darkness there was true black and viscous. The girl she was shadowing had turned to the right. If she had taken the left route Agnes doubted she would have had the physicality to follow. She had already surprised herself with her stamina and endurance rates, but the harshness of the decline into the pit was one that should only have been attempted with the appropriate climbing gear.

Heading up to the right, Agnes saw that the vent was at least twice the width as the shaft she had been following. Her chest loosened slightly, it was as if she could breathe normally again. The various factors of location, darkness and unknown threat had dwarfed her, usually substantial, fear of confined spaces.

Taking into consideration how long she had been walking, and the general direction, she deduced that she was somewhere within the vicinity of the abandoned mine. If a shaft had been tunneled out below the cabin that connected to the main mine then there was no telling how many other tributary tunnels could be littering the mountains interior. She could be heading towards an exit, or a never-ending labyrinth. She crossed her fingers and prayed it was the former.

The girls footprints became less widely spaced, the toes leaving little drag marks with each foot fall. She had run out of steam. The prints veered towards one side of the cavern, then the other. She was looking for a hiding place. She was going to ground. Agnes focused; the girl could be nearby.

In her mind, Agnes could picture the poor girl, frantic and erratic in her bid to find asylum, exhaustion sapping all the energy from her aching muscles; her fingernails scraping the rocks as they searched in anguish for a nook big enough to squeeze in to. Mingled into the musty smell of fungi was a distinct odor rising up from the vent behind Agnes. Sulphur. The stench of rotten eggs was an offense to the senses, and yet its appearance came as no surprise - Agnes was in hell after all.

A bead of sweat trickled down from her brow and tickled her cheek. It wasn't conjured by her nerves, this time, but by a change in temperature that she hadn't registered before. Something told her that, had she ventured down the left passage, she would be feeling a considerable heat rising from the bowels of the earth.

Agnes heart quickened when the weak light from the torch

highlighted some sinister shapes standing erect further up the path. Swiftly, she shot a hand up to cover the light before she was spotted. She had only managed to catch a fleeting glimpse of the shadowy figures, they had looked like people in long, dark robes. Leaning close to the tunnel wall, she stayed as still as a statue. Any moment, she expected to hear the footfalls of a search party. They would hunt her down, hurt her, kill her.

But nothing came for her. No alarm was sounded. No wild call of bloodlust cried out. She dared not move for some time as she was sure their silence was a trick, a trap to lure their quarry out of hiding. She found herself at a stalemate, neither party willing to make the first move. Her knees began to tremble from squatting for so long. Eventually, an accumulation of the strain in her legs and the trying of her patience overwhelmed her and she reluctantly dropped her hand.

Let them come.

A yellow wave of light spilled out and washed over the lurking sentinels. Agnes relinquished a long breath in relief. Cold stone - formed by minerals deposited by droplets of water over aeons of time - nothing more. From the high, cathedral-like ceiling, hung their mirror counterparts. In some places the stalagmites had bridged the gap and connected to the stalactites to form hourglass shaped columns.

The vent had led her to a natural cave deep inside the mountain. Its immense size was practically incalculable by the light of the head torch. Agnes fished out the camera from her pack and powered it on. A beam as bright and as powerful as the sword of the archangel Michael pierced the darkness.

The disruption caused an immediate reaction in the domed roof as thousands of bats took to the wing in a flurry of rage and chaos. Undeterred by the fury of the swirling tempest above, Agnes shone the light over huge shelves of rock, veins of iron ore, and claustrophobic burrows. Every surface was strewn with evidence of human interference; wrought iron supports held aloft some of the larger rocks, a wooden walkway had been erected to reach the higher segments of the cavern, and strange, ominous symbols peppered the walls between hundreds of handprints.

Although possibly lost until the arrival of the white settlers, the cave showed signs of being a highly visited place; perhaps even pre-dating the indigenous tribes. Indeed, many of the handprints looked misshapen, as if not created by homosapiens, but by an earlier ancestor, one not long out of the treetops. Had she not been functioning at a heightened state of fear, Agnes would probably have found the site quite fascinating. Weaving a path between the rock formations, she took the time to illuminate every nook and hollow, the miners had carved many shallow excavations extending away from the cave. Agnes thought it was more like an archaeological dig than a standard mining development.

The stone floor made tracking the girl considerably more difficult, many of the decisions Agnes made were purely crafted on intuition alone. The shrill coming from the bats overhead had lessened and when she shone the light up she could easily see their numbers were more than halved. It stood to reason that there was an exit hidden from view that they used for their nightly hunts. Agnes hoped there was an exit suitable for elderly ladies too.

The center of the hollow was void of stalagmites, the rock strewn ground moderately flat. Dark tarnishes showed where campfires had been lit over the centuries. It wasn't hard to imagine Paleolithic hunters taking shelter from the terrors of the night in their world of tooth and claw.

A man-made shaft led out the other side of the cavern, although it was entirely possible the girl had found a dark recess to crawl into, Agnes felt sure she would have pushed onwards at the sight of a possible exit. She repacked the camera to preserve its battery and went back to her faithful head torch.

...

The tunnels were scarred with the furrows left by cart wheels; a rotten rope lined one side as a make-shift handrail, hooks hung from timber roof supports where lanterns would have once provided a dismal glow. When the mineshaft split in a three-way fork, Agnes found she was frustrated more than she was frightened. It seemed the hostile world she had come to inhabit was one that relished challenging her, pitting her determination against its own resentful bitterness. None of the passageways showed any evidence of being recently travelled but that did not mean the girl had not come this way.

Agnes had a difficult decision to make, she could turn back and try and pick up the trail (an option she felt would be fruitless), or she could pick one of the tunnels and hope it led to either the girl or (even better) an exit. Her sense of direction had become skewed within the maze of stone corridors, she would have liked to have selected the path closest to where she believed the mouth of the mine to be, but she had become turned around. Instead she put her trust in the ancient technique of taking the left, and continuing to do so until either freedom or death greeted you.

Several of the left turns took her down abandoned shafts; twice she found her path blocked by cave-ins. When this happened she would about-turn and retrace her steps, all the while running her hand along the wall to her left. In places where the path dipped momentarily, mushrooms and puffballs sprouted from the moist floor, their spores drifted sickly green in the torchlight.

A gradual incline underfoot raised her spirits slightly; it meant she was getting closer to the surface, away from the sulphuric belly of the mountain. The mine itself contained more timber here; the walls were marked heavily with the scores of metal tools. Agnes didn't want to speculate too much, but in her mind this meant she was nearing the main hub of the network, the official mine – not some primordial hidey-hole.

She stooped low; flicked off the light. Waited...

She had allowed her mind to wander. She wasn't focused; hadn't been paying enough attention.

'Damn.'

She should have heard the noises up ahead before now.

...

Agnes sat in the dark. The sudden absence of light had left patterns of phosphenes dancing behind her eyelids. She blinked and squeezed her eyes tight to try and adjust to the impenetrable dark. Due to the shape and nature of the mineshaft she could not determine the distance between herself and the source of the sounds. Frowning, she tried to decipher the peculiar and muffled audio that resonated towards her.

Sobbing...gibberish...laughter..?

It sounded like a one-sided conversation, (something Agnes had become quite accustomed to); it had to be the missing girl. The varying changes in pitch implied to Agnes to approach with caution. The girl sounded like someone right in the middle of hysteria. Not wanting to alarm the girl and warrant a volatile response, Agnes removed the head torch and pointed it to the dirt. Its ever-diminishing glow provided a small spotlight to guide her way. She crept forward; ears pricked so to pick the correct direction. Another left then a sharp right and the incoherent mumblings slowly became clearer.

'...never even wanted... am I dead? ...mother?

Crying.

'I'm so sorry...'

Laughing.

'Well Gavin, you got your story! Hahaha...It tore Tony apart!'

Agnes wanted to wait, to announce herself gently when (*if*) the girl had stopped rambling. Foolishly, she had forgotten about the halo at her feet.

'Hello, who is there? I can see you!' the girl screeched. Agnes couldn't find her voice. Her lip trembled but no sound came out. 'Is it *you*? Please don't kill me, I didn't even want to come!' the girl broke down, her sobs sounded deep and wretchedly painful. '*I didn't even want to come…*'

Agnes raised the torch, slipping it back into position on her head. 'Michelle…Is that your name honey, Michelle?'

'Yes, yes… but… but how do you know my name? Mother… is that you, mother?'

The girl was delirious and Agnes had been separated from society for too long to know how to handle such a delicate situation. 'My name is Agnes. You can call me Aggie, if you like. I've come to help you.' Agnes slowly edged closer. The tunnel had several passages sprouting away from it, Agnes did not want the girl to become spooked and attack her because she felt cornered.

Slow and steady…

'Are you part of the rescue team? But no one knows we're here. We ended up miles off course. How long have we been missing? Did my mother call?' Agnes shone the light down the first junction. Nothing but rubble and dirt. Move on.

'No dear, I'm not with a rescue party. I live… nearby. I heard you and you're friends and though you might be in trouble.' *(No sense in going into detail about dead husbands and ancient monsters. Not yet anyway).*

The girl's fragile grey matter was desperately trying to claw itself back from the fringes of insanity. Fretfully, she tried to process the information she was hearing above the chaos of her shattered mind.

'But that's impossible, no one lives out here. It's isolated. It's uncharted, for god sake! The last town we passed was miles and miles away… you *can't* live out here!'

Agnes peered around the next open space. The girl was there. Flat on her stomach; she had tried to squeeze under a fallen support from an adjoining passage and had gotten stuck. Agnes could smell the sweet undertone of her floral perfume. For the first time, their eyes met one another's.

'It is for those reasons,' Agnes said, assuredly, 'that I most certainly *do* live out here.' The girl's eyes brimmed with tears. 'Besides,' the old woman added, 'I said *nearby*. Ain't nobody living in *this* shithole.'

…

It took some time for Agnes to calm the girl down. She listened as Michelle yammered through her story, much of which was either indecipherable or meant nothing to her. There would be time for 'how's' and 'why's' later, right now getting the girl out the safety of the homestead was priority one.

When Michelle started showing signs of slowing down, Agnes placed a small grey hand on the girls shoulder. She stopped mid-sentence and looked up at Agnes with wide brown eyes that seemed to ask, *'I'm sorry, was I rambling?'*

'Listen carefully, dear. I know you've been through a lot. Trust me, so have I. You can tell me everything later when we are back at my cabin, but for now, how's about we focus on getting you out of there?'

The girl nodded, dumbly.

'Ok,' Agnes smiled, warmly. 'Let me see if I can pull you out.'

Agnes managed to hook her slim hands under the girl's armpits. Sitting in front of the girl, she was able to brace her legs upon the offending beam of timber. 'Okay, I'm going to pull now.' With these words she leant back and heaved with all her might. Michelle slid forward a couple of inches and Agnes was awash with relief. Then the girl screamed.

'Stop, stop. I'm stuck!' Agnes let go. 'Something's cutting into me. I can't go forward!'

Agnes racked her brains. '*What to do…what to do…*'

She stroked the girl's curly, burnt-auburn hair and reassured her. 'Don't panic. I'll try and *dig* you out. See…' she brushed at the dirt below the girl, 'it's soft. I'll dig you out.'

She tossed her backpack on the ground and began rummaging, Wilson always carried a small trowel on his trips ('*for burying the unmentionables,*' he'd say). While she emptied out the contents, Agnes tried to engage the girl in lighter conversation. 'You have lovely hair. Mine was the same color when I was younger - much younger.' Michelle smiled for the first time. Agnes had not realized what a pretty girl she was. 'What could possibly have enticed you and your friends to come way out here?' Agnes added, 'Sorry, I don't mean to be rude…'

The young girl shook her head dismissively. 'Not at all,' she said. 'I've been asking myself the same question. The short answer would be – Gavin. It was his project.'

Agnes found the trowel and set to work scooping the dirt away from under the trapped girl. 'Go on, I'm listening.'

'We all met at college, film studies. Everyone in the class thought they were going to be the next big thing in documentary film-making; myself included, I suppose. We all dreamt of Sundance, you know?' Agnes didn't know, but she smiled anyway. 'Gavin, however, was the only one with real potential. You could tell as soon as you met him that, not only was he driven, but he had the skills to match. We were partnered on an assignment and, although often difficult to work with, I realized how passionate he was. We came out top of the class and decided to pair up. We started a blog online, it went viral, and we've been doing it ever since.'

Agnes opened her mouth to ask what a 'blog' was, then thought better of it. She wasn't even sure she knew what 'online' meant. Instead, she asked, 'So you came here to make a film?'

The girl nodded, enthusiastically. 'That's right. Our show is about unsolved mysteries. Unusual phenomena: the great unexplained. Our researcher, Tony, found some strange documents at a yard sale. I wish I could show you them, they are really neat, but they're in my backpack, which is beside me on the other side of this stupid barrier. They appear to be a mix of charter notes and correspondences between two military forts. We delved deeper and it seems during the time this area was being explored and mapped by the early settlers, hundreds of people disappeared, just up and vanished.'

Michelle gave Agnes a quizzical look which the old woman shrugged off. 'It's ok,' she said, trying to catch her breath. 'I just need a minute. My arthritis is killing me,' she joked, leaning back and rotating her wrist. 'So you came here to find out what happened to the missing people?'

The girl, perhaps blinded by her unspoken love and admiration of the great Gavin, seemed unaware that she shared in his passion. Indeed, when she spoke it was with the fervor the heart usually reserves only for its fondest subjects.

'At first, yes,' she said, excitedly. 'But the more research we did, the more we uncovered…and it got weird. Initially, when folk first started disappearing off the trails, the finger of blame was pointed right at the local indigenous people. The military up at Fort Eustace had been stationed there for 4 years and, apart from a few minor incidents, had been living side by side with little conflict. They even welcomed the Indian fur traders into the camp. A party was sent to speak to the Indian chiefs to see if they knew anything, it wasn't uncommon for tribe members to go rogue. I mean, who could blame them, right? Anyway, the chiefs were all very cooperative and willing to help, some even offered the assistance of their braves to aid in the search parties; until they were shown where the travelers had vanished.'

Michelle was grinning. Agnes couldn't fathom how the girl could still be so enamored with the tale - not now that she was a part of it. She supposed the line between ambition and obsession was a fine one; one that often allowed the two to meet and become intertwined. Yes, once you muddied the water it was nigh on impossible to separate the silt.

On the other hand, she was grateful for the excuse to take a break from digging. Her wrist was on fire. Agnes spoke solemnly, 'Let me guess... it wouldn't have been within this vicinity, would it?'

The girl gave her a coy look. 'You'd think so, wouldn't you? But no, not exactly. You see, the natives avoided the Great Mountain and everything around it. To them the entire place was cursed. Their ancestors had many legends regarding the area, none of which were especially pleasant. They believed something lived - or was trapped, we couldn't find out for sure - inside the mountain. I guess it was like their version of the devil or something. So the soldiers showed the chiefs terrain maps with the locations of all the disappearances, the known ones anyway, and they all start freaking out. Not in a hostile way, but cold and dismissive. Without so much as a word, the soldiers were escorted from the Indian camps and sent packing back to their base empty handed.'

Agnes could see the girl was enjoying recounting the story to her audience, she wondered if Michelle spent as much time in front of the cameras as behind them. She certainly had a flair for it.

'So, several months go by. The native tribes go unusually quiet. It's almost as if they've gone into hiding. For some, this comes across as an admission of guilt, and on the rare occasion when they are encountered it more often than not ends in confrontation. And yet, still reports of people going missing roll in. The soldiers are at a loss, patrols are sent out to comb the untamed land under the authority of one General Joseph Sutter. Have you heard of him?'

Agnes had, but it didn't come to her straight away. The name was so familiar, but her mind had drawn a blank. 'I have...I'm sorry. My memory's not what it used to be. Who was he?' she uttered, embarrassed by her age-driven condition. The way the girl looked sympathetically at her made her cheeks flush, it felt as though she had been caught out; trying to hide a shameful secret. Michelle's face softened, Agnes got the impression she wasn't the first mind-addled pensioner in the girl's life.

'Joseph Sutter liked it so much out here that when he eventually retired from the military, he settled down and built a ranch. It was prosperous and attracted many workers, with the workers came trade and land development-'

'-Sutter's Mill,' interrupted Agnes. 'He was the town's founder. Sorry it just came back to me.'

The girl shot her a wink. 'Bingo. Before he established himself as Mayor of the ass end of nowhere, he was a decorated and high-ranking military man. His superiors sent him out here because of his reputation for getting things done. It was all done on the hush-hush, a lot of wealthy men had plans for bringing 'civilization' to the valley and mountain range and news of disappearances would have been bad for business.' The girl shifted her weight with a grunt. 'Getting real uncomfortable in here. Would you mind? I'd really like to get out now.'

Agnes was intrigued by the girl's story but as much as she wanted to hear the rest of it, she had to agree, it could wait until later. She set the trowel to work, after a few minutes of awkward silence she asked the girl if she would mind continuing her tale. Michelle didn't need much encouragement.

'Where was I?'

'Joseph Sutter...'

'Ah yes, General Sutter. Even with him in charge, the case was getting nowhere. We couldn't find any information as to why, but it turned out some of the soldiers had gotten spooked after returning from an area described in Sutter's journal as 'a dense swampland hidden in the mountains.'

Agnes grunted a response. 'No prizes for guessing where that could be.'

'Many of the men went AWOL, hooked up with gangs, or headed back towards the coast. Sutter was getting frustrated; he prided himself as a man who got results – and the folks down south were losing patience. His big breakthrough came when a young brave rode into Eustace. He had been exiled from his tribe for disobeying the chiefs' ruling; he felt it necessary to get the information to the white men whatever the cost.'

Agnes was trying to hide her frustration; she hadn't expected the freeing of the girl to be so taxing on her joints. The dirt was clumpy and packed with stones, breaking through it was much harder than she had anticipated. She was making progress but it was by raking the thin layers of soil. She had hoped to have the girl out by now.

Michelle kept the words flowing from her mouth as though she were reading them from a script, Agnes was no psychiatrist but she understood it to be a coping mechanism; by narrating, the girl was excluding herself from the scenario and therefore rendering herself immune to the consequences and horrors the unfortunate cast might face. If playing this role kept the girl on the right side of sane then Agnes would encourage it.

'What did the brave say? Did he know where the missing people were?'

'Not exactly,' Michelle beamed. 'But he did have information that Sutter felt was worth investigating. You see, it turned out some of the local tribes had been keeping tabs on a particular group of pioneers that had rolled into the neighborhood. Unlike the usual travelers they saw crossing their land, these wore strange robes and carried long staffs with religious symbols on top. The natives had grown accustomed to the white man's Christianity and their tales about the man Jesus, the sign of the cross decorated many of their buildings and trinkets, but this group carried an entirely different sign. That made them suspicious-'

'-a crescent shape, like a moon?' Agnes chimed in. 'I saw it on the church spire. So they were like a cult?'

'Oh they were a cult alright. Simon – he's our cameraman but also a shit-hot researcher – he found out a whole bunch of crazy stuff about them. When we get out of here we'll find Simon and he can tell you all about them.' The girl's eyes were like frosted glass, she had retreated inside, back to the safety provided by the veil of denial. 'Gavin too. He ran into the swamp. He's probably on his way back with help as we speak…' Agnes could actually see the moment reality injected a flicker of its grim truth into the girl's thoughts. '…but not Tony.' Michelle's expression tightened, she looked like a porcelain doll. 'It got Tony. Tony is dead.'

Agnes stroked the poor girl's hand; the girl returned the gesture by clasping her hand around Agnes' and squeezing tightly. Agnes managed to fake a reassuring smile. 'We'll find your friends, sweetheart. Soon we will all be sitting in my safe, warm cabin. I'll light the fire and fix everybody some hot cocoa. Now that sounds good, doesn't it?'

The girl slowly lifted her head, her eyes found Agnes but the light that had burned so brightly in them had gone out. Perhaps, this time, for good.

'That sounds really nice.'

Agnes wiped a solitary tear that spilled down the girl's cheek.

'Why don't you finish your story, dear?'

The girl stared vacantly at a patch of dirt, or more likely, through it; her damaged mind like a projector casting visuals of a memory better forgotten.

'No,' said the girl, softly. 'I'd just like to get out now. Please.'

No words of comfort came to mind, so Agnes returned to digging in silence.

CHAPTER 26

Few sounds carried in the subterranean world. Somewhere in the dark, water droplets fell into a puddle with a *'plonk...plonk...plonk...'* Occasionally, you could hear the hushed scurrying of rats, the angry squeals when they encountered one another and proceeded to brawl. The most persistent noise in the underground was the scraping of Agnes and her trowel. The old woman wanted nothing more than to be done, the episode over.

Since the girl had gone quiet, an air of discomfort had settled in. She had frozen, Agnes felt as though she were digging out a mannequin, not a living, breathing creature. Agnes had never seen someone so... *so still.*

She was treated to a minor consolation when a rock the size of a large potato came loose enough to be removed.

'Michelle,' Agnes whispered, not sure the girl was still cognizant. 'I think you might have enough room to wiggle out. If you want to give it a go..?' The girl looked as if she had woken from a dream. Agnes couldn't remember seeing her eyes close in a long time. She blinked repeatedly, a red rim scored her sclera from lack of moisture and the exposure of the dusty mineshaft.

'Huh?' she mumbled, sluggishly becoming aware of her surroundings.

'I think you might manage to get out now,' Agnes said, gently. 'Why don't you try and wriggle out?'

The girl took a moment to register the conversation and nodded. She tried to scoot forward, but the obstruction that had foiled her earlier remained a burden. Agnes suggested the girl try and get her arm underneath herself and reach through to try and dislodge the offending item. With much stressing and pushing to the limits of the girl's flexibility, she finally managed to get her arm down one side.

'I can feel it,' she snarled. 'It's a broken spar of wood. I think the end of it is partially buried. I'm going to try and dig it out… if I can at least loosen it enough to-'

She was cut off as a bloodcurdling roar sounded throughout the cavernous tunnels. Agnes couldn't tell if the girl had finished her sentence or was simply drowned out by the perverse call of brutality incarnate.

Agnes watched as the girl's face morphed into that of a scared child, her wide doe-like eyes too young to bear witness to such horrible circumstances. Even with her many more years on the earth – Agnes considered herself too young also.

The girl's pout quivered with unbridled fear, sweat beaded on her brow and dampened her hair, matting it to her face in straggly strands. 'It's here,' she sobbed. 'It's come back for me.'

Agnes resumed her digging with a renewed fever. Trowel and hand raked furiously at the dirt. The old woman didn't even notice when two of her fingernails snagged on debris fragments and were ripped free of her fingertips. Nor did she notice when her blood streaked the soil red.

The girl was lost in a frightful state of delirium. Out of sight, beyond the timber barrier, her solitary hand trembled terribly as it clawed at the dirt around the wooden spike. Whereas Agnes had the minor misfortune to have lost a few nails, the girls fingers were shredded, deep lacerations allowed her blood to pour freely over the grainy earth.

A hideous shriek of wicked excitement penetrated the warren as the unseen hunter picked up the scent of its horror-stricken quarry.

Faster and faster, blood and dirt, young and old.

Together they attacked the soil and rocks. Sweat and dust combined into a layer of grime that stained the flesh. The harder they worked the more the beast relished their odor, its depraved cries echoed throughout the maze.

Agnes recoiled in agony as a fiery jolt shot up from her wrist. Such a burst of pain caught her off guard to the extent she was thrown backwards cradling the treacherous limb.

'No, no…help me…*help me…*' the girl pleaded, frantically, as the walls trembled with the thunderous approach of something wicked. Agnes feebly stretched out her one good arm until their fingertips touched. The girl gave her a weak smile of commiseration. The approaching ruckus stopped, suddenly.

The two woman looked at one another, silently asking the questions – Where is it? Who has it come for? They faced each other in the milky glow of Agnes' lamp, fingers entwined and waited.

The silence was no less terrifying than the cacophony of *Its* arrival. Their wait was drawn out deliberately; another of the beast's games. Somewhere in the darkness it waited and watched, feasting on their terror like an appetizer.

The girl went to speak then froze rigid. Her face creased into a grimace of despair. Agnes mouth hung open. The girl nodded through her tears.

'I can feel its breath.'

Those were to be her last words. Agnes' heart broke; she mouthed the word 'sorry' and squeezed the girl's hand. She could do no more.

A vicious, malevolent snarl boomed from the other side of the boards. The girl screamed, first in terror - then in agony, as the unseen horror tore into her. Agnes could only watch as the girl's blood spilled into the groove they had spent so much time digging out, all for nothing.

'Sorry...I'm sorry...I'm sorry...'

Blood erupted from the girl's mouth in a shower that covered Agnes' face, blinding her with red. She tried to wipe it off, but the girl's hand had clenched upon her own in a deathly spasm. Agnes felt as though she were drowning, she had to clear her face!

She threw herself backwards as hard as she could. Although she could not see, she could hear that the girl had ceased screaming. The only sounds discernible in the shaft were the girl's gurgling, death wheeze and an unsettling slap and snuffle that Agnes did not want to think about.

She had to break free. She spluttered as her own mouth filled with the bitter taste of the girl's blood and launched herself away once more. This time she broke the grip, the girl's nails scratched her wrist and palm. She landed with a thump, her shoulders taking most of the impact. There wasn't time to be winded. Frantic, she used her hands (and when that didn't work, her sleeves), to remove the viscera from her face.

With her vision cleared, she looked up to face the girl and was met by her cold, wide-eyed glare. Lifeless. In her last ditch effort to pull free, Agnes had partially succeeded in dragging the girl from her predicament. *Partially.* There was a considerable gap between her upper and lower body, a separation joined by a bridge made of entrails and gore. Not only had the poor girl had to endure such a horrific and violent death but, to add further insult, Agnes could still hear the stomach-churning noises coming from the other side of the boards. It was eating her.

Agnes reached out and touched the girl's cheek. 'I'm so, so sorry,' she whispered. She cried quietly for the girl, yet also for herself, for having witnessed such a tragic act. Now was the time to move though, while the beast was… preoccupied.

She stepped as quietly as a mouse, backing away from the scene. When she rounded the corner, she leant against the damp soil wall. Images played across her mind; The Stag, The Wolf and his Pack, The Head in the Swamp and The Pretty Stuck Girl.

'No.'

Agnes' jaw flexed as it dealt with grievance, hate and rage.

She checked her rifle.

'Her name was Michelle.'

CHAPTER 27

*O*nwards. Onwards. Into the labyrinth…
Her feet pound the earth. Through the ancient dust and mushroom spores. She ducks under rotten beams that creak and groan and threaten to give way. The tunnels are flooded in parts, in one passage the water has risen almost to the ceiling, she wades through it. The water gets in her mouth, her nostrils. It burns her eyes and when she breaks through to the other side her hair stinks of putrid eggs.

The need to be quiet is over. It has finished its meal, it has detected her, now it craves seconds. She has not seen it behind her yet, but it has made its presence (and its intentions) known by squealing in twisted pleasure.

Agnes comes to a junction.

'Which way?'

The tunnel on her left is partially boarded up. She considers climbing through the obstruction then remembers the girl.

Michelle.

She shudders and throws up. Acrid bile hits the soil just as the boarded tunnel palpitates, something is applying pressure on the old wood - something is trying to break through. The old woman watches as the beams are hit again. They puff out streams of dust as they bend but do not break - Yet.

Her blood races through her veins; her legs, her heart. It thumps a militant beat across her skull; the pressure threatens an aneurism.

Onwards she runs. Never more urgently.

Away from the creak and whine of splintering pine. The narrow corridor walls twist and spiral as they did in Logan's Pass, except here the pursuer is all too real. The ever-ascending gradient sets her calves on fire. Her knees and hips, already so worn, will never be the same again; should Lady Luck grant her the privilege of escaping this level of hell.

She runs and runs and runs. Then a blessing and a curse presents itself right before her. A wall of stone rubble blocks her path. Had it not been for the razor shard of moonlight that pierced the cave-in, and the waft of surface air that cleared the stour from her lungs, she would have lain down and let the beast take her.

From the tips of her fingers to the throbbing joints in her toes, Agnes is on fire with pain. She claws and pulls at the stones between herself and the outside, all the while reminding herself that it could be worse. A constant image of the 'Girl in Two' swims in her peripheral vision. Yes, it could be a lot worse.

With each rock that she scraps loose, each stone that clatters painfully against her shins, the promise of freedom draws nearer. One more large boulder and the hole will be big enough for her to fit through.

The orchestral rhythm pounding from down in the warren behind her is increasing in its velocity. Agnes' blood runs like ice water when it reaches its explosive crescendo. The destructive shattering of timber is accompanied by a triumphant victory holler.

Digging deep to find a strength she is unaware she even possesses; Agnes attacks the rock with all her might. Spittle flies from between her clenched teeth as she gouges the sediment holding it in place. As soon as the stone has enough wiggle room, Agnes thrusts her hands over and behind it and pulls.

The battle between old woman and rock is strenuous; Agnes only wins through sheer determination. The boulder admits defeat by allowing itself to be toppled onto its fallen brethren below where it cracks into two pieces. As Agnes shoves her pack through the gap she notices that the interior of the stone is mainly comprised of gold. Being someone whom has never known a lust for wealth nor money, Agnes barely gives the nugget a second glance.

Onto her belly she scrambles.

...

Her head emerged into the open; the sudden rush of clean oxygen filled her lungs and made her head giddy. Straining her neck upwards she lay eyes upon the stars and moon and could have wept. She had been positive she had seen them for the last time.

The thunderous roar in the caverns behind her grew louder. The creature was closing the gap; soon it would be upon her. For a frightful moment Agnes found herself wedged around her shoulders, not wanting to face the exact same fate as Michelle, she persevered and, at the cost of a few layers of skin, managed to free herself. She slid like a ragdoll over the rockslide and came to an uncomfortable stop upon her backpack. A brief respite.

Agnes, laying on her back and unable to comprehend just how she had managed to escape the labyrinth, watched the tiny hole she has just squeezed through. She could hear no sound coming from inside and could not tell if this was because of the fallen rocks muffling the monsters approach, or if the beast had come to a stop.

Her chest rose and fell heavily as she struggled to recover from her ordeal and the exertion it had required. Just as her breathing began to settle and her heart stopped trying to break free of her breastbone, she was presented with another pulse-racing fright.

A roar, filled with bile and fueled by rage, bellowed out of the gap like a foghorn in the night. The nightmare stood just behind the stone barrier. Agnes felt electric, to be so close to death, and yet just out of its reach. It may have been able to smash its way through the wooden obstacles inside the shaft, but surely it could not do so to solid stone? Silence returned. Agnes listened as the beast weighed its options.

'Yeah, that's right!' Agnes shouted at the creature. 'How'd you like that, huh? I hope you rot in there!'

The beast responded, but not in the way Agnes had anticipated. At first it sounded very much like the animal she had regarded it to be – a raspy chuffing. Then the chuffing morphed into something almost rhythmic, calculated. There was no denying that the hoarse, guttural noise was the creature's form of laughter. And how wicked it sounded. Agnes sucked cold air through her teeth as she watched in horror as a sinister shape curled from the hole.

A dark and sinewy tendril, neither of smoke nor solid but something in between, probed the night air. Agnes watched in shock and awe as the end of the unnatural proboscis became denser, firmer. From its hardening tip grew four smaller protuberances that ended in sharply pointed spikes. This creature was an entirely different entity to the beast she had believed she was up against. This was no mere animal, nor was it some mindless, primitive spirit. It hunted its prey with purpose and intent. What the purpose was, Agnes could not say, but she sure as hell wasn't sticking around to find out.

She scrambled to her feet and gathered her bag and gun, careful to steer clear of the searching arm with the spear-tip fingers. As she was backing away, her foot caught on something that sent her crashing down on her buttocks. Her hip popped painfully in its joint and she cried out. The serpentine arm swung round directly in line with her. It darted, striking at the air like an enraged viper.

Agnes was grateful to have tripped out with its reach, but she could have done without a new pain to add to her ever-growing list. She filed her grievance by kicking the rail track that had caused her miss-step. Back on her feet she shouldered the rifle. If the smoke-tentacle looked solid then maybe it could take a bullet. She took aim and fired. The forest still was shattered by a whip-like crack. The vaporous appendage dispersed in a sooty cloud. Agnes sneered, 'Got you, fucker. Direct hit.'

Her victory was short lived. The particles that had been blown apart began drifting back together the way iron filings are pulled towards a magnet. Within a matter of seconds the wispy mass had reformed itself into the ominous clawed hand.

Before she could react, the jagged fingers had grasped a stone from the rock pile and hurled it at her. The stone collided with her forehead; the collision carried enough force to send her reeling. The rifle clattered to the earth.

...

Agnes must have been hit for six. She regained consciousness lying sprawled in the mud; high above the Milky Way swirled like silt in a pool as her vision tried to correct itself. Gently, she touched her latest wound with tender fingers. Her hair was plastered to her forehead and cheek with blood. Agnes felt sick. Struggling more than normal, she rose up into a sitting position and, upon laying eyes on the mine's entrance, sprang to her feet.

While she had been taking an involuntary nap, the smoke-arm had been busy expanding the hole she had started. Already, the gap was more than large enough for any human to fit through. Agnes was positive the beast on the other side was of considerable size, but at the rate the ghostly limb was dissecting the rockslide, even it would soon be free.

She hurriedly gathered her supplies and took off in the direction of the settlement. Until she took care of her head injury she had no chance of out running the monster. She had to find a hiding place.

She looked over her shoulder only once, when the beast roared its awful roar. Deep in the shadows of the mine she caught a glimpse of the creature; a hideous silhouette, a glint of tooth or tusk, and one crimson eye that glowered after her, smoldering with unbridled hate.

CHAPTER 28

Accompanying her own footfalls, the chirrup of insects, and the bubbling of the swamp, was the tumbling of stone, as the beast tore down the blockade.

Sweet Christ it was fast.

Agnes staggered almost blindly into the hikers' camp. Taking refuge in one of the tents would have been down-right stupid - she had already seen how that one played out. She thought maybe the well could present a possible hiding place, but upon quick inspection, found it had been sealed with a thick iron cap, huge rivets held it firmly in place.

'Where…where…where…?' she chanted, desperation constricting all other thoughts. Most of the buildings were impenetrable ruins and she certainly did not fancy revisiting the last property she had explored.

Her best option was the one she dreaded the most. The town hall/church - whatever the hell those lunatics had built - was a portentous silhouette back-lit by a sickly, yellow moon. The wrought iron spire with its pagan symbol cast a long witchy shadow at her feet. The first flakes of the latest snowfall drifted slowly down like ash. If a storm rolled in she would be stuck here, and for how long was anyone's guess.

Another dull rumble signaled the falling of another stone being removed from the cave-in. Against her own will, Agnes crossed the swampy ground towards the church.

Around the halfway point, Agnes had to navigate around a particularly large smear of blood and worse. The pile of gore was indistinguishable; there were no recognizable body parts, only chunks of organs and pieces of flesh. This, she believed, must have been the remains of the one called Tony. To hazard a guess, she could only assume the rest of him was in the belly of the beast.

'What a terrible and violent way to go.'

To die in such a horrific way made Agnes glad she had the gun, if it came down to a bullet or – *that*, she would happily put the barrel in her mouth. At least it would be quick. A thought crossed her mind and she used her fingers to name them off.

Gavin, Michelle, Tony…

There were four hikers. Her mind, whether rattled from its latest bump or due to the illness that robbed her train of thought like a bandit, could not recollect his name. But he was *real*, and he had fled in this direction. She was sure of it.

The building stank. Bio-matter such as fungi and moss spread up and over its outer shell from where it had begun to sink into the bog. Several feet of the structure lay below the water line. The swamp was, for all intents and purposes, eating it.

Unlike the other properties in the encampment which were made exclusively from timber (bar their rough brick fireplaces), this one consisted of stonework with a wooden frame and roof. The heavy duty oak doors stood ajar. Agnes curled her hand around one and gave a gentle tug. It opened easily. But her hand *did* come away slick with blood.

Recent experience had taught her not to get her hopes up. Sure, the missing hiker could be alive, injured but still breathing. But Michelle had been alive too, and that hadn't exactly ended well.

Standing in the doorway, Agnes tried to take in the scene before her. The entire back corner to her right had sunk into the swamp. The roof was little more than a few remaining spars and beams. Its apex had been destroyed at some point in its history when, as the swamp had tilted the structure, the bell had broken free and crashed through its belfry and smashed through the roof below. It still remained where it had landed, on its side amongst the shattered pews it had come to rest on. On its way down it appeared to have collided with a second story balcony, snapping its log beams where it connected to the stone wall creating a wooden slope. If Agnes could find a way behind it, it could be a suitable hidey-hole. Not dissimilar to the *bivouacs* Wilson had used on his hunting trips.

The interior was considerably more spacious than its outside appearance let on, many rows of pews lined up in front of a raised platform where the town's speakers would address the flock. At the far end, behind the pulpit, were two parallel doors that may have led to small sanctuaries or a priest's quarters. Tall, three-pronged candlesticks made of cast iron stood, or leaned, at various points around the nave.

Agnes noticed something odd about the grime on the floor below her. Using a gloved hand she wiped the thickest of the mess to the side. It was hard to make out, but there was definitely some kind of mosaic covering the majority of the stone floor.

Agnes grabbed a stick that ended in a wide spread of small branches and used it like a brush. After only a few minutes of sweeping she had uncovered enough of the tiles to see they depicted some kind of story.

The images were faded, worn away by layers of muck, but she was still able to make out bits and pieces. People in strange robe garbs kneeled before a huge hog-like deity. An alter where priests performed grotesque human sacrifices took center stage. The carcasses of the damned piled high in a pyramid of flesh and bone.

A long corridor cut into a mountain, at its lowest point the same robed figures formed a circle around what appeared to be a doorway or portal of some kind. A swirl of black, as dark as the night sky, crept forth and wove itself around the figures.

Whatever god these people had come to worship was one that reveled in chaos and carnage, the floor was littered in depictions of violent deaths. The last image Agnes uncovered raised more questions than it answered, but it did shine some light on the monster that pursued her.

Again, the demonic boar-beast was shown, but this time it had changed, evolved. It was much larger now, its originally primal features seemed sharper, cunning. From its body swept the wispy arms of smoke, they too had undergone a transformation and were denser, harder looking. Its swollen belly and sides were covered in what Agnes believed to be faces, human faces. Agnes may have been misinterpreting the evidence but it looked as though the cultists had been absorbed into the beast's physical form. They were a part of it. They were its most dangerous part, the part capable of spite and hate – the human part.

A triumphant roar shattered the still. The last of the stones had been removed. Agnes sucked cool swamp air through her teeth. The beast had escaped.

...

Agnes bounded across the hideous tiles and rammed her way behind the collapsed balcony. Her pack restricted her progress and she swiftly removed it and tossed it into the gap. Side-stepping, she edged along behind the rotten wood slick with slime and swamp muck. The boards had large enough spaces between them to allow her to see through without fear of being exposed.

The awkward angle she was to the bag meant she could only reach it with one hand. As inconvenient as this was, it didn't stop her from pulling out a bandage from her medical supplies and binding it around her increasingly painful forehead.

Heavy footfalls paraded around the ruins of the church. Through the cracks in the boards Agnes could see the flicker of its immense shadow on the opposite wall as its bulk blocked the moonlight. Several times it circled the building, when it passed behind her, separated by only a thin layer of stone and mortar; she could hear its hungry snorting as it tried to pick up her scent. It may not have known her exact location, but it knew she was nearby.

The wall that pressed against her back trembled as the beast bumped into it. Dust billowed into the room as ancient stone crumbled. Thinking quickly, Agnes hiked her scarf up roughly over her mouth and nose, her tear ducts burned with the invasion, but at least she wouldn't give away her position in a coughing fit.

Grey powder rained down upon her, amongst it bird droppings and spider webs (complete with spiders). Frantically, she shook her head in a bid to shake off the worst of the down pour.

The monster demonstrated its patience by skirting the church at a leisurely pace; after all, if it could rest for centuries what was a few more hours, days, months? What it perhaps hadn't considered was that Agnes would happily starve to death behind the dilapidated make-shift wall compared to risking a desperate break for freedom. She slumped as far down the wall as the narrow space would allow. It looked like she was stuck here for the long haul.

She was just away to rest her eyes when a white orb caught her attention glinting in the moon glow from the doorway behind the pulpit. A face as pale as the snow outside stared right at her with eyes turned red from an endless stream of tears.

CHAPTER 29

S imon had been the one who had suggested they get some sleep. The hike had been long and tiring, but his reason for recommending they get some shut-eye was purely based on the fact he did not, under any circumstances, want to see this ghastly place after dark.

He had been friends with Gavin long enough to know the way he excitedly raced from one ruin to another, jabbering wildly into his Dictaphone, that his companion would push for some nocturnal footage, and probably a midnight ramble. The abandoned house with the creepy cellar they had found would definitely be the first stop on Gavin's Late Night Tour of Dread. Thankfully, he had caught the others' eyes first, and with a few conspiratorial nods, they made a silent pact. It was time to turn in.

Gavin, as usual, was defiant. He argued his perspective using his regular over-the-top spiel – 'Look at this place!' 'What a significant discovery!' 'We'll be famous!' etc, etc, etc. But for the first time ever, his colleagues put their collective feet down. Besides, they persuaded him, it would still be here come morning, and the equipment was playing up, it would need a looking over.

Gavin had actually been the first to retreat to his tent, citing: 'I *am* pretty shattered, to be honest. See you all in the morning.'

Simon knew it was because their director was rubbish when it came to the technical stuff.

The others had followed not long after, except Simon. He sat on a dry(*ish*) patch of dirt beside the campfire nervously watching the tree line and the vacant windows of the remaining buildings. Something about this place was... '*off*'. It wasn't the eerie structures (*although that church thing did give him the willies*), or the mystical looking swamp gas that curled gently around them, nor was it the sinister forest they had trekked through to get here.

A crow perched on the church spire and cawed loudly.

No, it was all of these things together, and yet something more, something unseen. Everything around him was just a backdrop, a setting, cheap scenery meant to distract from the real villain of the play.

As a young boy Simon had often felt himself susceptible to the influence of forces beyond his understanding. Not necessarily ghosts, he had never seen anything paranormal and if asked would claim to be an unbeliever – but he *could* read a room. If he found himself in a location that made him feel panicked or anxious chances were that, after a little investigating, he would discover it had been the scene of some form of tragedy.

This old settlement was raising too many red flags.

Through habit, he still carried his old inhaler wherever he went. It had been years since his last attack and yet, since entering the gnarled woodland, he had been puffing away like crazy. There was also the feeling (or was 'sensation' a better word?), that they were being followed. He didn't want to use the word 'stalked' or even worse, 'hunted'. Every sound or shadow had him on edge.

He kicked some loose dirt over the fire and had one last look at the sky before entering his tent. It was going to be a long night.

...

Sleep would not come. Simon had tried to switch off; lord knows he was certainly tired. His muscles ached from the long journey. What he'd have given to be have been back at the van! He was no stranger to camping, even before teaming up with Gavin and his crew he had done his fair share of spending the night in creepy places. He felt drawn to them, places that were meant to be haunted by spirits or harbored legends amongst locals. He enjoyed delving into their history and uncovering truths, therefore becoming a part of said history.

So what was it about this particular site that made him want to high-tail it through the trees and not stop until he was back in the safety of Sutter's Mill Roadside Motel?

He was sure he was not the only one sensing the woeful undertones. Michelle had said how she thought the 'air was full of menace,' and Tony, who rarely spoke anyway, hadn't really said a word since they crossed the rickety old bridge out of the swamp. Maybe in the morning the three of them could persuade Gavin to get the hell out of Dodge.

He lay in his sleeping bag staring aimlessly at the domed, nylon ceiling. Beside him Tony snored gently. Tony who rarely spoke: but feared nothing. Simon would never have admitted it, but he idolized Tony. Tony had survival skills. Tony could fight (and on some of their previous escapades, had). Tony could get the girls. Lying here wasn't going to be enough to coax sleep. After several minutes of internal debate, Simon came to the conclusion that he did, in fact, have to piss.

Being considerate of his snoozing companion, Simon shuffled out of his sleeping bag, laced up his boots, and stealthily unzipped the tent. The cold mountain air made his teeth chatter. He went to pull on his coat over his boxer shorts then decided against it, for all the time he would be it didn't seem worth the struggle.

The last aura of twilight was fading fast. The world was awash with an alien ambience that made Simon fell lonely and ethereal. Maybe it was he who was the ghost? His eyes settled on the village well they had decided to camp next door to. 'They': meaning Gavin. Michelle had expressed her opinion on the campsite very vocally, Simon, as usual, remained quiet and obedient. He looked to Tony for guidance. Without a word, Tony had briskly surveyed the area and nodded. Strategically, it was the best spot.

Two votes against one and one neutral. It was decided, beside the creepy-as-fuck well it would be. He could still see the look of disappointment on Michelle's face when he closed his eyes. Why did he have to be such a chicken shit?

He cast a moody glower at Gavin and Michelle's tent and wondered if they had fucked before going to sleep. If he had just had the balls to ask her out way back when - well, it could have been him sleeping beside her instead.

Simon realized how weird it would be if anyone saw him staring longingly at the side of a tent and returned his focus to the watering hole. The metal covering had been bolted down tight; something told him it wasn't to stop people drinking the bog water. And don't think he hadn't spied the long, deep scratches that crisscrossed over it.

When they had first arrived Simon had thought he had heard strange sounds coming from below, muffled noises like the grunts and snarls of wild animals. The others had left him to set up the camp and had gone off to explore the church and the entrance to the mine (which was sealed by a cave-in, thankfully). Simon, not wanting to sound like a nervous ninny, had dismissed the sounds as being anything other than your bog-standard, run-of-the-mill, abandoned well sounds. Simon was always the first to freak out, he had promised himself that this time would be different. So he had kept his concerns to himself. An act he was seriously starting to regret.

He walked around the curve of the well and unbuttoned his

shorts then thought against it, he was still too close to the tents for comfort. Plus it felt rude to urinate so close as to where others slept. Instead, he crossed the open in the direction of the church, tripping over the log walkway twice.

His bladder felt full to the extent it bordered on painful, yet it was a good few minutes before it released its burden. This place had really gotten under his skin!

He watched as a chunk of ice broke away from its place on the churches dilapidated roof and slowly slid down the eaves. As the ice gathered momentum, Simon became aware of a slight, but noticeable, shift in temperature. The air had already been frigid but now his breath hung in a white cloud before his face. The little iceberg, along with the slush it had accumulated, tumbled from the roof and landed on the ground beside him with a wet 'plop'. Simon turned slowly to face the campsite because this was not the only sound he heard.

Nothing moved.

The world was eerily still.

Behind the village well he could see the twin apex's of the tents - one yellow, one blue. The ruined buildings remained desolate; shadowy sentinels to a Shangri-La of the Damned. Beyond them the serpentine sculptures of the tree line waited like poised snakes. Towering over all, looming like some ancient leviathan, was the Great Mountain.

It had probably been nothing to worry about. This was a secluded pocket of natural wonder, after all. An owl or some other nocturnal creature had likely made the noise as it went about its business.

Simon told himself to get it together, to stop being so god-damn jumpy, and started the short walk back to the campsite where he could stare blankly at the nylon until either sleep or daybreak arrived.

Around the halfway point he stumbled again on the walkway.

The logs had been buried so that only a fraction broke the surface of the ground; just enough to give cartwheels some traction. He hit the dirt with just enough force to warrant a moments recess. He sat on his ass and rubbed his knee. Tiny pinpricks of blood oozed to the surface of the graze. Simon, the notorious bleeder, was going to have to cover the wound quickly, as once he started bleeding it was usually a chore to get it to stop. His hand and forearm were already turning red. What a klutz he was. He flexed the joint, it was tender but he doubted it would swell. Then he saw the mud already beginning to cake on his thighs and buttocks.

Great.

Could this excursion get any worse? It was then he saw movement from the corner of his eye and knew that yes, it most definitely could.

...

If Simon had not only recently emptied his bladder, then he would have now. Had he not fallen, chances were the thing lumbering across the bridge would have spotted him first. Instead, it seemed focused on the brightly colored tents. Luckily for him, the circular wall of the well blocked most of his body from sight.

Simon was paralyzed. The thing was gigantic. It had to be a bear! He could do nothing as the thing lowered its huge head and took a step into the moonlight. No bear had a maw like that.

Simon found his voice which came out in a strained screech. 'WAKE UP! RUN!'

The creature charged. Behind its head emerged a bulk far larger than Simon had thought possible, and what the hell were those transparent *things* coming out of it?

A furious flurry of movement erupted from both tents. Michelle was the first out. She didn't stop to look around, like a woman possessed she ran full pelt towards one of the abandoned buildings and disappeared inside. Simon wondered if, she too, had been lying awake, just waiting for an event like this to occur.

Gavin had been next. He had flopped out of the tent like a newborn calf, eyes wide and full of alarm. He clocked Simon lying mostly naked in the dirt and, after following Simon's gaze, took to his heels and sped off into the marsh. He did not know what that thing was, and he sure wasn't sticking around to find out. Every man for himself. Good night and good luck.

The beast had arrived at Simon's tent when he finally gathered his wits enough to stand up. He watched aghast as the monstrous face tore into the side of the tent. Its fierce tusks and teeth annihilated the fabric. Tony (*who Simon had expected to be the first responder*), had not been resting on his laurels. Upon awaking, he had instinctively reached for his rifle and loaded a shot.

The blast was deafening, (*had Agnes been 100ft closer she would probably have heard its muffled sound bounce off the walls of Logan's Pass*). Simon's ears rang. A hole tore through the creature's cheek, spattering the ground with thick globs of blood and shards of bone. The beast cried out. Had Simon been able to hear it, he would have heard it was not of pain but pure, festering rage.

It snatched the rifle in its huge mouth, along with Tony's forearm, and swung its head back and forth, dragging the young man in agony from his tent. Tony was tossed through the air like a child's play thing. When his body landed on the well's covering, Simon had thought he had broken free of the beast's grip. It was only when the other man stood up and stared unbelievingly at the bloody stump where his arm had once been, that the truth of the situation became apparent.

Tony only now became aware of his friend standing idly in his underwear. Simon, although still unable to hear past the ringing in his ears, could read his lips perfectly.

'RUN!'

Never one to question Tony's authority, Simon spun on his heels and raced towards the church. When he reached the heavy oak door he stole a look back over his shoulder. The beast had finished guzzling down Tony's gun (and his arm), and was bearing down on the running man to finish the job. With one look into Tony's eyes, one last look, Simon knew his friend was about to expire.

Tony slumped to his knees. His shoulders slouched and his head lolled back. Simon prayed that whatever life-force exists, be it soul or otherwise, had exited his earthly vessel before the monster had thrown its mouth over his upper body and bit him in half. What was left of Tony remained kneeling in the filth as the enormous beast crunched noisily on the rest of him.

Simon felt a liquid warmth run freely down his legs. His bladder had spilled its reserve. The beast swallowed its meal then, still consumed by its bloodlust, turned its attention to Simon.

With a speed unnatural to a creature of its size, it barreled down upon him. Simon clamored inside and shoved the door shut with all his might. The beast collided with the outside wall, launching Simon clear across the room. He ricocheted off of the pews and landed in a dazed heap beside the opposite wall just in time to see a section of the balcony above him come crumbling down.

•••

When he regained consciousness, two things immediately struck him. One was that he was still, somehow, miraculously alive. The other was that he could hear again. When he heard the monster return to devour the rest of his friend, he wished he had stayed deaf.

CHAPTER 30

The young man looked at Agnes with disbelieving eyes. Agnes returned the same look; neither of them had expected to see another living soul. The man's chapped lips trembled as he leaned further into the light of the moon. He stood in the doorway, disheveled and partially dressed. Agnes spied the soiled underwear and felt a pang of heartache for him. His friends were dead; he had to be freezing, and to top it all off, he had been robbed of what little dignity he had. His mouth opened to speak. Agnes raised a finger to her lips and shook her head. He flinched as though she had physically struck him. Any trace of the man he had been was gone; all that remained was the fractured mind of a child. The experience he had somehow lived through had not made him stronger but left him perpetually terrified of anything and everything.

The pale moonlight made him look like an albino. His body was too thin. Agnes pondered on whether or not this was his regular appearance, or if it was some form of reflection of the situation he had found himself in.

More dust rained down as the beast pressed its colossal weight against the exterior walls. Agnes had learned a lot from studying the behavior of the forest's animals over the decades and she was happily confident that she knew its motive. It was testing the structure, circling the walls, looking for the weak spot.

The walls shook and the boy cried out. Agnes shot him a burning look. She did not want to chastise him *(hell, he had been through enough)*, but it wasn't just his position he was going to give away. It wasn't just his life on the line.

The beast stopped parading around the building. Agnes listened past the thud of her own beating heart to see if she could hear its tell-tale snorts. Silence. Had it given up? Fucked off to ruin someone else's evening? Agnes very much doubted it. More than likely it was taking a moment to reassess its tactics.

Movement across the room caught her eye. She turned her head and saw the semi-naked figure of Simon edging slowly towards her. His hair was matted across his forehead with sweat. His left eye blinked and quivered with a nervous tick. Something had come unhinged.

Agnes shook her head frantically, shooing him away, pleading for him to go back, to stay hidden in his recess.

Simon was nodding and smiling (or grimacing, Agnes was unsure which). He had taken the cease in the beast's onslaught to mean it had retracted, the fool was so desperate for it all to be over he had persuaded himself it had actually wandered off. He reached the center of the long room. He stood in a halo of moonlight between the pews, one arm out-stretched towards where Agnes hid, beckoning her to come to him. In this unholy chapel, he was offering *her* salvation.

One by one, but in quick succession, the candlesticks ignited. Agnes was sure there had been no candles on them when she had entered the church. They hissed into life with the puff of gas catching a flame. Each one appeared in a fireball before receding down to a gentle flicker. They did little to lighten up the room; Agnes knew this was not their purpose, this was another of the beast's theatrics, another move in its repertoire to instill fear.

It worked.

The smile fell from Simon's face; the glow of the candle light it made it look like his features were melting. He crumpled to the stone tiles as his knees gave out. From beyond the buildings crumbling veneer came the insidious, throaty laughter of the monster. Simon looked at Agnes for guidance; all that was visible of her was two nervous eyes staring out from between the wooden slats. He twisted and rotated on his buttocks and hips, unable to move from the circle of moonlight. His body was as weak as a new-born deer's and the moon's glow had him mesmerized like the hypnotic glare of a truck's headlights.

He had been reduced to the primal condition where an animal associates the dark with certain death. Agnes watched him pirouette and knew there was nothing she could do to save him.

A tumultuous gale rose and blasted up and over the buildings framework. The candles reacted and danced accordingly, but none of them extinguished. The wind died out as swiftly as it had been born. Simon cradled himself in a puddle of his own piss. Another of the creatures tricks. It relished instigating fear on others. Feasted upon it.

Agnes could see through its smoke and mirrors, its parlor tricks, but she was not foolish enough to think it didn't have the capability to back up its illusions with genuine acts of horrific violence. Stripped of its magic it was still a deadly foe – Michelle could attest to that.

Trudging, methodical footsteps approached the church. Simon, sprawled across the dusty tiles, gazed towards the direction of the advancing threat.

Simon looked too vulnerable, too exposed. He may have placed himself in the center of the room, but the combination of the moon's shine and the ominousness of the candelabras made him look just like an offering. Agnes could not shake her eyes off the sacrificial lamb, nor was she surprised when the ancient pagan deity rose up to claim its tribute.

The wall that pressed against her back groaned under the weight as something significant scaled its perishing stonework. Agnes could hear its perverse, raspy breath as it scurried up the flip side. It was so close she could smell it. Hell, she could practically taste it. A fragrant aroma of rot, sickness, and death.

Thankfully, the balcony's collapse had created a barrier between Agnes and the monster which now crowned the walls summit directly above her. Her own view was obscured (she could only make out its size and a few bristly hairs from between the spars), but Simon's terrified expression painted a clear picture of the nature of their nemesis.

Simon found himself once more locking eyes with the spawn of his very worst nightmares. The beast's enormous head and broad shoulders loomed over the collapsed wall like it was a nosey neighbor peering over the garden fence to discuss the latest gossip.

What scared Simon more than anything, more than its ghastly appearance, more than those long, sharp tusks, was the glint in its eyes. That glint showed this was no mindless predator; it had cunning and understanding in its arsenal. It was motivated by blood and carnage, and if it could understand him (which Simon believed it could), there could be no reasoning with it, no bargaining, no deal to be made.

Simon watched in equal shares of awe and repulsion as the beast opened its maw and a thick, black tongue lolled out. The vile thing was slick with globs of mucus which dropped off it and landed on the wooden planks below. Agnes flinched as some of them fell through the gaps and landed on her coat. The tongue slapped noisily off its chops. Simon realized it was salivating at the prospect of its next meal, namely - him.

Feebly, he began to plead for his life. 'No…no…please. Let me go…please… Please let me go… I don't want to die!' Tears flowed and snot bubbled from his nose and down onto his lips where he spat his words through it. When he saw his words were falling on deaf ears he resorted to screaming. His shrill voice, so pitiful and forlorn, bounced around the valley walls. The beast, in an act of ice cold cruelty joined his cry with one of its own, mockingly.

Simon, on his knees, his hands clasped together beseechingly, looked to Agnes for help. She could not meet his imploring stare. She turned her head to the side and squeezed her eyes tightly shut. Whatever was about to unfold, no matter how horrific, Agnes prayed it would be over quickly.

The young man's demeanor changed. Agnes snuck a peek and saw a terrible wave of acceptance wash over him. He stared at the dirt, his head nodding slightly like a man who has been told his disease is back, and this time it is terminal.

Simon knew he was done for; this was his finale, no encore. He hoped death was painless and that the monster would make its first move a kill shot. He thought of his mum and dad and felt sorry for them. It was unlikely they would ever find out what had happened to him. They would have a ceremony, eventually – once they had given up on finding him alive, but it would just be for show, there would be no body in his casket. Not unless they raked through the monster's shit. Simon closed his eyes. Better to not see it coming.

Agnes did not want to watch, but morbid curiosity prevailed. Every time she tried to look away she found herself being drawn back to the macabre spectacle. Simon knelt with his palms turned skyward. Agnes miss-read the gesture, she thought he was offering himself to the beast. Had she been able to ask him without giving away her own position, he would have told her it was a gesture of impatience.

'Come then… Get it over with, you bastard!'

The beast watched its prey surrender. Simon had hoped the monster would be satisfied knowing it had won. It tipped its Goliath-sized head back and roared in outrage at the moon. He didn't understand how, but he had somehow enraged the beast.

Agnes knew.

It had been denied the thrill of the fight. She also knew that it would punish him now. And punish it did.

From behind the creature rose the ghostly tendrils, four of them. They crept up and over its bulky mass and slithered down into the sanctuary of the church. Agnes froze in horror as two of them crawled down the boards she hid behind. She was close enough to see they had some substance to them, an almost viscous, milky liquid appearance. She could not see the other two and nearly got herself into a panic, what if they were coming for *her*?!

She did not have to wait long to find out.

On one hand, it was a relief to know she remained undiscovered - on the other... poor Simon.

The other two creeping limbs had snaked along some of the rafters and were slowly dangling down to hang on either side of the boy.

All four struck as one. Each took hold of an arm or a leg and with astonishing speed the young man was hoisted up into the rafters while the four constrictors tightened their grasps. His arms were pulled outwards in a blasphemous depiction of faith. Agnes heard a crack as one of his arms was twisted free of its socket. The lower ghost-arms tugged his legs downwards so violently, so *lustfully*, Agnes could see his skin stretch drastically over his ribs and abdomen.

The phantasmal appendages pulsed with whatever other-worldly force powered them. Each grotesque throb made them swell like fat worms, with each beat they became less like apparitions and more physically substantial.

Simon had hoped there would be a brief moment of pain followed by a veil of nothingness. His beliefs had never found a place for Heaven to be realistically considered, but now - as he faced the inevitable - the concept of pearly gates and harps was becoming very appealing.

Sadly, the beast had other plans, it was going to delay Simon's passing over until it had sated its diabolical penchant for violence.

He had managed to keep his eyes closed as he was raised upwards *(much to his own surprise. But then, the whole weekend had been one long surprise, had it not?)*. It was when his arm had been twisted and the sound of tearing muscle occurred by his right ear with resounding clarity, and the accompanying pain dragged him right back into that awful moment, it was then that his eyes had shot open and he was greeted by a vision of what Hell awaited.

At first he thought he had been apprehended by a mass of writhing snakes, until he laid eyes on their peculiar extremities which he could only describe as being fingers. They were too long and too sharply pointed to be considered human, but they had the same characteristics and dexterity of man, which repulsed Simon more than the drooling monster looming hungrily at him from its perch on the wall.

With each breath he expelled from his lungs the constricting limbs tightened, pulling and stretching his shoulders and torso. Looking at the beast's venomous glare, Simon knew it could end him easily if it wanted to; this was nothing less than a heartless act of retribution. In his life he had never imagined he would welcome death so gladly.

He wanted to call out, to beg the old woman for help. He knew there was nothing she could do, but the urge was nearly overwhelming. In a final moment of bravery, maybe to atone for his friends who he could not have saved *(but could have tried)*, he consciously avoided even looking in her direction. If the monster caught her, it would not be because of his actions.

Something inside him *twanged*. A frightening numbness crept down his spine, into his buttocks and throughout his legs. He struggled to draw a breath, a queer sensation of liquid warmth flowed around *inside* his midsection.

In the shelter of the rotten timber, in her own private booth, Agnes shuddered at the prospect of what was about to happen. Her mouth had filled with acrid bile when the monster had pulled apart the boy's spine. She could tell something terrible, and unrepairable, had happened by the unnatural shape his body had been contorted into. He had been stretched, his legs twisted to such an extent that both his feet nearly faced the wrong way around.

Simon's mouth started to froth as the death convulsions started. White and pink spittle spurted from his lips as his cries rose to an agonized scream. The beast joined him with its frenzied bellow. Its hideous wail became one of ecstasy as Simon's torso split, first on the left under his ribcage, and then rapidly spread across his stomach. The demon hog rejoiced as its monstrous tendrils pulled his arms free from his body. The air itself seemed to be misted in crimson.

Simon, in his wildest dreams, could never have imagined such pain. His head slumped forward and his brain could not process what it saw. Where once his legs had been there was only threads of gore and viscera hanging down in slick, ropey strands. A mess spattered the stone tiles below him in an ever-growing circle, but there was no part of him that had walked Suzy Dexter home after school, or danced with Grace Malone at his senior prom. Where were the legs he had been so fond of?

Dying and confused, he lifted his head meekly for the last time. The last thing he saw was the freakish ghost pythons feeding his lower half into the mouth of the abominable beast. They were free to wander, now that he had been tied up and suspended by his own intestines.

Shame.

Then his head lowered, the lights dimmed, and the world went away. The infinite nothingness was bliss.

CHAPTER 31

S o this was Hell.

Agnes felt cold and distant.

She hated the monster. Such cruelty had no place in this world; which probably explained why it wasn't from here. The evil fucker must have been banished long ago. She stood in the shadow of the fallen balcony and listened to the pitter-patter of a young man's insides decorating the floor. She prayed death brought peace – for all their sakes.

The beast had devoured most of the boy's thighs directly over her head. The life source had rained down upon her leaving streaks of red war paint in lines down her face.

The creature had hauled the remaining hunk of meat over the wall and carried it off into the swamp where it noisily crunched and chewed in delight. Agnes had no doubt it would finish every last morsel and then return for the rest. She had to make her break for freedom while it was… distracted.

As quietly as the crumbling wreckage would allow, Agnes gathered up her supplies and edged out from behind her shield. In the open she felt as naked as the dead boy. The frigid air stripped her of the imaginary security blanket the balcony had provided. She felt exposed on all sides *(and with those ghastly appendages on the prowl, maybe she was).*

Even though she could still hear it gnawing on bones, hers eyes darted wildly, checking for signs of an ambush or a sneak attack from a stray serpent *thing.*

She began to shoulder her rifle then changed her mind, from now until home it would be cocked and ready to go. Looking down the sights gave her confidence a nudge in the right direction. Putting a bullet into the beast's repulsive face would give her no end of joy. Even if it proceeded to tear her apart.

Fragments of glass from some long ago destroyed stained window *(no doubt depicting something horrendous)*, crunched under her feet as she crept towards the exit. In her haste to secure the building, she had inadvertently shut the door behind her, and now faced the predicament of trying to sneak out without alerting the monster.

The wrought iron ring handles were stiff and brittle. Agnes was reluctant to apply the necessary pressure to get them turning, lest their screech reached the beast's ears. It was no use; she couldn't get them to budge. When she had slammed the door in behind her she must have caused something in the mechanism to jamb. One last firm push resulted in her hand slipping down the sharp metal; she recoiled at the sight of the blood spreading out across her mitten.

'Fucksake!'

Not only was she trapped in the slaughter church, but now she was bleeding. She raised her arm out in front of her to stop the blood from running down her sleeve. Agnes didn't know how good the beast's sense of smell was, but she didn't want to be wandering about smelling like bait. For all she knew it could be picking up her scent right now, like how a shark hones in on a bucket of chum.

'Dammit,' she cursed her own clumsiness. 'Way to ring the dinner bell.'

Luckily, she had Wilson's first aid kit in an easily accessible pouch on the front of her pack. Within minutes she had wrapped the hand up nice and tight. Content her field dressing wasn't going to loosen, Agnes reassessed her current situation. She had dealt with problem number one, but problem two was a doozie - she was still stuck in the rotten, old building. Agnes had to find another way out. Carefully, she traced a route around the churches interior, looking for any signs of ruin that might signal a crawl hole big enough for her to shuffle through. She made a point of giving Simon's splash zone a wide berth.

The room in which she had first laid eyes on the near-naked boy was much smaller than she had expected. It was empty of all contents and charm. A thin sliver of a window built into the stone was the closest thing to decoration and it was far too narrow for Agnes to attempt an escape. If this room had indeed housed a priest in the village's hay-day then he must have lived a life of minimalism.

'…and been a real prick,' thought Agnes, contemplating what sort of asshole would worship such an evil deity.

The only other objects of note in the room were signs of Simon's length of stay hiding from his nightmare. Agnes had put the smell down to the putrid swampland. Now she knew how shit-scared he had been. She turned her back on the steaming excrement and left the small room to fester.

The other door was practically inaccessible. Agnes could see no way around the shrubbery and debris that had smothered this quarter of the building. Squinting into the darkness of the doorway (she dared not shine a light source), she could make out the vague shape of rising stairs. Most likely this meant that the only place that room led to was the top of the crumbling belfry. The fall of the bell had created enough carnage and destruction to the towers structure to completely dismiss the idea of forcing a way up from Agnes' mind.

Besides, what would she do at the summit, jump?

Her old feelings towards enclosed spaces were returning. Her chest was tightening. For a brief moment she considered scaling the lean-to balcony she had only just made use of, but promptly crushed such foolish thoughts. She could probably scramble up and over it with considerable effort, but to what avail? The beast had skulked off from here and she didn't want to go leaping straight into its waiting *'arms'*.

A 'eureka!' moment chimed into her head. Maybe the floor had a trapdoor; it had been the solution last time!

Nothing.

Not on the areas she could see or reach anyway. She even went back and checked the little room with the big turd. In the main room, a quick glance under Simon's guts clarified that it was not going to be an exit through a passage of blood. For that, she was thankful. Then it came to her. Of course...

Her head turned slowly, pivoting to look at the furthest corner of the hall. The darkest corner. The one that had sunk into the moldering mire of the swamp. That inky water had to have got in somewhere. The question was, had it seeped in over the course of years due to deterioration, or had it crashed in when the bell had pulverized the building below? Agnes walked down the center of the candle-lit pews to find out.

CHAPTER 32

The back corner had sunk a lot more than she had first thought. Without the support of a solid terrain holding it up, the weight of the stones and timber had begun to pull the structure apart. Stepping into the shadows, her eyes adjusted to the dim light, it was easy to see how precarious the standing remains were. It could happen a hundred years from now or in the next few minutes, but at some point, this entire quarter would collapse in on itself and be swallowed up by the black ooze of the bog. Overhead, the log roof trusses were dangerously splintered; many beams had come free from their joints and hung aimlessly in the air. The slightest nudge could bring the whole thing crashing down.

Agnes took her first step into the murk with a tender foot. The slick gloop came up to the top of her boot. Its icy chill seeped through the material and froze her toes almost immediately. She was going to have to bite the bullet and do this quickly. Her muscles tensed rigidly in preparation of what was definitely going to be a bitter cold experience.

She waded in and it came slurping and frothing up to her knees. Her boots overflowed and became leaden; each step was a strain on her efforts. Her head bumped against a dangling spar and she braced herself for the inevitable cave-in. She stood for several

'Mississippi's' with her head cradled in her folded arms. When she eventually reappeared from below her little canopy of weak bone and flesh, she brought with her the expression of someone who can't believe they are still alive. Well, for the time being. If she didn't start moving again soon she would likely give herself hypothermia.

Under the viscous soup her feet bumped against various unseen objects, some of which felt organic by nature. Agnes shuddered at the image of being surrounded by swamp rats. Pointed yellow teeth searching for something soft to sink into...

Instead of randomly submerging and prodding blindly at the walls, Agnes had the idea to softly *(quietly)* push the fetid stew at the stonework with just enough strength to create an air pocket. Her hopes were, 'Where there's a bubble, there's a hole'.

She sloshed the slimy water with her boot towards the closest segment of the wall. The ripples crossed the surface, hit the stone and came back to her, but in lesser numbers and without gusto. No bubbles rose to the surface.

Agnes readjusted her position and repeated the process, this time forcing the slurry into the corner where the two walls met. Her toes were simultaneously going numb and stinging with ice fire. Again, no pocket of trapped air revealed itself.

She aligned herself with the last section of wall; her movements growing increasingly sluggish. Her dry, chapped, trembling lips uttered something akin to a prayer, and she shoved the crud filled sludge with all the effort she could muster.

'Please, please, please...' she pleaded, fingers crossed, as the swell crested and broke against the moss covered stone. A few ripples returned to her, but nothing else. She was done for. No exit – no hope. The icy grasp had climbed her legs to just above her knees. She turned to wade out of the chilly pool of muck.

'Ba-Loop...'

Her neck shot round so fast she nearly unscrewed her head. The surface water ran in a furrow towards her. With bated breath she waited, and watched... the internal thud of her heart beat so hard she could swear she could feel the rhythmic pulse of blood traversing her veins. *'Come on...*

...

... please...'

...

... 'Ba-Loop!'

Agnes, had she had the strength, would have jumped for joy. A fat, oily bubble surfaced and popped right beside the wall where she had disturbed the mulch. In the depths of this revolting pool, maybe, lay an opening to the midnight world beyond. The temptation to hurl herself towards it was one that could only be dampened by the terrifying possibilities that lay on the other side. For all she knew, this could very well be one of those *frying pan/fire* situations.

From where she stood in the recess of the church, she could no longer hear the beast dining. Although it could be as simple as being out of earshot, she wasn't going to kid herself that it had gone away. Any moment it could appear over the rise, seeking to claim the rest of its feast.

An image of a white face peering at her from the middle of a swamp rose up in her mind and she had to physically shake it away. If this did indeed turn out to be a fruitful venture and she found herself out in the open, then she would have to tread with extreme caution. Let Gavin serve as a warning to what a mad dash could lead to. Her fingers crossed, she slid through the dark water to investigate.

CHAPTER 33

Agnes nearly lost her footing as the floor beneath her feet dropped away in a radically steep gradient. The stone tiles here had been washed away and now she treaded on broken banks of silt and gravel. The murky water took no time in submerging her up to her armpits; the sudden descent, along with the frosty weight of the icy bog water, constricted her chest and stole the air from her lungs. Instinctively, she raised the rifle above her head, her backpack was not as lucky as it disappeared into the tarry blackness.

Agnes fell to her hands and knees when she reached the stone floor again. Well, that had been unexpected. She couldn't risk the rifle filling up with scum, to try and venture back home without it seemed, not only perilous, but nigh on suicidal. Surprisingly, the contents of her pack had faired their dip in the slime quite well.

Shaking off as much gunk from herself and her equipment as she could, she went to the wall where the jammed door stood. It was situated at the furthest point from where the boar-faced demon had made its grand entrance. If she could throw her stuff up and through the gaping hole where the roof should have been, then she should be able to retrieve it on the other side without being detected. But first she had to make sure she had an exit.

(*Something that only dawned on her as she was preparing to launch the rifle. Damn, that would've been stupid*).

Leaving her gear leaning against the old oak door, Agnes, with new found purpose, waded into the frigid water. She thrust both hands into the thick brew of stagnant slush and mulch. Her fingers grazed many an unpleasant encounter as she frantically searched the stonework for an opening. The process was taking much longer than she had expected, she felt her window of opportunity shrinking smaller and smaller.

As if to sum up her fears, a ferocious roar shattered the still of the forest. The buffet was open for seconds.

Agnes kicked it up a gear; fingers clawing in frenzy at the wall below the surface. She slipped forward, clattering her chin against the bricks; her left hand reached out and fell upon nothing. So there *was* a hole? Her other hand plunged to join its counterpart and, sure enough, there was a gap. A big, beautiful gap.

No time to celebrate. Agnes rushed back to her gear and tossed them over to the flip side. The backpack landed with the dullest of thuds, but the stupid rifle found a rock, its clang sounded, to Agnes anyway, loud enough to wake the dead. She didn't wait to see if the beast was going to investigate.

Back at the hole, Agnes didn't hesitate. She sucked in a lungful of air and allowed herself to be completely consumed by the dark ooze.

Blind.

Deaf.

She had expected to be in a panicked state, what she had not anticipated was the serene, almost comforting absence of senses. Under the blanket of the swamp she felt almost safe, tucked away from the monster that prowled the surface world. What worried her more than anything was the acceptance she found she had, if this was what awaited in death, maybe it wasn't so bad?

Such a dangerous thought had to be banished, which she did as she pulled her body through the hole. The stones were coated in enough slime to allow her to pass through without gouging herself, although a few managed to leave little scrapes along her back.

She was nearly clear when she felt a tug on her right leg. She kicked out; knowing one of the beast's serpentine tendrils had her. Throughout her entire body a warm rush of blood circulated, it seemed to even heat up the surrounding mire that '*glooped*' and bubbled in her panicked thrashing. She could not quite get her head high enough to break the surface and draw air. Her lungs burned. She waited on the sharp withdrawal the beast would give her as it dragged her backwards through the gap. After all the effort spent trying to elude the monster, she had failed, she was going to be chewed up and devoured anyway. But no sudden jolt came, Agnes wanted to scream at herself. Foolish, foolish old woman! Dottled fool!

The creature had not snared her, her foot had just became snagged on some unseen obstruction; probably nothing more than a root or creeper vine. Agnes stretched back through the hole and managed to free herself with ease.

Her head emerged from the frothy pond, slick with scum and debris. It trickled down her face in gooey, black syrup. She inhaled loudly, never before appreciating the necessity of the pungent swamp air. With the balls of her fist she cleared the majority of the sludge from her eyes and peeled her hat off. She saw the moon and the stars, the shadowy trees draped in the finest lichen, the yellow eyes of an owl. Such a view was filled with ominous mysticism, but to Agnes, at that moment, it was the most beautiful sight she had ever seen.

CHAPTER 34

A wind from the west was gathering momentum. It spiraled through the trees in little outbursts like a child throwing a tantrum. Amongst the gales were the fine particles of sleet, the kind that never looks to carry much threat, and then proceeds to soak you to the bone.

Agnes moved against the weather as she made her way through the forest of warped trees. She could see very little through the thick, twisted canopy, but the world was getting lighter, she believed night was becoming day. With each step she put more and more distance between herself and the cursed settlement.

'And good fucking riddance.'

She retraced the route she had come in on, but not going at such a speed that would be careless; nothing looked familiar, just endless swampland. Her clothes, already leaden with a dense coating of muck, seemed to absorb the rain and sleet and were getting heavier. Combined with the fatigue that drained her, the combination was swiftly becoming a volatile mixture.

It was the warming thoughts of hot cocoa (spiked with a generous measure of whiskey), warm clothes (not caked in blood and dirt), and a roaring fireplace that kept her kicking one foot in front of the other-

-And Wilson. She had a lot to speak to him about. So many questions...

The falling water was gathering in pools all along the already precarious pathways. The swamp rose up to meet them, in some places it had already spread itself from one side to the other, spilling into puddles and conquering them like an invading empire.

Fresh streams swept away the topsoil, uncovering crooked roots that tried to catch her boots like snare traps. Twice she passed the bleached skull of a ram, she had to believe it was *not* the same one; she could not be traipsing in circles. *Could not.*

Light, up ahead...

Cloudy yellow, like a swirl of curdled milk, but light nonetheless. It was still some way off - the winding path would make it even further - but hot-damn if that wasn't the way out! The sickly shimmer, no more than a vague glimpse caught between the gnarled and knotted trees, was enough to refresh Agnes anew. Home was still a hell of a hike away on the other side, but at least she wouldn't die in this fucking swamp!

The faintest of smiles quivered upon her thin lips. She had to restrain herself; otherwise she knew she would breakdown. There would be time for all that later. Time to reflect. Time to slide into a therapeutic nervous collapse.

Faster and faster she navigated the marsh, leaping over roots and puddles with vigor then-

-then...

'Oh no. Nonononono...'

The creamy light suddenly obscured. Swiftly, Agnes dropped to her knees (their crack audible over the rainfall). She peered through the undergrowth towards her only known exit. Her senses were on red alert. Something had passed in front of the dim-but-present daylight; its enormous girth obstructing the dingy glow, reducing it to little more than a few lackluster streaks.

The silhouette it formed, to Agnes, was unmistakable. Its magnitude, together with the boorish way it shook its head and shifted its feet, meant only one thing. The beast had gotten ahead of her and was waiting. It had cut her off at the pass. Its hunt was not over.

...

It was as if the entire woodland held its breath. Not only in anticipation to see what the old woman would do next, but also in fear of provoking the beast. It emitted malice the way oil spreads over water. Even the trees near it seemed to shrink away, aghast at the appalling fetish for violence that oozed from it.

From a perch high above her head came an unexpected cackle, Agnes flinched as a crow cried out and took off into the safety of the vast sky. The treacherous bird kicked off with such a careless retreat that the upper branches shook and trembled enough to break free a handful of twigs.

Agnes wasn't watching the small sticks raining down around her; her focus was on the behemoth that glared in her direction, its crimson eyes lit by hate.

'Thanks for that, you flying bastard. Why not just stick up a flashing neon sign? *She's over here!*'

She had expected the monster to charge, bringing with it a fiery tempest of rage and brutality. She had certainly not expected it to lower its head and slowly, yet methodically, start sniffing the ground like a bloodhound.

It *was* coming, though. If she stayed here it would be on her sooner than later. She had to move, stealthily. Looking over her shoulder at the dark and sinister path, she promptly binned the idea of going back to the settlement. That was a chapter she would not be revisiting. No way, no how.

This left her with a very limited set of options. The waters were still rising around her; it could be possible to navigate the little islands and peninsulas if she was careful. Again, that stark image of Team Leader Gavin's rat infested head poo-pooed that idea. She was sick fed up of hiding. Waiting. That left her one route. And boy, was it a doozey.

CHAPTER 35

A ridge had opened up, exposed by the cascading rainfall. It snaked from tree to tree like a prehistoric creature's spine. It was narrow and surrounded on either side by deep, deep pools. It was precarious, but in light of the alternative, it shone like a golden path. Agnes tried to spy the beast through the swampy foliage, she couldn't see it, it had moved beyond her line of sight. Keeping as low as she could without seizing up, she tiptoed across the flooded path to the ridge. Her thought being that if she could just keep a reasonable distance between her and *'It'*, there was a fair chance she could find a way using the tree roots to circle around the beast and escape via the entrance.

The roots were slippery, slick with sleet and slimy algae. Every footstep had to be carefully placed as to avoid the many knots that protruded from the branches like buboes on a plague victim. Eyes bobbed from below the black water, watching her curiously. Agnes prayed they belonged to frogs or toads and not *something* new. One fucking monster was proving to be more than enough.

She lost her footing and skidded down, her left foot plopped into the mire. Her shin smacked the knobbly wood and she had to stifle a yelp by biting down on her hand. Any noise she had made had not carried far enough to alert the beast of her position. Still, she waited, listening...

Only when she was confident nothing was going to come barreling down upon her, did she (painfully) get up and push on.

The pain in her shin was a non-issue. She was getting used to the bumps and scrapes. When she came to a section where all the roots were submerged and hidden from sight however, it suddenly became something to think about. She was sure she could make the leap but...

But if her shin should cause her to buckle on the other side she might find herself in real trouble.

Between her side and the other was an expanse of murky water just over a meter across. To most people, this would amount to not much more than a simple step, to an old woman riddled with arthritis and a plethora of other ailments, well; it could just as well have been the Grand Canyon.

Agnes braced herself; she could feel her legs vibrating involuntarily as her aching muscles went into spasm. She pushed off. She saw (in that strange slow motion reserved for moments like these) herself gliding through the air in the oily reflection of the scummy pond below, as graceful as a swan. She landed delicately on the other side, feet together like a gymnast.

She felt the weight of her pack bounce off her back. She felt gravity do its thing. She felt herself fall backwards into the bog with a splash.

For the briefest of moments, no more than a second, her head bobbed under the tarry surface. The unsavory water invaded her nostrils and filled her mouth. Her eyes, which had not had time to close, viewed the canopy through a shimmering filter of brown and yellow. She bolted upright, sputtering and coughing out the muck. Her revulsion caused her to momentarily forget about the bigger picture and she sat wiping the crap from her arms in disgust.

A deep, gravelling snort, much like laughter, brought her back to the present with a thud. It was like a punch to the chest. Her head spun over her right shoulder and there he was. No more than a hundred meters away. Vermillion eyes jeering at her. Plumes of white vapor puffing from his massive snout. She had given herself away. Bingo. The hunter had his eye on the prize, now he just had to line up the shot and…

'And not fucking today, you insufferable bastard!'

Agnes shot off like a rocket, no longer treading lightly, nor carefully. Her boots stomped a path across the balance beams made of roots and branches, it no longer mattered if it was done with grace and poise, as long as she was in motion.

Behind *(too close!)*, came the earth-shaking charge of a ravenous boar. Close enough now to catch a whiff of its carrion odor. The stench attacked her eyes and throat, still she raced on. Her heart leapt up into her mouth, damn it all to hell if she hadn't gone and trapped herself!

A towering wall of briar stretched out in front of her. The dynamic of its curvature made it appear to not only be infinite, but also as though folding in on itself to form a trap, a pen of which there was no way out.

She could not about turn and face the beast; if needs must she would ram her way through the seemingly impenetrable tangle of thorns until she was torn to ribbons. Which is exactly what she did.

As luck would have it, some other animal had already carved its own path through the jumble of sharp branches. Just as Agnes was preparing to throw herself upon its mercy (literally), she spotted the small, round burrow at the foot of the wall. Swinging her backpack off and in front of her in one beautiful, fluid motion, she dropped to her stomach and furiously army crawled into the dark hollow. To say it was a tight squeeze would have been an understatement, the barbs that jabbed and raked at her made her all the more conscious of the confines of the space.

With each nudge forward she moved deeper into the overgrown thicket. The rifle, burden that it was, repeatedly became entangled in the thorny mess, but due to previous events, Agnes was reluctant to relinquish said burden.

No light could penetrate far enough down through the underbrush. The darkness was exquisite, yet also terrifying. Agnes could not decide whether she felt the fear of being enclosed, or overly exposed in a vast expanse of space. When a barb snatched at her hair and tried to scalp her, she settled on the prior. She had lost her hat. Was it in the bog or back in the mines? She had no idea, only that it was no longer on her head. She had a vague visual in her mind of wringing it out after she had escaped Simon's tomb. She wondered why she even cared. In her current crisis, what the hell did it matter? A few paces further on, and she realized there was something else missing: the weird-looking cassette player. It wasn't in her pocket anymore. She wondered if she had lost anything else that she wasn't aware of. She had hoped to hear the rest of the recording, now all she had was the camera.

A cataclysmic collision erupted behind her. The beast had not only caught up, but using its incredible strength and thick hide, was planning on making one hell of an entrance.

Agnes ignored the persistent needles that whinnied for her attention with their incessant pokes and prangs. Opposed to the chaotic thrashing sounds that travelled down the burrow behind her feet they were small change.

On and on… deeper and deeper…

Agnes had lost all sense of direction, she could not tell if she had swung left nor right, she wasn't even sure which way was up. All that she was certain of was the beast was behind her, and as long as that remained a constant, then the bastard wasn't going to be suddenly popping up in front of her like some hideous Jack-in-the-box.

The branch-shattering impacts came in 3 second bursts as the beast charged back and forth relentlessly trying to bash its way through to her. To Agnes' dismay she found herself in a section of tunnel that was considerably narrower than the rest, she practically had to lie completely prone and shuffle forward dragging her face through the dirt. Before she had managed to squeeze her bony hips through the slender passage, she became acutely aware that the barrage had seized. Her puzzlement did not last long. Grunting wildly, she shimmied onwards as fast as she could, well aware of why the monster had stopped.

Her feet had barely cleared the tapered section of the crawlway when she felt the desperate, grasping fingers brush her heels.

She scuttled away until her back was pressed against a wall of weaved bracken. She had emerged in a den of some sorts. A natural gap in the coarse network of vines and branches overhead allowed the faintest rays of light to feebly spill down to her. She could see she was in a dome-shaped clearing no bigger than a two-man tent. The floor was littered with gnawed bones and scat, but neither seemed fresh, Agnes felt sure that whatever creature had called this home was long gone.

Her eyes danced over the opening she had sprung forth from. Although grateful to be sitting in the little well of light, her vision needed to readjust to the darkness of the tunnel once more. She swallowed her breath and blinked repeatedly until the blackness revealed its secrets.

It came slowly, almost timidly. Agnes saw its muted luminosity drift like a ghost into focus. It slivered like a fat albino python, except where a head would be there was something perversely like a human hand. As it crawled blindly into the dim morning light, Agnes could make out all the details that made it so alien and unnatural.

Fingertips like little daggers carried the palm as a spider carries its body. Each extremity bore an extra knuckle. The finger-like appendages reached out on their own like an insects feelers, probing the dirt, sensing shifts in the air. Agnes forced herself to not react upon her revulsion. The scream in her throat had to remain lodged where it was.

The way it took its time showed it was confident she was trapped; it would drag her out kicking and screaming when it wanted to.

Agnes hugged her knees to her chest. The 'hand' was crawling left to right, sweeping over the ground until it connected with the walls of the den then going back again. Searching...

It was almost upon her. She placed the rifle upright between her knees. Her finger hovered near the trigger. She had decided. If she felt it snatch her she would put the barrel in her mouth and **BOOM!** Nighty night. That's all folks. No hesitation. No second thoughts. No 'ifs', no 'buts'. Just like turning off a lamp before bedtime.

Ok? Ok.

She squeezed her eyelids tightly shut and tried not to think about the inevitable. She pictured Wilson's face. The face she had known in life – not the shabby night visitor she knew now. His gentle eyes creased with laughter lines, his rosy cheeks, chubby and friendly. The smile that welcomed you before infecting you with its contagiousness. She could almost smell his scent, musky, but with the cleanliness of old pine.

'I'm coming Wilson. I'm coming...'

...

The wait was excruciating. What was taking so long? Was the beast toying with her?

She allowed herself a quick peek and had to stifle a hysterical outburst of laughter. Less than half a foot away, inches from the toe of her boot, the ghostly hand pawed at empty air. Behind it lay the snake-like arm, stretched out to maximum length. Agnes grinned like a maniac, her face contorted by the madness that threatened to consume her.

'Well ain't that a stroke of luck, you miserable bastard? Didn't quite measure up, did ya?' she spoke in a stage whisper, before clamping her hand over her mouth. If she kept quiet maybe it would think she had escaped.

Careful to not accidentally drift into its reach, Agnes edged up the thorny wall until she was as close to upright as the cramped space allowed. She had been too focused on finding a way out on the ground level she hadn't noticed the opening beside her head. The 2 foot wide gap sat at shoulder height and looked to lead into another tunnel. This had to be it; she could exit by the backdoor!

There was only one problem. To get through to the passage she would have to crawl over the briar, and those thorns were razor sharp. There was no way she was getting over it without being torn to shreds. While she pondered her dilemma she absent-mindedly took a careless step in the wrong direction. The fingers of the ghost-arm clawed at her boot cuff, attacking like a spider strikes at its prey. She kicked out at it, stomping down hard on it with her other foot. From overhead came the sound of snapping twigs. She looked up in horror as a second ghost-arm slivered down through the light shaft. Free of the beast's grasp, she shed her heavy coat and threw it roughly over the thorn covered shelf. She loved that coat but her continued survival required its sacrifice.

She tossed her backpack and gun through the hole and clamored over the jacket. Even though it took the brunt of the punishment, a few thorns still managed to snag her skin and penetrate her flesh like needles.

Agnes fell face first onto her rucksack, her boot heels kicking the back of her head. She flopped sideways and lay in a crumpled heap. That was a sore one, her back was going to feel it tomorrow – if she should live that long.

Groggily, she stood up, having to stoop to avoid raking her scalp against the roof of the burrow. She turned to retrieve her coat, but couldn't shift it. The thorns had it hooked good and proper. The second ghost hand dropped into view and Agnes flinched at its close proximity. The fingertips brushed against the coat and rapidly assaulted it. Within seconds, the jagged fingers had sunk into the thick material and were hauling it up and away through the shaft.

'You can keep it,' she thought, smirking at the rage the beast would have when it realized the coat was empty.

The tunnel narrowed, but not as severely as the first passage, here she could wear her pack as long as she hunkered down. Although there was no way to tell if she was headed towards a way out, she had to maintain that it would be likely – especially as turning back was no longer a possibility. The depth of the undergrowth did well to muffle the beast's fury but Agnes could still hear its manic temper tantrum. The burrow, not quite as dense as before judging by the slight increase in light levels, was spectacular in its intricacy. The weave of thorn covered branches coiled in a seemingly never-ending spiral. Agnes had no clue as to what forest dwelling creature had constructed it, but she was eternally grateful to it.

She felt she was a safe enough distance from her pursuer to be able to use the head torch and pulled it from her pack. It blinked twice then died. She tossed it aside and continued on in darkness until she remembered the camera she had stashed in her bag. The rucksack had proved itself invaluable, even after fully submerging in the putrid swamp it had managed to keep its contents (mostly) dry. Agnes fumbled with the side panel, first turning the machine on, then powering up the torch beam. On the little display window the screen was pale blue as nothing was filming or playing back. A small white symbol was flashing in the bottom right corner though and Agnes (although not particularly *'tech savvy'*) knew exactly what it meant. The battery was running low. It still showed three of the six possible bars, but the cabin had no charge points, let alone the required cables to power the damn thing. She had a choice to make here, either use its remaining juice to light her way, or view the tape later. It wasn't just the possibility that the camcorder could contain some vital clues or information about her monstrous adversary, it was also because she wanted, craved, to feel a part (even if it was just as a voyeur) of the group of young filmmakers. She felt she owed them that at least. They had died for their art, after all.

She switched it off and carefully replaced it, almost ceremoniously, as though she were handling sacred remains, which, in some way, she was. She had made it this far in the dark, so why not a little longer?

CHAPTER 36

A little longer turned out to be a considerable distance; the burrow wound a crazy path through the spiny brush. Her sense of direction had been well and truly obliterated. To add to her confusion, she found herself going up a gradual incline. Just where in the *blue blazes* was she going?

She could no longer hear the beast, she could hear no sound at all, except for her own scurrying across the twigs and tiny bones that lay scattered around. This could mean several things, none of which were particularly great. The monster could simply be out of earshot, frantically throwing itself against the fortress of thorns, lost in a blind and savage rage. But what if it wasn't, what if it was following the perimeter, searching for the tunnel from which she would eventually emerge? Only time would tell, Agnes mentally prepared herself for the worst.

An oval disk of light rose up ahead. Agnes let loose a deep sigh of relief. The closer she got to the opening, the tighter the space became. The final stretch required her to crawl on her hands and knees. The temperature dropped with each foot she advanced on the exit; she hadn't noticed until now how warm the interior of the burrow had been.

White flakes pirouetted down from the skies and came to rest on her slender shoulders. She sure missed her coat. She stretched, straightening out all of her limbs, and sucked in a gracious breath of crisp mountain air. She was back out in the great, wide open and it felt as refreshing as a dip under a waterfall.

She was taken aback to find herself so high up on the mountain side. The meandering burrow had taken her up and over a ridge that completely by-passed Logan's Pass. From where she stood she was able to look out over the sprawling treetops of the forest she called home. Even though the sky was grey and the view was washed out of color, Agnes thought it had truly never looked as beautiful. She still had a fair amount of ground to cover, but seeing the familiar landmarks and mountain tops made it seem plausible. The cherry on top came with the observation that there was no sign of a certain hog-faced monster prowling around below. Now she just had to figure out how she was going to get down…

Luckily, whatever animal had created the burrow had also carved a rough path that rambled down-slope towards the wagon trail. Agnes blessed the wonderful creature. If it had appeared before her she would probably have given it a big, wet kiss. Pack on, rifle ready, she started for home.

…

The journey back to the cabin was arduous. The falling sleet had caused the snowdrifts to thaw enough to create slushy streams of run-off that careened downhill like interconnecting veins. The sleet had been a precursor to a much heavier storm; Agnes had barely crossed the halfway point when she found herself snow-blind in a whiteout. Fortunately, she knew this part of the woods well enough to avoid getting lost. All the while, she could not shake the dire possibility that somewhere (and maybe closer than she cared to think about) there could be a living nightmare tracking her down. After all, the wolf had ended up at her door…

Now was not the time to be pondering such horrors though, with the knowledge that home was within reach, Agnes had her blinders on and pushed on like a mule.

The familiar sight of the cabin materialized out of the whitewash. Agnes lost the strength in her knees, overcome with a flood of emotions she had no defense against. The edges of her vision turned black and her eyes began to roll up into her skull. She realized she was going to pass out. She was unconscious before her face fell flat into the fresh snow. And to think, she had been so damn close.

CHAPTER 37

The storm continued its relentless bombardment. The snowdrifts that had started to defrost were soon twice as large as they had been to begin with. The rivers and streams froze where the currents were weak and became mirrored sheets of ice. Sky and earth shared the same palette of white and grey making them indistinguishable from one another. Far from the other humans who took refuge in the homes and bars of the cities and towns, an old woman was waking up in the middle of a great forest. But she was not alone.

It was cold. The sound that broke her from her involuntary slumber was the *chitter-chatter* of her own teeth. Although she tried, she could not quite muster the strength to open her eyelids. Her entire body, from her exposed scalp down to her worryingly numb toes, felt groggy; as though trying to wake from the deepest of sleeps.

She had a vague recollection of passing out. It had brought with it the sensation of sinking under water. She remembered the snow and the storm that carried it. But she had collapsed outside in the thick of it, why then was she still alive and not a frozen, dead Popsicle? And more importantly, because even though her eyes could not open she could still tell, was she now under shelter?

The recovery process was a slow one. Her body, after all the turmoil she had put it through, was desperate to shut down and sleep. Pins and needles fluttered down her arms and legs making her muscles twitch and spasm in uncontrollable bursts. Gradually, she began to feel in control again, and not like a passenger in her own body. As her senses awoke, she became distinctly aware of a peculiar sound coming from behind her head. She frowned and forced her eyes to open.

She was lying on her back, above her ran rows of neglected timber, eaten away in places that allowed individual flakes to fall through and gently land on her face. The smell of damp wood was strong, but not enough to mask a secondary scent, something organic and familiar, something like…

Agnes' eyes shot open, wide and fearful. She knew that smell, and also where she was. Keeping still, but allowing her eyes to confirm her hypothesis, she took in her surroundings. To her left, a stack of branches, some smaller twigs ideal for kindling. On her right side a rickety old wooden door, slick with mold and moss. Through the gap she spied a snowy flurry that was slowly covering the red-stained ground.

Somehow, she had ended up on the wrong side of the woodshed door. Something soft and furry brushed against her hair. The wolf was right behind her.

...

Making a break for it was not on the cards. Agnes still lacked the strength to fire up and take flight. The wolf would have her before she had even gotten to her feet. This was a precarious situation best handled delicately. She thought it wise to alert the animal to her waking presence through soft murmurs and very restrained movements. Anything too raucous could be perceived as an act of threatening behavior, or even worse, as lunch trying to escape.

The animal had taken to her well enough in the short period of time they had spent in each other's company, but *that* wolf had been weak, *that* wolf could barely move, *that* wolf had been *fed*.

She closed her eyes and pretended to be rousing from sleep, making little whimpers as if coming out of a bad dream. *A bad dream indeed!* She felt the fur behind her shift. The wolf had taken an interest.

She had to keep her little play rolling; a forced yawn and a (*slowly!*) stretch would hopefully sell it. A blast of hot, meaty breath was promptly followed by a dripping wet tongue that ran from her temple down to the point of her chin. It was done purely as an act of affection. There could be no mistaking it. Agnes opened her eyes and saw the wolf's inverted face looking down upon her. He looked even bigger than she remembered; she couldn't help but think how her entire head could probably fit inside its mouth.

'Hello, boy,' she croaked through a dry throat. 'How ya been?' The wolf cocked his head to the side, the dark fur of his eyebrows sloped in a comically puzzled look. 'Nice to see you remember me, buddy. For a moment there I thought maybe you were lining me up as a snack.'

Agnes managed to sit up. Beside her she found her backpack. One of the arm straps had been torn along the stitching. The frayed edges were slimy with wolf drool. She rolled onto her side so that she was level with the animal.

'You saved me? she asked the wolf. 'You did, didn't you? You pulled me in here.' She grinned at him. 'You wonderful, magnificent beast!' She could see from where she slouched that his wounds were healing nicely. 'I guess you could say we're even now then.' She gave him a wink and rubbed his ears. 'I'd love to stay and chat, believe me when I say I've got a lot we could talk about, but I need to get inside before I die of exposure.'

She stood up. A wave of light-headedness came and then passed momentarily. She was more than ready to curl up in Wilson's chair and sleep like the dead, but before she did she had one thing she wanted to do.

'I owe you my life, you giant lug, so let me get you something to eat as thanks.'

There was some dried venison strips in a jar in the kitchen. They would have to do until she managed to defrost some meat from the freezer.

CHAPTER 38

A vast expanse of white covers the world. A bleak and unforgiving landscape made all the more hostile by a new and unwelcome presence that had settled in and made this world its home.

From far above, at the origins of all storms, a speck of light can be spied in the center of the frozen mural. Swollen flakes spiral down towards it as if attracted like moths to its enticing glow. To peer through the frost-encrusted windows of the little cabin is to steal a glance at a scene from a Christmas card. The fireplace is roaring, its flames lighting and warming the room. The snow outside the windows shimmers with the orange reflection of the dancing flames.

Inside, curled up under a patchwork quilt, upon an old and worn out chair, sleeps an old woman who had faced the hostilities of this frightening world and survived. In the corner of the room, in a dark spot that could never be considered natural, a figure watches her sleep. The figure has grown weaker; he knows soon he will no longer be able to cross the void between this world and the next. He has much to discuss with her; matters of urgency that would need to be addressed as soon as possible. But for now he lets her sleep. He smiles at her from his personal darkness. She has *earned the rest.*

...

The world was completely devoid of color when Agnes stirred back to life. Every muscle ached, deep pain, bone pain. The fire had snuffed out, but the heat it had generated while she had slept had flushed the cold spell from out of her flesh. It felt good to be free of the wintery grip.

Her movements were labored, her joints stiff. Areas of her skin, particularly on her face, felt tight and crusty. It took her a moment to remember the cuts; she had still not washed the blood and pond scum off. Evidence of which remained congealing on Wilson's chair and quilt.

'Great,' she groaned. 'That'll take more than soapy water to scrub clean.'

In the meantime there was nothing stopping her from bathing herself.

The old tin bathtub filled with water while Agnes peeled off the layers of clothing that were plastered to her body. The outer layers were wrecked and deserved a cremation; the barrel drum in the yard was to be their final resting place. Amen. God bless.

At first she was horrified by the amount of blood that streaked in smears across her limbs and torso then – rational thinking kicked in – chances were the wounds were mainly superficial.

The warm water stung like hell, but once submerged for a few minutes Agnes almost found herself welcoming the sting, it felt cleansing, as though not just cleaning her body, but her soul as well.

She allowed herself to slip down into the cozy liquid; completely covered she opened her eyes and stared blankly at the obscured timber ceiling. She stayed in suspended animation, deliberately depriving herself of her senses, until her lungs burned and cried out for oxygen.

...

Including Wilson's pocket watch, there were four timepieces in the cabin. A cuckoo clock in the hallway *(which had called its last nigh on a decade before)*, the carriage clock in the living room, and a twin-bell alarm clock that sat on the bedside cabinet. None of them were working. A possible coincidence if it were not for the fact that each clock face displayed the exact same time: 03:37.

Agnes did not know, nor did she want to, what this signified. All she knew was that she now had no way of telling the time. The season had brought with it a permanent state of twilight. A world awash in shades of blue and grey. For the next two to three months, neither day nor night would claim entirely over the skies.

Agnes had to treat one or two of her more vicious scratches (the gouge on her head was particularly nasty), but all in all, she had gotten off lightly. After bathing and bandages came food and rest. She struggled with the exhaustion; the endless predicaments she had kept finding herself in had really done a number on her. Someone of her age should not be out having life-risking adventures and fighting monsters.

Once rested to a degree that she felt tolerable, Agnes busied herself with cleaning the cabin. After a voyage through a rancid swamp, Agnes didn't want to lay eyes on even a speck of dirt again. Period.

The difference she made in only a few short hours was staggering. Worktops were scrubbed; bric-a-brac was shoved behind cupboard doors or buried at the back of closets. The last area to be cleaned was the most symbolic.

Agnes stood motionless at the foot of the bed. The time had

come. Piece by piece she removed the clutter that had come to rest where she should have been sleeping. Once cleared, she stripped off the covers and changed the sheets.

She climbed into the bed and fretted. As comfortable as it was *(and cozy, boy was it cozy)*, Agnes' big worry was the vacant plot by her side. The whole reason for avoiding the bedroom was she didn't want a constant reminder every night of her loneliness. She traced an affectionate hand over the spot where Wilson had used to lie. She smiled, but it was not a happy smile. Not really.

She had forgotten just how nice a bed could be, much better than the seat in the living room; it felt real nice lying with her back out flat. Her posture would thank her in the morning. She was quite tired, not just from her escapade, but cleaning the whole cabin had been a fairly large job. Maybe she could just rest here for an hour, only until she had gotten her strength back.

A fat, yellow moon, full and low over the mountain tops, had dispersed the cloud cover and conquered the heavens by the time the visitor came to stand at the foot of his old bed.

CHAPTER 39

Agnes had been stolen away into a deep and heavy sleep the likes of which she had never encountered before. Her eyes fought against the crust that had sealed them shut. Even through the warm padding of her duvet she could detect a notable shift in temperature in the bedroom; like someone had opened a window and let Jack Frost sneak inside.

When she had crawled into the bed she had done so by the light of a hanging lantern, now the room was fully dark. The lantern gently swayed, caught by a subtle breeze, its glass panels still fogged with the residue of its blackened wick.

Even though the moon hung in the night sky beyond the window, its yellow light barely lit much more than a single skewed square on her bedding. The rest of the small room was thick with the now comforting darkness that signaled the coming of her deceased beloved.

'Hello, Wilson,' she greeted the shadows. 'Step forth won't you? I can't see where you are.' A whisper of movement, painfully slow and drier than dust, came from the corner opposite the door. His wheezy chest had gotten worse, each breath was laborious, his airways sounded clogged. 'Are you alright, Wilson? She asked, aware of how ridiculous the question was. 'You sound...*worse.*'

The shape that separated from the darkness was a far cry from its previous manifestations. Agnes had gradually come to accept Wilson's new look, but this incarnation was frightfully unexpected.

'Wilson, it *is* you…right?'

The shape seemed to be having trouble keeping upright; its shoulders slumped downwards as though the weight of gravity alone was too much to bear.

'It is me, Aggie,' it rasped. 'I'm afraid this will likely be my last visit.' Wilson lifted an arm that resembled a branch stripped of bark and made a '*follow me*' gesture. 'Come,' he croaked. 'Let's talk.'

He about turned and shuffled rigidly out of the door into the hall. Agnes tailed behind, the stunted pace made her feel like she was in a funeral procession. As Wilson progressed, so his darkness followed, snuffing the candles in the hallway lanterns as it went. Just enough midnight light remained to let Agnes see that he was naked. In her youth she had learned of the POW camps, the horrific pictures of those poor people, mistreated and starved to such inhuman extents that their emancipated forms no longer resembled living men and woman. Wilson's degradation took this to the next level. His muscles and fat were all but gone. Agnes could see through the thin membrane of skin between his bones. If he were to return another night it would be as a skeleton, she was sure of it. He paused in the doorway of the living room, his back to her when he spoke.

'Give me a minute, will you, love?' His voice was so strained and thin she struggled to hear it.

'Of course, Wilson. Take your time and call me when you're ready.'

Wilson entered the room leaving her standing uncomfortably in the hall with only her reflection in the brass framed mirror for company. The woman in the mirror looked tired, battle-worn and permanently scarred. The warm glow on the reflections face disappeared. The living room had been plunged into darkness. The fireplace extinguished.

'Come now, Aggie.'

She had been summoned; it felt like being called into the doctor's office, where the only news is bad news. The room was bitterly cold, the smell of ash lingered in the still air. Wilson stood in front of his old chair, the quilt wrapped around him like a burial shroud. He had it pulled up over his head like a monk's hood, only his lower jaw was visible. The lips were taut and his gums had receded to show the yellowed roots of his teeth.

'I thought I'd try and preserve my dignity. I hope you don't mind. I know you love this thing,' he said patting the patchwork.

Agnes shook her head softly. 'Don't be silly, I made it for you. I'm glad you're using it. Why don't you sit?'

'Can't,' Wilson said. 'My joints won't bend enough. I'm afraid if I take a seat I won't be getting back up again.' His usual jovial tone was gone. Where once he would have made light of a bad situation, he now sounded tired and defeated. If Wilson had lost hope then what was left for Agnes?

'I tried to save them, Wilson. I truly did. I just wasn't...wasn't-'

'-I should never have sent you,' he said, cutting her off. She bowed her head, teardrops overflowing and dripping from her lower eyelids. She couldn't look at him. She had failed. All those young people had been relying on her and she hadn't been able to help them. Hadn't been strong enough. 'Don't you dare blame yourself,' he wheezed. 'You, Agnes, went above and beyond in your efforts. I should have told you to leave, to take the truck and flee, get as far away as possible. Instead I made you play the hero and it nearly got you killed. I'm such a fool.'

Agnes sat on the arm of the couch, a little light-headed, it was as if an enormous pressure had suddenly been removed, leaving her feeling weightless.

'You're not a fool for having a golden heart, Wilson. It always was your most outstanding feature. It's why I loved you - and why I continue to do so.'

'Either way, I put you in danger. I'm sorry.'

Agnes stood up and crossed the floor to where her backpack had been discarded. Crouching down, she unclipped the twin clasps and drew back the zip.

'It wasn't all for nothing,' she said, as she rummaged through the contents of the bag. 'I learnt a little of what we are up against...' she grunted as she hauled the camera out, *(along with some rope that had gotten tangled around it)*. 'The campers were documenting it, they already knew about it from some urban legend or myth, or something... I don't know. Whatever the case, they went to that swamp to solve a mystery and got a hell of a lot more than they had bargained for.' The cool white light lit up her face with a ghostly glow as she powered up the screen. 'They dropped this; I figured there might be something on it that can help.'

She saw Wilson nod.

'It was wise of you to bring it back here; sadly I don't think I have the time to watch it with you. Put it to the side, preserve the battery, you should watch it in the morning.' She did as she was asked, leaving the camera sitting on the mantelpiece. 'Come tell me what you found.'

...

Agnes told him everything, saying her account out loud helped her piece together parts of a story she had not had the time or frame of mind to consider until now. She told him of the ominous settlement *(he remembered it well, even though he hadn't seen near as much of it as she had. He told her the sight of the crumbling church had given him the willies*). She recounted her journey through the labyrinth of tunnels in the abandoned mine, the natural cavern with its handprints - an archaeological wet dream.

It seemed so obvious to her now that she had time to reflect on it, the citizens' of the town hadn't dug out the mine searching for gold like so many other pioneer settlements, they had been looking for something much, much more powerful. Something they had not only found - but also unleashed; now it roamed the land she called home fucking shit up and killing its way up the food chart.

As she told her tales of bloodshed; the girl in the maze, the head in the bog, the boy in the church, so she was given the pleasure of reliving the nightmare she had hoped was behind her. Wilson patiently waited while she calmed herself with a generous swig from the liquor cabinet before pushing her to continue.

She spoke of the sinister murals that decorated the town's worship hall. The blasphemous depictions that gave praise to an unholy deity. Finally, she ended her story with her miraculous escape through the briar patch where she had been reduced to little more than a scurrying animal fleeing from an apex predator.

'Alright,' croaked Wilson. 'This is much worse than I thought. Agnes, come morning I want you to pack a bag. You can't stay here.'

Agnes started to protest. 'But... but this is our home. Besides, I left that...that... *thing* miles away. Let it have the swamp. It's not going to come-'

'-Agnes!' Wilson's voice was powerful; the effort shredded his vocal cords. 'Don't you get it? It's already been here. The stag, remember?'

Agnes didn't, not to begin with. The deer she pictured was the wounded doe and her twin babies from long ago but then, like pieces of a jigsaw, the image of the stag's rotten carcass formed in her mind.

'Yes,' she said in a small voice. 'I'd forgotten about that. But we don't know that it was that beast that killed it, it could have been a bear or...'

Wilson sighed. 'But is that a chance you are willing to take? You've already made yourself known to it. You have to leave Agnes, before it comes for you. It sure seems like a vengeful creature, and the fact that you've managed to best it several times already means it's no doubt pretty pissed off. You can bet your ass its planning some dreadful consequence for your defiant actions.'

Agnes bit back her frustration. 'But Wilson, I don't want to leave. I don't want to leave you. How am I meant to survive out *there*? This cabin, this mountain, the forest and valleys – it's all I know, Wilson!'

Wilson understood. He had been lucky, he got to die. Even if he hadn't, he had maintained *some* contact with the small town of Sutter's Mill, not a lot but enough to likely be able to find his way back into society. Mr. Brautigan at the general store would have helped him; old Shep at the bait shop had always been friendly and would certainly have lent a hand. Agnes had no contacts, no friends to guide her, she would be on her own, either swallowed into the states bottom-rung care homes, or tossed out into the streets where her mind could deteriorate until she was just another forgotten, mad old woman. Abandoned and alone. Nevertheless, at least she wouldn't be monster chow.

'You must be strong, Aggie. Stronger than you've ever been. You've already proven you've got some serious grit, but it ain't over yet. Those kids had families, Aggie. If they were your kids wouldn't you want to know what had happened to them? The *truth*?'

Agnes glimpsed a memory of Gavin's head rolling backwards as the water rat swam away with its belly full. No, she probably wouldn't want to know, not if the truth was so vile and perverse. But Wilson did have a point.

'I have to go…' she said out loud, but to herself, not Wilson.

'Take the truck. Go to town. You'll have to tell the authorities. They won't believe you; you'll have to leave out the crazier details, but they *will* come for those kids. The best you can do is persuade them that it is dangerous up here. The rest they'll have to find out for themselves.'

Agnes was conflicted. 'But I could end up putting so many lives in danger. What if it kills someone that comes to investigate? That'll be on me!'

Wilson did not answer. His figure, draped in the quilt, was as still as the stone stalagmites in the mineshaft cave.

'Wilson..?'

This time he answered, but it was as though he were a mystic coming out of a prophetic trance. 'If you don't, Agnes, many, many more will die. This thing is big, it's mean, and it isn't going to go away. It has to be stopped.'

They spoke some more, reminiscing about the past, avoiding any conversation about death and what comes next. Agnes was sure Wilson could tell her all about the afterlife and the secrets revealed upon cashing out, but she didn't want to know. That kind of knowledge could easily alter how you lived out your days and dangerously skew your perception of mortality. She could wait.

'This is it, isn't it?' Agnes asked. Wilson's condition was getting worse. He could barely move now. His make-shift hood bobbed up and down stiffly.

'It is.'

He raised an arm and pointed towards the window where snow was banking on the sill. The quilt slid back to reveal a forearm that resembled a chicken's foot.

'Will you help me outside, please?' his parched throat made the words sound brittle. Agnes linked arms with him, no longer repulsed. Just like the doe all those years ago it was clear to her, the shell didn't matter, it was still the man *inside* she loved.

The pair slowly made their way down the narrow hallway. As they passed the mirror with its streaks and smudges, the front door swung open as if struck by a through-wind. It bounced gently against the wall and came to rest. Agnes knew there was something more than a westerly breeze at play.

They stepped out into a pool of moonlight; the garden was a dream-like wonderland where snowflakes sprinkled down like flour sifted through a sieve. The hedgerows and bushes topped with a thick layer of icing sugar.

Agnes was taking in a spectacular view of the stars above when she felt Wilson pat her arm gently asking to be released. She let her arm slip free of his indecisively, this could be the last time she felt his touch. His name bubbled on her lips.

'*Wilson...*'

He kept moving forward, he didn't turn around to look at her, whether it was because his fragile neck wouldn't allow it, or if he was now being guided by that magical force, she did not know.

'*It's okay, Aggie,*' came his voice, but in her head, not from the husk. '*Don't worry about me. Remember what I said, follow the plan and you'll be alright.*' Wilson raised his arms skyward, the quilt-robe bunched up at his shoulders revealing stick-like arms as dark as beef jerky.

Agnes felt something akin to excitement run through her. It was the same sensation she used to get standing on the rocks at the drop-off. The rush of being as close to nature's power without succumbing to it. The thrill of 'what-if?' The titillation of indulging a secret. She felt drawn to the night sky again, and when she let her eyes drift from Wilson to the heavens she was gifted an insight into one of those secrets.

The snowflakes had ceased, the cloud cover vanished. Above, the night sky was a window to the universe and beyond. It started as a thin line, no more than a smoky ribbon. Agnes could not decide if it was coming from a far off region of space, or if it was materializing from particles in the upper atmosphere; she dismissed the line of thought, deciding it was irrelevant either way. The ribbon curled and rippled like waves across the sky, its green tones strikingly beautiful against the blue hues of the world.

The Aurora Borealis, the northern lights, flowed through the air like a stream. A silent river that ancient gods sailed upon, guided by solar winds. The longer she watched the more vibrant and majestic it became. Where the green light ended, multiple tones of pink and purple took over the reins.

Eventually, the formerly matte azurite blue midnight sky was a kaleidoscope of color and pattern. The palette of colors began moving together as one in a spiral, the four winds meeting and creating a whirlpool of light. Agnes stood in her little garden feeling dwarfed by the display. The entire sky seemed to have taken on the persona of a living entity, something so prestigious and gargantuan that Agnes could not escape the feeling of her own insignificance.

The swirling sky had all the makings of a storm, an incandescent hurricane of Greek fire, but the night's cool air remained muted; only the call of a loon broke the still. The spiral formed a circle, the eye of the soundless storm positioned over Wilson's welcoming form. The circle gained momentum and started to bleed downwards as a tornado reaches out towards the earth. Wilson embraced its approach with his outstretched arms; he looked to Agnes like the conductor of nature's orchestra.

The green threads wove across the garden, close enough to Agnes that she could have reached out and allowed them to run through her fingers, had she been brave enough. She expected to feel the draft from their movements; however the force that controlled them seemed to be entirely self-contained.

Wilson let the quilt fall to the ground, Agnes saddened at the sight of his withered remains. She was grateful he had his back to her; she didn't think she could stomach the front view. The celestial lights whirled around him like party streamers. Their embraces were non-threatening, almost playful.

'I love you, Aggie,' said Wilson, his voice no longer raw and scratched. His voice seemed to come from all around as though carried on the colorful winds themselves. It was the voice of a pre-death Wilson, it made her heart swell. Agnes felt her reply leave her lips, whether Wilson heard it, she knew not.

He was laughing now. Joyous at the sensation the swirling particles of light had as they glided across his naked form. A sensation of life, of being warm of body, of flesh and blood, and of something more – the next step in the cycle of life and death – a profound and complete understanding of all things. It was wondrous, a level of ecstasy the likes of which he could never have conceived. The winds were reclaiming him; piece by piece he was turning to dust, first his hands, then arms. There was nothing violent or horrifying about the scene. Agnes thought it may have looked like the most wholly natural display she had ever seen.

The atoms that had been Wilson's body corkscrewed upwards with the cosmic dust and spread out far and wide across the infinite sky, the only thing that remained was a slightly scruffy patchwork quilt lying in a crumpled heap in the middle of the garden. Agnes watched as the last green hue faded into the heavens. She stood alone, truly alone. Somewhere an owl hooted.

'I love you, Wilson,' Agnes replied.

CHAPTER 40

*T*he morning came and went without Agnes being a part of it. She had gone to bed with an odd mixture of emotions running rampant through her mind, these paired up with a queer numbness that came in waves and shut her down for short periods, making her feel incapable of anything; above all else she felt tired. Really, really tired. She had lain tucked up with the covers under her chin watching the starry sky outside of the window for the faintest flicker of green magic, she saw none and was not surprised. And yet she continued to look until her eyelids could stay open no more.

While Agnes drifted in an ocean of sweet dreams and ghastly nightmares, a new storm rolled in; the biggest of the season so far. It eclipsed the stars and devoured the moon, when the winter sun dared to rise over the horizon it was banished to a cell of impervious thunderheads. It was slow moving, sluggish, due to its magnitude, even the gale-force winds that came calling over the Southern Ridge did little in the way of moving it on. The pitch black clouds only showed their exquisite details when sheets of lightning tore through the spaces between them.

The region, and indeed four of its neighboring counties, would log this one down as the heaviest snowfall in a 24 hour period *since records began. Snow gates were enforced on the worst of the mountain roads, rescue vehicles waited near all the major highways with bated breath – hoping for a quiet shift, but expecting the worst. Men and woman sat in cabs sipping coffee in polystyrene cups, bleary eyes watching the swish-swish of the wipers, toes numb despite doubling up on socks. Their loved ones, safe and warm at home, fretted should they wake to the comforting weight on the other side of the bed, or a phone call concerning an accident and a ditch.*

...

At some point in the late afternoon, Agnes woke up. The bed she lay on felt cold and empty. Her first port of call was to get a fire going, if her plan to leave went accordingly then there would be plenty of time to freeze her ass off later.

The weather presented a substantial obstacle; it had really blown in a whiteout. Agnes hadn't been prepared for the conditions to be as bad. She had only learned to drive from watching Wilson and even then she could count the times she had been behind the wheel on one hand. All those times had been during the warmer months – snow driving, the very thought of it, scared the pants off her.

The window she stared out of had frosted over; the intricate patterns distorted the view of the garden beyond. It was hard to believe the wonders she had observed there just a little while ago. Maybe it had all been a dream. Maybe, this whole mess was a dream.

Except...

Except the shiny chrome camcorder on the mantelpiece said otherwise. Its very presence was an affront to the time capsule of the cabin. Its modern design, smooth curves and clinical cleanliness stood out in alien contrast to the earth tones and cut-wood of her surrounding abode. Agnes saw no point in delaying the inevitable. Delays cost lives. It was going to be a difficult watch; the faces on the tape were those of ghosts now. No matter, she had to see this through.

...

Agnes carried the camera over to the dining table and set it down. The generator was known to be a tad unpredictable when the really cold weather came-a-knockin', so she lit up a few strategically placed candles in case of a power outage. The bare bulb hanging from the rafters placed her in its spotlight as if she were the star of a one woman show. When he was alive, she had refused to sit under it if Wilson was sat opposite; she despised the way its light showed her scalp through her thinning hair.

'Like the finest strands of silk,' Wilson would say.

'Like milkweed and pocket lint,' she'd reply.

It was a non-issue now, no audience – *no Wilson* – no problem. And that was when it *really* hit home. The grief she had carried for the last two years like a nursing child combined itself with the guilt she now harbored for the young strangers and, like a mule under a heavy load; she could carry the burden no more. She wept for over an hour, she bawled, she screamed (so loud that at one stage, the wolf in the woodshed joined in with his own mournful howl). She cried until her eyes turned red and the scratches and scores on her cheeks stung with the salt. She cried until the tears stopped flowing because she was simply all dried out and, with nothing left in the reserve, sat dry heaving until that too stopped. Eventually, after a period where she was as stony-faced and unmoving as the mountains outside, she was ready.

The camera '*dinged*' as it powered up. The screen displayed its blue background and the machine emitted a soft electronic '*thrum*' of static. Agnes didn't find the buttons as hard to figure out as she had expected; in no time at all she was drumming her thumbs together, waiting on the cassette to rewind. When she pressed PLAY she realized she had made a mistake. She ejected the tape and flipped it over before rewinding again. She doubted very much that this was the first cassette they had used on their trip, but this side of the tape would take her as far back as circumstances allowed. She figured if she was going to watch it all then it should be in chronological order.

The machine clicked, it was ready to go.

A nauseating opening shot jittered across the little screen, out of focus and swinging wildly. The camera settled on a picturesque scene of what Agnes figured to be a university campus. A familiar face beamed into the frame, smiling and pretty. That poor lamb had no idea of the tragedy that awaited herself and her friends. Gavin's voice came from behind the camera.

'Watch out, girl,' he said, playfully. 'You're huge head is gonna ruin my shot.' Michelle laughed, white teeth flashing like a movie star. She shoved him then skipped out of reach. Gavin called her back and she came to him, but in that silly foolin' around way that smitten teenage girls do, batting their eyelashes constantly as a reminder of their intentions. Agnes wondered if the girl's feelings were reciprocated or if Gavin just strung her along. She couldn't quite put a finger on what it was, but something about Gavin irritated her. 'Go on then…' said Gavin.

Michelle cocked an eyebrow at him. 'Go on what?'

'You want to be a star. Tell the camera who you are and where we are.'

The girl's composure changed immediately, it was so natural and fluid, she was born to be on film. Agnes had seen it for herself when Michelle has started her history lesson in the bowels of the mountain. A well-rehearsed mask of professionalism.

'My name is Michelle Dawson, production assistant for The Conundrum Club blog. We have travelled cross country to the campus of Elliedale University following a lead on a truly mysterious story. Currently, we are just about to join the rest of our research team in the library to see what new information, if any, they have acquired.' An impish smirk spread across her face. 'Who knows, maybe this time it won't be a wild goose chase.'

Gavin clearly didn't appreciate her attempt at humor. In a very deadpan tone he uttered, 'We can cut *that* out in post.'

Agnes paused the tape and set her kettle up to boil. This was going to take a while; she might as well get comfy. Returning to the recorder with a fresh mug of coffee, she was greeted by a black screen, for a moment she thought she had done something to break the camera, but then a blurry hand removed the lens cap. Panic over.

The interior of the library was quite basic; Agnes had expected grand antique shelving and detailed carved paneling on the walls. In the shot, a few faces gathered around an oval table. Stacks of dusty volumes piled high around them. Michelle sat in between the two researchers while Gavin filmed them.

The one called Tony (Agnes assumed, his being the only face she didn't recognize) was handsome and muscular, he didn't seem fazed by the interruption, but the poor boy Agnes had encountered in the church became fidgety and nervous when he spied the camera. The way his eyes darted as he stole sneaky glimpses at the girl beside him told Agnes that the relationships in the group were perhaps more complicated than they had first seemed.

Michelle smiled that dazzling toothy smile for the camera (*and Gavin,* Agnes thought), and started her interview. 'I'm sitting here with Tony Costa and Simon Andrews, regular viewers will recognize them as our elite researchers and, of course, our cameraman and scout when we are filming on location. So guys, what have you got for us?'

Simon looked to Tony to see if he was going to take the lead. He wasn't, in fact he didn't react to the question at all, he just kept scanning the book he was reading. Simon cleared his throat.

'Alright, well, quite a lot actually. For a start we now know quite a bit about the religious cult, or at least, we think we do. Right, Tony?'

'Mmm... yup,' Tony agreed without looking up. Simon had evidently hoped the other man would take over.

'Ok then... So we found some papers, many of them coming from much further afield than the mountain range by the way, that mentioned a creepy sounding preacher. Now, it's worth noting that back then wandering missionaries were pretty common, certainly not news worthy, so the fact that this guy made it into the local rags shows that there was something about him that the press felt necessary to document.'

Simon stopped to clear a dryness in his throat by chugging down most of a bottle of water. Tony had stopped reading and was paying attention now, but still showed no signs of contributing. To Agnes it seemed like he was deliberately leaving it to the other boy, to force him out of his shell. Michelle came to his rescue.

'Can I see?' she said, picking up one of the splayed volumes he had in front of him.

'Sure, look here,' he replied, pointing at a section he had marked. Michelle quickly glanced over it then read it out for the camera.

'This is a clipping taken from 'The Essa Times'. I've never heard of it. Have you?' she asked Simon.

'I hadn't, but I dug a little and found out it was a fortnightly spread for the town of Essa and its surrounding neighbors. The town and the paper don't exist anymore, but that's not unusual for frontier settlements. I do know it was around 100 miles west of here though.'

Michelle nodded then read the piece *verbatim*:

'March 15th 1823 – Residents of Essa were greeted by an

irregular spectacle outside the grounds of Parson's Bar & Cookhouse yesterday. The whole town, it seemed, came out to witness the arrival of the peculiar strangers who came down Main Street on foot with only one horse and one wagon between them, even though they numbered between fifteen and twenty. They dressed in baptismal gowns that had been altered to withstand the trials and hardship of life on the move and walked ceremoniously in pairs. Some carried long scepters or spears adorned with an unusual crescent shape at the tips. Many citizens will have noticed a growing number of travelling circuses and sideshows making their way west through the town in recent months, and many believed this to be more of their ilk.

Their leader, a curious fellow dressed in the garb of a Quaker – wide brimmed hat and all – smiled and waved at the residents of Essa. With so many outlaw gangs roaming the foothills in the region these days, one may have expected the Essa populace to be wary of such travelers, but it was only a matter of time before the town's children were playfully trailing behind the troupe and the community came to flock around them.

From their wagon, a carriage trunk was removed and positioned as a pedestal for their leader to address the town's folk. The man sported white whiskers and appeared much older *(than I originally suspected)* due to a long life on the trails. When he spoke it was in a loud and clear voice, and his tone, as opposed to the often grating and sanctimonious pitch of other wandering zealots, was both friendly and welcoming. For a religious man he certainly spoke with the charisma of an entertainer.

Although much of what he talked of revolved around faith, not a lot of it adhered to the familiar passages of our pastor's bible. Indeed, some of those who witnessed the speech *(while later discussing it at length in the Cookhouse)*, came to the conclusion that the man's dialect indicated he likely came from a land in Eastern Europe, if not further, where many different faiths are practiced.

The real draw to the preacher's show was the accounts of his travels. Tales of distant shores, and of the many exciting places his pilgrimage had taken himself and his followers, enthralled the young and old of Essa alike and filled their back-water heads with wonder.

The residents of Essa showed their hospitality that evening by assisting the troupe with the fixing of their camp, and donations of food and water were provided for the travelers. Come morning their site, the barren land beside Watterson's creek, had been cleared and left respectfully clean of mess.

Curiously, two men from the township appear to have taken up with the group: James Voss and Colin Roberts – who are both known to have suffered injuries working on Peterson's Ranch in the last year *(and for having landed on hard financial times)* – seem to have packed light, locked up, and left their dwellings before sun up. On behalf of the town of Essa, we wish our former residents well, and all the best in their new calling. If they, or the troupe, should return they will be greeted with open arms.'

...

Michelle handed the clipping back to Simon who placed it carefully back on the pile. The stack of books and notes wobbled then toppled off the desk and onto the floor. Simon, red-faced and flustered, got busy picking them up. No one batted an eyelid, it was so typically Simon; especially when Michelle was nearby.

'And you say there's a whole lot more of these testimonials?' came Gavin's voice from behind the camera. Tony nodded but it was Simon who answered, his voice muffled from under the furniture.

'Oh yeah. Lots more. Each one follows the same set up too. The cult enters the town, they are made welcome while their leader does his soapbox thing, the townsfolk rally around helping them out, then the next day one or two people are missing from the population, presumably left to join the pilgrimage.'

'So what do we think guys?' Michelle asked, her fingertips together like a classic villain. 'Is it foul play?'

'What do you think, Si?' said Gavin.

Simon adjusted his glasses, content the precarious heap was not going to drop for a second time. 'There's something else, something that throws shade on the foul play theory. Don't get me wrong, like you I instantly thought the cult were, you know...' he made a throat-cutting motion across his neck. 'But every single one of those who went missing was described as having been injured or lame. Some were born retarded-'

'-Don't say that word. I don't like it,' chipped in Michelle.

'Sorry. Simple, I meant born simple,' Simon's face had turned the same color as a London bus. 'What I mean is they were always the weaker members of the community. It stands to reason that they likely saw a better life for themselves amongst the cult's members. And let's not forget, cults can be *veeery* persuasive.'

'So what about the others?' said Gavin's voice. 'The ones just west of here? Do we think they were recruited into the cult's numbers? I mean, we are talking about possibly over a hundred people. That many folk couldn't go unnoticed, could they?'

Tony raised an authoritative hand and paused to take a sip of coffee from an Elliedale University mug. There was something about his mannerisms, the way he commanded respect, which made Agnes think he possibly came from a military background.

'Can't rule it out, but you're forgetting one important fact,' he said in a drawl. He went back to the coffee, apparently without the intention to elaborate. Or maybe he did, none of the others spoke; fellas like Tony might hold all the answers but tend to only trickle-feed them to you – and in their own time too. He looked at his friends over the rim of the mug with one raised eyebrow.

'Really?' he said, surprised no one else had thought of it. 'The massacre sites, guys. They might not have found the bodies, but they sure as shit found parts of them.'

CHAPTER 41

Agnes paused the tape. Her stomach ached and was cramping in a way she hadn't felt since she was a woman young enough to receive her monthly blood. She had sat down on the toilet just in time; cursing the coffee with every name under the sun. She did not feel good. The smell was atrocious. God only knew what sort of disease and bacteria she had come into contact with in the forsaken swamp. Agnes used the time spent confined to the lavatory to switch out the worst of her soiled bandages. The wounds on her forehead and the cut on her hand were the main offenders. She couldn't see the condition of her back, but going on how much the bath water had made it sting, it was safe to say it was probably a mess.

The pain in her stomach eased off but only when her bowels had been completely evacuated. She began the clean-up procedure and froze, something was wrong. The paper felt soaked through, she brought it round front to confirm her suspicions.

'Well… shit.'

It was sodden with dark crimson blood. Absolutely end-of-the-line saturated. She could hear it dripping from her *plip… plip… plip…* There was no reason to look at the water in the bowl, she knew exactly what she would see – but she looked anyway.

...

It was what it was.

Fact.

In truth, Agnes wasn't even surprised. How could she be? So much had occurred in her life recently, was it really little wonder her body had been affected so? She bore the scars of her turmoil indeed, her skin was a testament to her epic story; it only made sense that the damage done would extend beyond her flesh and into the organs and entrails inside. What could be done? What could *she* do anyway? She hadn't rolled over and gave up when the monster had come calling, she hadn't quit when the forces of nature blocked her path and made her crawl through miles of shit on her belly, so she sure as hell wasn't going to call time now. If she had one positive to say about her misadventures, it was that they had made her find in herself a strength and resilience that had lain dormant her whole adult life. It turned out the beast wasn't the only one with teeth and claws. No, this bitch could bite too.

Agnes shuffled back to the dining table a little phased and shook up, but not so much at the shock of it all, but through concern at the various ways her latest ailment might hinder her progress in her attempt to leave. It was entirely possible that the passing of blood was a one-off, a purge of sorts, her body's extreme way of resetting. Agnes did not believe this for one second, but it could not be ruled out, and for that purpose she saw no better course of action than to return to the video tape and wait it out.

Before committing herself to the rest of the recording, she swung by the liquor cabinet and fetched herself a brandy, fully aware of the negative effect it was bound to have on her stomach, and fully not giving two fucks. It was cold, and the auburn liquid had certain unique warming qualities, besides – it was what it was.

The only thought in her head that stirred trouble, the only niggling little voice that hammered home its point and made her sip her beverage slowly, was one that repeated the phrase: Blood in the water, dinner bell for the shark.

...

When Agnes resumed playing the tape there was a two second interval of black screen before the picture continued. A time jump had occurred as the filmmakers now wore trekking attire, *(Agnes recognized the black and purple waterproof Michelle was wearing, it was the same one she had on when she had been killed)*. The setting had also changed; the library had been replaced by the interior of a small van. Tony was at the wheel, Gavin and Michelle sat beside each other in the back, Simon *(no doubt grateful to be behind the camera)* sat swiveled around from the front passenger seat.

Agnes watched the tape like a fifth wheel. The group laughed and discussed trivial things as friends do. Simon's recording was purely for filler material – and for prosperity, of course. Old Aggie smiled softly, enjoying the sounds of their jovial conversations and playful ribbings at Simon's expense (which he took like a champ). Even if she did not care much for Gavin, she found him tolerable in the company of the others. In a different life she could very much have imagined being friends with the group – instead she was the sole witness to their demise. A plain truth that, no matter what, she could not come to terms with.

Occasionally, the conversation would return to the documentary and the nuggets of information they had found. Gavin, who was just as natural on film as Michelle had been, explained to the camera that they had found a name for the band of wandering zealots. There was no evidence that the name had come from the troupe, or if it had been coined by the newspapers of the town's they had visited, but whichever had started it had made it stick - there were at least six different mentions of it over a four year period within a hundred mile radius.

The Cult of Oeneus. Agnes thought it sounded Greek.

Simon and Tony had ploughed through many more documents, possibly thousands, since the recording at the Elliedale campus. Rifling through painstaking fragments and numerous dead ends, they had managed to form a loose backstory behind the cult and their motives. They believed the pilgrimage was actually a scavenger hunt. These people, each lugging along with their own disability, were searching for something, a mystical legend or deity that could cure their ailments; perhaps even grant them life everlasting.

Several accounts mentioned the diversity of the travelling clan; Spaniards and Turks, Central Europeans and Portuguese – even North Africans. It did indeed appear that the leader had partaken in an incredible recruitment journey.

Agnes allowed these snippets of information, along with her own experiences, to piece together, in her mind, what she considered a rather valid conclusion. The cultists had found that which they had seeked. Unfortunately for her, it had been lying dormant only a stone's throw away from her doorstep. The ancient monster had indeed granted them an extended life but, as with most deals with the devil, it had come at a cost. Those repulsive humanoid hands that snaked on phantom limbs from its equally vile body were just that – human.

Agnes wasn't able to come up with an exact explanation, but she believed that the cult's members had somehow been absorbed into the beast. They were a part of it, and it a part of them. If they had once been good people then that goodness had been stripped away and corrupted, tainted by the creature's malice. If Agnes was right *(and for reasons unclear to her she truly believed she was)* then the cultists now existed within the monster like a hive mind;

no longer surviving as individuals but as grotesque appendages or tools for the beast to utilize at will for its own gain.

It seemed entirely plausible that what had started out as an honest and noble cause, a proposed treatment for those in need, had escalated beyond their control, and in their haste to procure a solution to their suffering they had unwittingly unleashed a monster. Hell, they had *become* the monster. Wilson was right, something as powerful and wicked could not be allowed to exist. Unchecked, this diabolical creation would bring this land to ruin.

On the video, Tony was slowing the van down. Simon rotated in his seat so that the name of the rest area was captured on film. Reekie Falls – Agnes knew it, although if this was where they had begun their jaunt through the wilderness, then they had crossed a much greater distance than she had first thought. She had intended to go to their van first, to what end – she did not know, it just felt like the right thing to do. Maybe, she reasoned, there would be more answers, more information to help her piece together the puzzle she was living in. Nonetheless, Reekie Falls and its magnificent plunge pools and beauty spot were in the opposite direction of Sutter's Mill, Agnes would consider herself lucky if she could make it in one piece to just one of those locations. The authorities would have to deal with it; at least she could provide them with a place to start their investigation. And really, even though she was at the nexus of the mystery, was it so bad of her to want to pass it on and wash her hands of the whole miserable chapter? Her torn up mind and body didn't think so. Not one bit.

The team used a picnic bench *(the exact same bench that, 15 years ago on a day trip, Wilson had carved W+A ALWAYS into. Agnes caught a glimpse of the faded epitaph surrounded by the crudely cut love heart and wasn't surprised in the least. Coincidence is folly; everything is eventual)* to unload and check all of their gear.

Gavin was speaking to Simon in the background; arms

gesticulating wildly, Simon looked like a schoolboy about to receive the lash. Tony intervened, a firm hand placed on Gavin's chest as a warning to cool it. Their conversation could not be picked up by the camera's microphone at such a distance, but Agnes had enough knowledge of the group, and each members place in its hierarchy, to speculate at a possible scenario. She imagined Gavin was trying to force Simon to share the rest of his findings on film, a situation that, after the awkwardness of the library, Simon as not comfortable with. When Gavin and Tony walked towards the camera and Tony sat before it, she knew she was right.

Tony may not have had the natural charisma of a presenter, but his looks, along with his bad-boy broodiness, carried his screen time well enough. What proceeded was a back and forth between the pair, Gavin asking the key questions and Tony giving a summary of the details they had uncovered.

'So tell me about Sutter,' Gavin said, clearly still harboring select feelings about their altercation. Tony, his persona systematically slipping into its own defiant time zone, made himself comfortable before delivering his spiel.

'The soldiers that came back from the swampland, remember them?'

Gavin said he did. 'Most of them disbanded, right?'

'That's right. And it was their reaction that, coupled with the Indian brave's information on the cult, prompted Sutter to start investigating around here. You see, the brave was a damn good tracker, and the wandering zealots had caught his attention. When something or someone new comes into your neighborhood you keep an eye on them, right?'

'Right,' Gavin agreed.

'Right. So recruiting the brave as a member of an expedition, Sutter formed a reconnaissance team to scout out the mountain range in search of this swamp area and the secretive cult.'

'Was Sutter a member of this squad?' Gavin asked, the earlier hostility forgotten.

'No. As I said, this was just meant to be recon, they were to locate and observe then report back.'

'So what happened?'

'Well, a few weeks go by with no word from the squad, but Fort Eustace is some way off, especially on horseback, so Sutter is not too worried. After a month he starts thinking something ain't right, and by the seventh week he realizes that he is going to have to take action, personally. See, the camp was getting restless, too many whispers for the general to ignore. Without at least some closure, there was a high possibility of Sutter having an uprising on his hands.'

'This is good,' Gavin said. 'Keep going. The camera loves you.'

Tony scoffed and raised a finger. 'Just give me a minute to hydrate,' he said, knocking back a glug from his canteen. 'Okay so, Sutter selects two of his top men - we have their names but I'll be damned if I can remember them - and sets off to find his missing platoon. It takes a while, but luckily Sutter has some tracking skills of his own. Eventually, they come across a fissure in the mountains, and scrawled across the rocks at the entrance is one word – LOGAN.'

'Logan? Remind me why I know that name,' said Gavin.

Sergeant Kurt Logan was Sutter's best war-dog and the expedition's leader. He had marked their path lest something happened to them. Good call, right?'

'So this is the same Logan you have on your map?'

'It is. Sutter saw fit to name the pass after him.'

'That was nice of him, I guess…'

Tony gave him a disbelieving look. 'You want a graveyard named after *you*?'

Gavin paused long enough to show he was considering it. 'No.

Not really.'

'I should think not. Anyway, they follow Logan's route and emerge…' Tony fumbles through his notes for the exact quote from Sutter's journal. '…in a dense swampland, hidden in the shadow of the Great Mountain.'

'Ooh… a lost world!'

Tony couldn't help but smile, just a little. 'Yeah, or a completely natural plateau. Whatever the case, Sutter knows he has found the place he has been looking for.'

From the front zip of his pack, Tony pulled out a laminated copy of a historical ordinance map. Although the original appeared to have been mauled by a pack of dogs, it was, for the most part, legible. The camera blurred briefly as it came into focus on the piece of paper. Tony used a pen to indicate two specific locations, both of which were marked the word 'LOGAN' followed by a question mark.

'As you can see here there are two possible passes that cut through the mountain range in this area that could be Logan's. We are going to try this one first and hope we get lucky because the other one is actually quite a trek away.'

'That's enough for now then,' said Gavin. 'I think we better get moving.'

Tony showed a white-toothed smile. 'What's the matter boss, not feeling lucky?'

Gavin laughed. 'Brother, I am luck personified.' Tony shifted, giving his gear one last going over. 'Oh Tony,' Gavin spoke in hushed tones. 'I ain't trying to wind Simon up, you know. I just want him to push himself a little. Will you speak to him; try to talk him into doing a bit more screen time?'

Tony nodded. 'I'll talk to him. But I can't promise anything.'

What followed were a collection of trail shots, scenic views, and the odd spot of group banter. Agnes didn't want to speed through any of it just in case she missed something of value. When the group finally came to the first passes location they were greeted by a wall of stone, at some point in the last hundred years or so the passage had collapsed in on itself.

'Well, fuck me. This is perfect!' Gavin was wailing, while Michelle casually sat on a boulder eating trail mix. 'What are we going to do now?'

'Gavin, calm down,' Tony intervened. 'We stick to the plan. You knew this outcome was a real possibility. No biggie. Why don't we have a rest here before going on? Simon could do his interview. Ain't that right, Si?'

Simon looked like a deer caught in the headlights of an artic lorry, but he agreed just the same. Gavin's demeanor changed completely. 'You'll do it, Simon?'

The boy's face was scarlet. 'Yeah, I guess so...'

It took a moment for Gavin to pick the right backdrop for his shot, but it wasn't long before Simon was in position and ready for his close-up.

...

'Ok buddy, so Tony has caught you up to speed with where he left off, yeah?' Simon nodded, uncomfortably.' Good, good. Alright then, begin in your own time.'

Simon cleared his throat *(which felt drier than a bag of sand)* and started talking. 'General Sutter and his two companions navigated their way through the swamp. Sutter remarks in his diary how '...the absence of the day's light was not only profound, but also augury'. It wasn't too long before one of the men, a soldier named Harris, I think, spotted what appeared to be a spire of a church through a gap in the foliage.'

Gavin cut him off. 'Yeah, you have a note about the spire, don't you?'

'Um yeah, give me a minute,' Simon said, flicking through his notes. 'It's here somewhere...' Agnes couldn't help but feel sorry for the young man. If he thought he was out of his comfort zone now... 'Here we go, found it. Yes, Sutter describes it as a sideways crescent moon but I think he got it wrong –'

'- How so?'

'Well, Oeneus was a Greek king famous for the story about the Calydonian hunt, you know the one?''

'Never heard of it. You can fill me in later.'

'Never mind then, it's just with the cult sharing his name and after comparing the few dozen sketches we found of it, I think the symbol is a bow and arrow. See here?' Simon held up a rough pencil drawing.

Gavin said, 'Aw yeah.' Agnes agreed. 'So come on, Si,' Gavin said, impatiently. 'Get to the good bit.'

'Alright, alright. The three men get to the little town hidden in the swamp expecting it to have riders on horseback, people milling about, kids playing in the street and so on – but it's empty. No welcome committee from neither the settlers or from the missing squadron. It seems Sutter and his men are late for the party, and by party I mean massacre. The rainwater collecting in puddles all along the street has taken on a reddish hue due to the amount of blood mixing into it. Chunks of mystery meat are spread across the sod in maggoty piles. Harris said something to Sutter about bears or wolves, but Sut' wasn't buying it. There could have easily been around fifty members of the cult by this point, add in his missing soldiers and that number was probably nearer sixty. And let's not forget that Sutter's scouts had come across quite a few similar butcher sites when they were out looking for missing people in the wilds. Sutter knew that it was highly likely that he had found his lost squad – well, parts of them anyway.'

'How deliciously macabre,' Gavin scoffed, clearly delighted at the bloody details. Gore-hounds were going to love this, which meant he had a hit on his hands.

'Sounds terrifying to me,' interjected Simon. 'If it's all true, that is.'

'You're kidding, right?' gasped Gavin. 'Simon, we have it in black and white. General Sutter's own words!'

Simon acknowledged this and appeared to ponder it for a moment. 'I know. I get it. I guess it's just so hideous, so... so *dark*, that it's hard to believe. We've really found something big this time, huh?'

'*Big*? Simon mate, we've uncovered the most significant mystery of this century!' Simon nodded slowly. He didn't share his companion's enthusiasm. 'Go on then, Simon. Tell us the rest.'

'The three men spread out. Guns at the ready. They searched the homes and buildings but found only blood, guts, and destruction. It was Harris who found the brave. He had gone to relieve himself in one of the outhouses at the back of one of the properties when he heard something moving inside. He called for Sutter who rallied the other guy, Stephens, to his side. The outhouse had been locked up with a huge chain that circled it many times. The men managed to bust the padlock off it and, ever so carefully, opened the door. The Indian was alive, but only just. He had been stripped and was covered in blood and shit. They asked him what had happened, why he had been locked up, but he couldn't answer.'

Gavin was ecstatic. 'Tell us why, Simon.'

'Because his tongue had been cut out.'

'Yes! Damn, our viewers are gonna lose their minds over this!'

'It sure is a story that sticks with you, I'll give you that.' Simon sounded like it was a tale he would rather forget.

'So how does it end?'

'Well, the general doesn't go into a lot of detail about that. He basically states that, although something has clearly gone down, whatever battle ensued is over. He has Harris and Stephens check the edges of the settlement for fresh tracks, but they find no evidence that any of the cult or his own men have left the township and so they get the brave onto a horse and leave – but not before blowing the entrance to the mine as a precaution. Sutter writes '...*if any of these devils sought refuge below ground then let it be where they remain.*' He also made a point of having the location wiped from any documentation and labelled as 'barren wasteland' on any later maps of the area.'

'Ha! He tried to erase it from history but that couldn't stop us, huh Si?'

Simon smiled a little, the story may have been a tad on the violent side for his tastes, but he was still rightly proud of his research skills that had brought it to light.

'Did you know Sutter never returned south? He sent word to his employers that he was retiring as soon as he returned to camp. He said '...*this land is safe now that it has been cleansed.*' Oh also, just a last minute bit of info that I found interesting – the brave stayed with Sutter working on his ranch until the end of his days.'

'Know what I think, Si?'

'No, what?'

'I think the Indian *did* talk. I think Sutter knew something and that's why he stuck around and why he made a point of keeping this place hidden from the world.'

Simon looked notably pale. 'Me too. But if he stayed to keep an eye on things that means he didn't believe it was truly over.'

CHAPTER 42

Agnes switched the camera off and sat contemplating her acquired knowledge quietly. Good old General Sutter had devoted his remaining years to playing guardian of the valley, but his lifespan was too short for him to be around when the beast had announced its resurrection. Why it had returned now, Agnes had no clue. Maybe some tectonic shift had occurred deep in the mountain's core that had allowed the monster to break free of its stone cell; maybe it had simply been biding its time. Evil has immortality and patience on its side. Simon's words chilled her, if only he could have known how accurate he had been. She wondered if he had felt something, like someone walking on his grave, when he had uttered what was really a premonition of sorts. An image of his crucified remains floated across her mind, a wide grin spread over his face that said '*I told ya so!*' she shook it off. What a clusterfuck.

A howling wind rattled the glass in the window frames. Agnes jumped and wondered if she would ever feel at peace again. The pit of her stomach centered on a dull, aching pain, not unlike when you haven't eaten anything in a long time. At least she didn't need to use the bathroom again. It would be no small mercy if her excessive bleeding were a one-time thing, but mercy was an attribute she was running low on.

Having no way of telling the time was getting to be a real downer. It made her feel as though she were living in a perpetual twilight, existing in a space outside time's dimensions. The world beyond her windows was never-changing, and yet she still deemed nightfall to be nearing. She could probably have gotten to the pick-up and made her way down the mountain, but there was no certainty that the night wouldn't bring with it a darkness that would inevitably present additional hazards that would fraught her plans. In the end, she decided the risk out-weighted the gains, instead opting to wait until first light to make her move.

From the bedroom she compiled a selection of fresh clothes for her trip. Her backpack had seen enough action and was still reeking of the bog so she swapped it out for the spare one that hung on a peg in the hallway closet. She transferred her survival gear from one to the other, checking the equipment as she went. If she made it out of this mess, she fully intended to write to the bag's manufacturer commending their fabulous product.

Somewhere in the distance an owl cried out, its prey shrieked before being silenced for good. Night had come. Agnes settled in on Wilson's chair. She had intended to climb back into the bed but, for tonight, the chair felt symbolic. It could very well be the last time she got to sit on its worn and tired fabric. There was a moment's dismay when she reached for the patchwork quilt and realized it still lay out on the lawn. By now it would be soaked through and carpeted with fresh snow. Agnes didn't dwell on it. It was what it was. Drawing her knees up, she curled into a ball and fell asleep in her nest. Her hands held her stomach which made all sorts of strange and concerning sounds which would have vexed her, had she been awake to hear them.

CHAPTER 43

It had been the pain in her guts that had roused her from sleep. It was in no way severe, she wouldn't have described it as agonizing or excruciating by any means, but it was serious enough to get her moving swiftly in the direction of the toilet. There was an unpleasant 'looseness' to her bowels that could not be ignored, a significant, physical metamorphosis taking place somewhere between her stomach and colon. She worried that soon would come a time when she would be unable to get to the toilet with what was left of her dignity intact.

Like the churning sensation in her abdomen, the urgency to void her bowels came in waves. For all its unpleasantness, this particular wave did not last too long. Agnes was able to be in and out of the little bathroom before her mind had time to mull over the gravity of her situation.

She wasn't sure if it was the equivalent to putting a plaster on a fatal wound, but it crossed her mind that she should take extra care to keep hydrated. By the wraith-like glow of a bare candle she entered the kitchen and filled a jug from the barrel. It had been a while since she had replaced her reserve with fresh water and it had taken on a slightly chalky taste.

A shadow played across the path of the night's natural

luminescence. Agnes instinctively stepped back so that she would not be visible to the eyes of any peeping Tom. She listened tentatively. A part from the metallic '*ting*' of water dripping and hitting a pan in the sink, the cabin was as quiet as a crypt.

But there *was* a sound, faraway, but getting louder. Agnes moved to the window. The snow continued to fall but, for now, it had toned down its assault to a mere dusting. The moon, although shrouded by clouds, made its presence known by providing just sufficient enough light to see the outline of objects.

That sound...

It wasn't thunder; its steady rhythm was too continuous to be a distant storm on the approach. Agnes wondered if it might be a rescue helicopter, perhaps searching for the missing hikers! She burst into action as she darted into the hall and snatched up her boots and coat. A snarling wind launched a sneak attack at her as she pulled the front door wide open, but she had been hardened to such assaults lately, and brushed its fury aside without a second thought.

Agnes stepped off the small raised porch and took three paces across the snow that crunched underfoot. She waited, straining to hear the sound so she could figure from which direction it was coming. She swatted the mist away as her frozen breath hung in the air. She looked to the blackened sky over the Great Mountain. There was neither a tell-tale flash of tail lights nor the piercing beam of a searchlight. If a chopper was up there looking for the documentary crew then it as not visible from the ground.

There was something else that didn't seem right to Agnes. The sound, now that she was out-with the confines of the cabin, did not seem to be emitting from the sky, but from the mountainscape itself; and it did not sound as mechanical as she had first thought. Also – did her ears deceive her, or was the noise getting closer? It almost sounded as if-

-*movement in the underbrush* - where her garden joined the

forest's frozen tangle, snatched at her attention. She sucked in the chilled night-time air in a reverse gasp. The cold made her back teeth ache. There was no time to retreat back into the embrace of her home. A split opened in a wall of rhododendrons as something approached. Agnes swallowed, the lump of air stuck in her throat.

The slender figure of a doe stepped over the threshold. Agnes could not control her thoughts as she conjured a thousand potential significances the appearance of such an animal could mean to her. Could this be the doe from her past? Had she come full circle? What sort of omen did it represent?

She ceased her whimsy when the deer, wide-eyed and terror stricken, bounded in a bee line right for her. She was able to avoid the collision but still landed on her rump as she threw herself out of its way. Over her shoulder she watched as the animal pogoed on its bandy legs into the thicket on the opposite side of the plot.

'Bloody thing!' Agnes hollered after it.

She got to her feet, muttering under her breath. Stupid creature could use a lesson in spatial awareness. With immediate effect, the rumbling sound grew louder. Agnes dusted herself off and had little time to react as the drumming barreled down upon her. A porcupine darted out of the shrubbery and raced past her, its bizarre, alien features even stranger in the dim light. Agnes had a peculiar moment where their eyes met. The quilled beast looked terrified. The spiked creature was not alone. Agnes backed up against the cabin's wall as her garden gave way to a procession (stampede) of forest animals. Deer ran parallel with foxes; winter hares and other small creatures scurried frantically across the flowerbeds. A mama bear herded her two cubs before her; to the two-leg she gave a look that asked, '*Why are you just standing there?*'

The sky darkened to even greater shades of night as birds of every variety swarmed in one never-ending flock, their shadowy wings creating most of the sound that filled the valley as their mass devoured the heavens. Agnes as not blind to the message she was being sent. *It* was coming, and every beast this side of the Great Mountain was its envoy.

She stood in the clearing as the last stray deer trotted by. 'Don't you worry,' she spoke to it. 'I'll be joining your exodus as soon as I can.'

CHAPTER 44

The dawn brought little in the way of change. The world maintained its bleak and harsh greyness, the white continued to fall from above. What Agnes would give for a brief spell of sunshine, a solitary ray of warming light to bask in. The only noticeable difference she was aware of was the complete lack of woodland noise. It appeared, beyond all certainty, that every animal and bird that had called the forest home had vacated for safer pastures. Agnes didn't blame them. The beast had already shown that it was not capable of making idle threats. Besides, wouldn't she be hitting the road less travelled herself in an hour or so?

All the items she intended to take with her had been neatly piled upon the kitchen table. She was loathe to leave anything behind, but instinct dictated she travel light. With any luck she would be able to return to all her sentimental belongings before too long.

The previous night she had taken some game from the freezer. Before she left the premises she intended to turn off the generator and instead of letting what was left of her meat spoil, she decided to give it to the wolf as a parting gift. He was no longer the invalid he was when he had first taken shelter in her woodshed and she knew he would likely take off on his on soon enough. The meat would be a nice send-off before he went to find his new place in the wilds. With the haunches of rabbit and grouse breasts resting in a tin bucket she went outside to pay her furry cohort one last visit.

The moldy, old door of the dilapidated shed hung wide open. The garden was a spider's web of animal prints, a crisscross tapestry of who's-who of the untamable woodland. One set of tracks started at the doorstep of the shed before lining up with the other fleeing paw and hoof prints.

Agnes couldn't bare goodbyes. The wolf's absence was one she found particularly difficult to deal with. A part of her had needed to go through the dissolution process in order for her to have closure. The bond they had formed in their short, but meaningful, time together had been more than two lonely souls coming together; it had literally saved her life. She could not deny feeling glad the wolf had joined the mass migration. She wished him well and hoped his new life would be free from tragedy and unspeakable violence but, when it came down to brass tacks, the truth of the matter was basic – she missed her only friend. From now on she was in this situation completely solo.

She dumped the bucket by the doorway; the snow around it was still tinted pink with the wolf's blood. If he should return then let it represent a candle in the window, a symbolic gesture to show he would always be welcome. If not, then sod it, let the scavengers feast.

...

Everything was set. Beside the tidy pile of provisions and weapons, Agnes had laid out a clean and fresh outfit which consisted of many layers to keep her warm. A breakfast of porridge and coffee would be sufficient; she also had a snack bag to take with her which contained a variety of nuts, fruit and jerky. She understood the importance of moving on and the time factor surrounding it but, against her own will (and better judgement); she could not bring herself to simply leave without some sort of fanfare. To shut the door behind her and walk away, possibly for the last time, felt *wrong*. These walls that had been erected by Wilson, with her help, had been so much more than just a house for the majority of her existence, they had been a home, and a bare and honest statement of a life well lived. She owed it more than that.

Agnes started filling the bath, reasoning it could only be a good thing if she got a heat in her before braving the cold outside. While the water steadily flowed, she took one last thoughtful stroll through each room. She checked all the windows were latched shut. She picked up ornaments and trinkets, giving each one a brief, yet loving, study before returning them to their places on their shelves or unit tops. A true home is filled with the wonders we are pained to leave behind. She would miss each and every item.

She checked the temperature of the bath water and, content it was just on the right side of tolerable, undressed and got in. For a while, she sat in a monk's silence watching the ripples spread from where the tap dripped. Nothing, she thought, could rival the serene peace and calmness of an uninterrupted bath. No distractions, no conflict, except those we allow our brain to acknowledge and consider.

She had no intention of getting her hair wet, it would only need a thorough drying which was an inconvenience she could not be bothered with, but the tips had already dipped into the water, so she let herself slide down into the warmth. She listened to the strange underwater sounds and found them soothing, like being back in a mother's womb. She could not escape the reoccurring thought that there was a certain beauty in drowning. The water came up the sides of her face so that her mouth and nose were just above the waterline. She remained placid, listening to the sound of her own breathing; she never wanted to get out. She could almost sleep...

Her eyes opened. She had thought she had heard something. She stared at the ceiling and waited to see if the noise came again. She must have imagined it. It was probably just the cabin's woodwork settling. After all the crazy shit that had been going on she figured she was allowed to be a little paranoid.

'*Thud.*'

Nope. That wasn't an ambient sound, and it wasn't coming from somewhere else in the house. It was far, *far* closer than she liked. Agnes sat up; her exposed upper half formed goose bumps where the cooler air chilled the water that ran off her. She sat naked and felt the creeping sensation of prying eyes. Stealthily, she started to get up. Her ears tuned to pick up even the faintest of sounds.

'*Thud.*'

Something had bounced off the bathroom window, she knew because she caught its shadow as it collided with the frosted glass. Agnes, even though she was constantly on edge these days, didn't panic. One certainty that she had learnt over the years was that if you built a cabin in the middle of the woods, then you were going to get birds flapping into the windows fairly regularly.

Agnes dried and dressed quickly and wrapped her soaking hair in a towel. Apparently not every bird in the forest had gotten the memo about the mass evacuation. Stepping into her boots she went outside to see if it needed her help.

...

The absence of the forest's living residents could be felt as Agnes rounded the cabin's exterior. The old pines, like columns in an ancient and forgotten mausoleum, gathered in mutual silence like mourners at a funeral. Agnes could quite easily believe she was the only thing with a heartbeat left in this neck of the woods.

The culprit lay half buried in the white powder that had accumulated in a drift below the bathroom window. Judging by the scarlet smears that it appeared to be caked in, Old Aggie was going to be playing funeral director rather than bedside nurse.

'Poor thing must've been in a fair hurry,' said Agnes aloud, more so to break the eerie silence than to commiserate the bird's unfortunate luck. Agnes saw that the creature had not died alone; two more of its kin lay in the snow nearby. Now that *was* an unusual occurrence. But perhaps not quite as unusual as the bird's physical appearance; Agnes had never seen birds that looked-

-Shit... *Not birds.*

Agnes realized too late that she had been duped. A trap had been set and like an old fool she had allowed herself to be lured right into it. Another 'thud' rang out in the quiet, Agnes felt the shift in the air as the object narrowly missed colliding with her head. The thing rebounded off the window and landed beside her feet. She tapped it with the side of her boot and rolled it over; when she saw what it was, she screamed.

The severed head of a young wolf pup, eyes mercifully closed, tongue lolling out one side of its mouth. She looked to the others and saw that they too were the missing heads of the pack's younglings.

Another projectile shot out from the conifers. Agnes clocked this one in the air and was able to avoid its trajectory. It splatted with a bone-crunching '*Thock*' against the log cabin's frame. Agnes took to her heels before it came to rest on the ground. She skidded as she tried to take the corner of the building too quickly and felt her brain rattle in her cranium as something impacted with the side of her head. She didn't have to sneak a peek to know what it was. For a fleeting moment her vision was doubled, but that didn't stop her from kicking open the door and slamming it behind her. Picture frames were knocked down or sent sideways as she stumbled down the corridor. She smashed into the kitchen table and snatched up the rifle. There was no need to check; she had made a point of having it loaded and the safety off.

Agnes, using the gun's sights to guide her way, cut a line through the house until she was in a position where she could see, not only the front door, but the majority of windows too. She should have left when she had the chance; the opportunity had been right there! Now she was stuck. The pig-faced fucker had arrived late to the party, but now he was here and he had his game face on.

Even here, surrounded by thick walls of timber, Agnes could smell *It*: a pungent concoction of shit, death, and Sulphur. Its stench churned her stomach and made her want to claw at her own throat. She had to get her head straight. She knew its tactics, had played its cat and mouse games before.

'*Think Aggie, think!*'

It would toy with her, wait her out. It would quite likely try and lure her into another trap. She could not afford to fall for its deceptions. She pictured it in her mind, trying to figure out its next move. She could envisage it methodically circling the cabin, slowly assessing the weak points, searching for a way to sneak its ghostly limbs in to attack her.

The chimney.

It had tried to snatch her from above before, this time she would take away the possibility before it got the chance. Racing into the living room, she tossed every available log into the fireplace. Not content with the stack, she broke down two end tables and threw their parts on as well. The fireplace was packed fairly tight, but this still might not deter the beast. For added measure, Agnes dowsed the wood in lighter fluid and struck a match. The instantaneous heat was immense. The whole room shimmered orange with the introduction of new light. Good. Let the bastard try and get passed that.

Making sure she stayed low so she wouldn't be seen through the windows, she performed a rapid, yet thorough, sweep of the property. She had to make sure she didn't miss any openings to the outside. There could be no margin for errors.

Returning to her vantage point, she squatted down and kept the rifle level, moving it in an arc back and forth that covered as much of the house as possible. There was nothing left to do, nothing she *could* do, but wait for the beast to commence its assault.

CHAPTER 45

Her eyes glowered at the hallway clock; it still ticked even though the hands stayed locked in position. It was as though she and the monster had stepped out of time to settle their quarrel. She asked herself what was taking it so long, why did it not make its move? But she knew the answer, plain and simple, because it could. It would have no problem staying in its reverie, thinking of all the horrors it could unleash upon her while the snow piled up on its motionless form. Simon had provoked the beast to carry out a heinous act of despicable cruelty; Agnes had done so much more. By eluding the monster several times she had put herself in line to receive the worst tortures it could come up with.

It hadn't been that long ago that she had considered trying to catch a bullet in her teeth. Eyeing the rifle now, she realized she was no longer considering this as an option. Every bullet she had in her possession had the creatures name on it.

A thought dawned on her that she could not believe she had neglected until now. A possible game changer that, although wouldn't give her the upper hand, could present an advantage and buy her some time. She was at home. That meant she knew the lay of the land better than the beast. She had already utilized the fireplace, what other weapons did she have at her disposal? The hall closet might hold the answer.

On all fours, she scurried towards the cupboard and very suddenly had to veer into the bathroom, her stomach had chosen a god-awful time to betray her. The only blessing to be had was that her silhouette would not be seen due to the position of the toilet in the room. Her teeth were liable to start shattering each other as she bit back the pain. It was like her insides were being burnt with a blowtorch. She shoved the side of her hand into her mouth and bit down until the dreadful bout passed. At any other point in her life her condition would have had her undivided attention; now, it was just an obstacle in her way that she had to overcome.

Expeditiously, she took care of business. Certain that, with her luck, the monster would pick this opportune moment to launch its attack. However this stand-off was to end, she had no intention of dying on the toilet. Once finished, she slid off the bowl and quietly lowered the lid. She didn't bother giving the contents a look; she had seen enough blood lately.

It was this thought that started an idea forming in her mind, but first she needed to prepare. Cautiously, she prowled back into the hall and resumed her mission. She had to be careful opening the cupboard as the movements of the door might have been visible from the outside. She pulled it out until there was just enough room to squeeze herself into the gap. Her eyes lit up as she took stock of her arsenal.

...

God bless Wilson and the duty of care he felt towards the beasts of the forest. Even though he had taken his share of their numbers as prey over the years, he would not have them suffer, and would not abide killing for anything other than sustenance and necessity. Acting nobly as ward of the woods meant that there were times when he would come across evidence of other hunters whose methods of procuring their bounty angered him and gave him cause to intervene. Hence why Agnes now had two vicious bear traps to play with. The steel jaws were lined with teeth that seemed to get sharper the more corroded with rust they were. Agnes sneered the full-mouthed grin of a maniac; the fucker was going to need more than just a tetanus shot if she got her way.

There were a few other items Wilson had confiscated, but Agnes couldn't imagine a scenario where she could trap the hulking, great monstrosity with a snare loop. That didn't mean the cupboard didn't hold some hidden gems amongst its clutter of crap. A coil of rope could definitely be put to use; the head of a pitchfork looked like it had deadly potential. Wrapped up and bound in a worn leather apron Agnes found something she had thought Wilson had disposed of a long time ago. He had found it in an abandoned campsite, a real *shithole* of a campsite, left by a bunch of city boys who might have known the ins and outs of the stock market, but couldn't get their collective minds together to clean up their own shit. An ornate rosewood handle supported a long, fat blade just shy of a foot in length. This was no hunters knife, Wilson had said, this was the wild card in a dick swinging contest. Somewhere, an office jockey had paid the price of a cold shoulder and a few nights on the couch after losing an anniversary present. A blade like this wouldn't just bring an animal down; it would likely cut it in half. Agnes touched the serrated edge delicately; maybe it had its use after all.

She had the components and the basis of a plan, all that was needed was some bait, and she had a toilet bowl full of it.

CHAPTER 46

Agnes' lip was bleeding. One of these days she was going to have to stop chewing her skin off when she was nervous. Her trap was set, she thought Wilson would have been proud, but it was still a longshot. For her plan to work she would have to predict the beast's movements and keep one step ahead of it. Not an easy task when dealing with an ageless deity versed in the art of cold, calculated evil. Agnes wasn't going to make the mistake of underestimating the monster's cunning, what she *was* relying on was the beast underestimating *her*.

The skies had really opened now which was going to make pinpointing the beast's position all the more difficult. Agnes didn't fret though, if she executed her plan successfully then the monster would make itself known soon enough. She cast her eyes to the grey slab that made up the sky and sighed; she had hoped the weather would hold off until she had made her escape. Surely she was due a lucky break by now? It was tempting to kid herself, to try and convince her own mind that the whiteout could be a blessing in disguise, but she knew that the monster would have far less difficulty navigating the snow-covered slopes than she would and that even a blizzard wouldn't hide her scent from its tremendous snout.

This was it then. The point of no return had arrived. Agnes' next move would set in motion a chain of events that there was no coming back from. There was no plan B, no calling for back-up, the cavalry weren't going to ride in and save the day at the last minute. This was to be her Alamo; her last stand. She felt like Ned Kelly, except instead of a make-shift suit of armor she had a broken garden tool and a horrendously dodgy tummy.

Agnes scooped out a mug's worth of toilet matter from the bowl using one of her favorite cups, screamed at the top of her lungs, and used the vessel to smash the bathroom window.

...

She could not see into the bathroom from her hidey-hole in the kitchen larder. She did, however, have a good line of sight to the front door, and if the beast did not fall for her trap she felt certain that this would be where it made its entrance.

The idea was simple; she wanted the monster to think she had, seeing no other way out, taken her own life. The crash of glass coupled with the bloody water that decorated the broken fragments looked convincingly like she had blown her brains out and if she was correct about the beast's bloodlust then it would not be able to resist diving in for a better look.

The larder door was only open a sliver yet Agnes couldn't shake the feeling of being exposed. With one nervous eye she stared at the front door and wondered when the fight of her life would begin.

...

She had misjudged one aspect of the creature's character, it had not come charging in at the first smell of blood like she had expected. In fact, enough time had passed since she had smashed the window that she was beginning to question if it was still in the area. Wisely, she remained hidden, and it was just as well too as was the beast's putrid stench not growing stronger? Something caused a din in the garden as it was knocked over. She had waited it out, now it was coming to investigate.

'Go on,' Agnes murmured. 'Go for the window, you son of a bitch.' A shadow filled the cavity of the front door. 'Come on, come on. Keep moving...'

Incredibly, Agnes got her wish. The gigantic shadow moved on. The cabin trembled with each plodding step the monster took. Agnes was able to track its progress by how much the pictures that hung on the walls bounced within its proximity.

The weak stream of light that spilled out from the bathroom into the hallway was snuffed out as something loomed into the scene. 'Here we go,' Agnes muttered as she braced herself for whatever came next.

She had grown accustomed to its snorts and grunts, not to mention its frightful roar, so this new sound stopped her in her tracks. It sounded like... whispering? Yes, she had heard correctly, breathy voices spoke to each other in hushed tones. A rescue party had come after all! She had to warn them, if the beast was still in the vicinity then they were in great danger! She pushed on the larder door and stepped forward with one foot. She froze with only her head through the doorway.

Wait.

She listened. Something was off about the way the search party spoke to each other.

'...where...is...she?'

'...tricked...tricked...tricked...'

'...find her...'

The voices spoke in unison. Their collective whispers sounded like the drone of a bee hive. Agnes had to strain to make out individual phrases amongst the chatter.

'*...the blood...the blood...the blood...*' one voice that sounded slightly feminine repeated excitedly.

When she focused her hearing on one particular voice, much gruffer than the rest, she understood that this was no band of fabled rescuers. This was the unified murmurs of the cult. The deepest voice was the raspy breathing of the beast.

...

'*Go in...enter...find her...*'

This had the potential to throw a spanner in the works. Agnes had set her trap up believing her victim to be driven by its animalistic intuition, not the formerly human minds of a diabolical hoard. With their combined cunning there was a real possibility that they would see right through her deception.

If she ran now, there was a chance she would make it out the front door, but then what? How could she expect to out-run such a relentless adversary? She didn't like it, but the best course of action was to remain in her lookout and pray for a miracle.

The brittle sound of crumbling glass resonated from within the tiny bathroom. A display cabinet's door in the hallway had partially opened when the monster had made the building shake. Reflected in its glass front, Agnes caught a glimpse of the creature as it forced its enormous mass through the broken window. Along with the boar-like head came dark, spidery limbs that clawed and stretched across the walls. They were no longer translucent and ethereal. They were solid and *real*. The monster had evolved.

The beast's snout got to work, gleefully inhaling the aroma of her troublesome bowels. The voices became boisterous and the sound of splintering wood heralded the destruction of the outer wood. They had let their sniffer dog off its lead and now nothing could get in its way. The little bathroom was obliterated to the sound of whispered hollering; the beast was inside.

'...*stop...look there!*'

Agnes felt a pang in her chest, she had been rumbled.

'...*the fool...cast it aside...*'

There was a metallic clatter as the bear trap she had left in the center of the floor was discarded as though it was no more than a minor inconvenience. The creature had broken through her first line of defense; luckily, she still had an ace up her sleeve. Along the hallway leading to the bathroom was a waist-high sideboard; on top of it Agnes had placed a long, wooden pole that she used for holding up her washing line, on the far end of it she had duct taped the head of the pitchfork.

Dry, nasty laughter filled the bathroom. Agnes could see flakes of snow billowing into the hall from the cabin's new entrance.

'...*the fool...the fool...*'

'...*we will make her pay...*'

'...*find her... she is near...*'

Agnes assumed this last voice was addressing the pig-beast. If she was going to fight, then it had to happen now.

She slammed all of her weight against the larder door. It banged loudly against the kitchen cabinets but it didn't matter, the time for being quiet was over. The force she left her little nook with caused her to crash into the opposite wall, the impact hurt her shoulder but the pain was good; it fueled her on. The raucous she had created had served its purpose and gained the monster's attention. The boar's head screamed with delirious excitement and was joined by rapturous cheering from those who dwelled under its skin.

It pushed its maw into the hall. Agnes could not fathom the sheer size of the monstrosity; the door frame buckled and cracked under the pressure. This was the first time Agnes had gotten a proper look at it and her idea of its grotesqueness proved to fall short of accurate. It was far more repulsive than she could ever have imagined. It was like the three little pigs had a secret fourth brother; one who wasn't invited to family gatherings, one who made his house out of the bones, skin, and hair of others. Part of its face was missing; a gory hole, ragged and charred, exposed the inner workings of its mouth. Someone had gotten a decent hit on it and that gave Agnes hope. But damn if she couldn't take her eyes off those teeth…

The monster chuffed like a bull as it tried to use its bulk to widen the doorframe. It stretched out one foreleg in front of it to gain purchase and went to reach even further with the opposite foot. Agnes threw herself to the floor and tugged sharply on the rope she had placed along the length of the hall. The rope, which lay in a straight line right to the other side of the bathroom door, was tied to the second bear trap. When Agnes gave it a yank, the makeshift weapon skidded across the wooden boards and came to rest directly under the beast's descending trotter. The trap's metallic jaws slammed together, its shark-like teeth biting deep and viciously into the monster's flesh. The giant cried out with a pathetic yelp that turned into an even more pathetic squeal.

A long-fingered hand the color of charcoal curled around the woodwork. It was joined by two more; one clawed above the doorway, the other took leverage on the other side of the wall. Their sinewy muscles tensed as they sought to force the beast through. In the confusion she had created Agnes saw her moment and, consumed by a bloodlust all of her own, seized it with both hands. She grabbed the wooden pole and thrust it along the sideboard with all her might. A battle cry that would have made history's mightiest warriors quiver in fear erupted from deep in her chest.

The beast never saw it coming. Agnes relished the terror in its eye as the fork's tines punctured its face. The voices of the hoard all cried out in horror.

'...*No!...No!...What have you done?...*'

Agnes screamed back, 'I've fucking killed you! I got you, you bastards! I fucking got you!' but she wasn't done yet and now she was on a roll she felt unstoppable. She had left the rifle leaning upright against the display cabinet, throwing herself to her knees she snatched it up and took aim. The monster glowered down at the little old woman on the ground below it. She had hurt it, and that offended it; made it furious. It drew its fat jowls back and opened its gaping mouth to strike. Agnes shoved Old Bess into the opening, lined her sight up with the soft pink flesh of the roof of its mouth, and pulled the trigger.

Chunks of rotten meat splattered the ceiling and rained down upon her, they were infested with maggots which, in a bizarrely calm moment of clarity, Agnes thought explained the beast's stench. Almost all of the monster's face had been disintegrated, all that was left was its lower jaw which protruded limply from its body with its tusks jutting out.

The beast stood upright for a moment longer before collapsing in a dead heap. Agnes had done it; the frail old woman of the woods had slain the monster. Agnes crawled away from the piles of flesh and viscera and lay flat out on the hall rug. She couldn't quite believe the plan had actually worked. Now that the beast was dead she could admit to herself that she had expected it to be a suicide mission. But here she was, worse for wear but still kickin'. Pulling herself up so that her back was supported by the sideboard, she asked herself the all-important question: 'Now what?'

How was she going to clear up the mess? What were you meant to do with the festering corpse of a goliath hell spawn, anyway? The bathroom wall was letting one hell of a draft in, so that would need fixing. And then there was the issue of her stomach…

The monster twitched. Agnes flinched. Probably, it was just gas escaping from its insides. Christ, she hoped it wasn't going to add to the carnage by shitting itself.

The humanoid appendages that had gone limp when the beast had *bit the big one* started jerking and flailing about. From inside its husk came a roar that sounded like the infinite rage of a thousand damned souls. Its flesh rippled and stretched; shapes pressed against the membrane of its skin from the *inside*. Agnes could not move, the shock and awe had her nailed to the spot. Its skin kept pulling tighter and tighter, the arms that had adorned its hide were soon joined by other body parts; heads with the skeletal outlines of skulls, torsos with jagged ribcages that split the flesh. Agnes could see the frightened faces of animals that had fallen to the beast's reign of terror bubbling under the surface. If she saw any sign of the young campers in there then her mind would snap and be lost to madness. The random body parts that stuck out of the dead pig at odd angles began working together. On hands, forearms – whatever it could use – it raised itself up from the floor. She may have killed the carrier, but the parasitic beings inside were still very much alive. It was not over.

CHAPTER 47

As with the most traumatic moments in nature, Agnes found herself unable to look away. Such incredible horror holds our fascination and demands to be studied; to be observed and analyzed. A sight such as this grabs our attention and insists we bare witness. It would be this need to see what terrors were developing that would summon Agnes' demise, unless she fled now.

One of the skeletal heads, one that perched on a torso that grew from behind the ruin of the beast's skull, turned to face her. She swore it grinned at her from under the veil of flesh.

'*I... see... you...,*' it croaked in a guttural snarl. Agnes knew this figure that had risen up to take command of the shape-shifting knot of flesh and bone. It was the same one who had started all of this in the first place. The wandering preacher stretched out a sinewy arm and pointed at her. '*You... are... too... late...*'

'Fuck you,' Agnes spat, masking the tremor in her voice.

The leader of the cult threw his head back; his arms spread wide, and shrieked a rage filled cry that rallied his flock into action. Agnes found herself inches away from a barrage of clawing fingers; the thing's speed was staggering. Had it not been for the door frame holding it in place, she would have been diced up like raw beef. She hated the monstrosity with every ounce of her being; the way it reached for her face showed the feeling was mutual. She shimmied backwards away from it and tried to stand, immediately halted by a piercing jab in her guts forced her to her knees. She looked down to where her hands held her stomach expecting to see a gnarled, knife-like finger jabbing into her abdomen, but it was just her bowels going through whatever-the-fuck situation they were dealing with. The pain caused her body to curl up, never mind running, she couldn't even walk.

The creature wanted her, and was exerting all of its phenomenal strength in reaching its goal. The doorway started to buckle; cracks appeared and spread over the walls. It was going to bring the whole house down!

The sound of breaking glass joined the cacophony, but it came from *behind* her. Agnes sensed the arrival of a new player in the game approaching from the rear and braced herself for the impact of its attack. She anticipated sinking teeth and tearing claws, so when she felt the gentle brush of fur glide across her cheek almost affectionately, she opened her eyes in bewilderment.

The sight of her white knight in all his glory nearly sent her heart into overdrive. It turned out the wolf could not simply walk away from his past no more than Agnes could move on from her own. He looked proud and noble, but more than anything he had a steely determination in his pale eyes that burned like ice fire. The look he gave Agnes in passing was up for interpretation, but to Agnes it said two things: 'Now, we are even,' and 'Goodbye.'

His front end dipped low, his shoulder muscles tensed, as he coiled up in attack mode. He gave out a deep, 'fuck-you' growl and made a point of showing his teeth to his enemy. The oddity did not know how to react to the lone wolf, the various heads looked to one another in bemusement. What was one canine to the newly crowned King of the Mountain?

It turned out, quite a lot.

This revolting mass of condemned souls, using their hog-faced weapon, had not only wiped out his entire pack and ravaged his homeland, they had killed his young, and if there is one thing you don't do, its incur the wrath of a father scorned.

He leapt at the nearest throat in a full frontal assault. They had taken everything from him, left him with nothing left to lose. Which suited him fine, without fear to hold him back he could put his all into ripping chunks out of this abomination. The two-leg had shown him compassion and got him back on his feet, he carried in his veins an inbuilt sense of loyalty to the pack. *She* was his new pack, and he was going to do everything in his power to keep her alive.

The creature's shrill cry rang throughout the little cabin. The wolf swung by its jaws from the neck of a cult member, Agnes was sure the whole conjoined group felt its agony as one. To hesitate now, or to attempt to join the fight in some foolish act of honor, was to consign them both to death. The wolf was giving her a gift, one that she took, not only respectfully, but with gratitude. She snatched up her rifle and high-tailed it to the front door. Her pack was beyond reach. It would have to stay behind. Before she exited the building she stole one last look at the gladiatorial battle between wolf and beast. Her companion was in a fight he could not win, and she knew it. As he launched from limb to limb and the creature screamed, she thought to herself, at least he was going to leave it with a taste of its own medicine. And if he could transfer some of the pain it had inflicted back to it, then all the better.

CHAPTER 48

Plumes of slate grey smoke gathered and intermingled with the frosted mist that weaved between the trees. Agnes hadn't been aware of it while in the cabin but, in fairness, she had been focused on other matters. Outside, at the garden's perimeter, she watched as everything she had ever loved, everything she could ever say she owned, was taken from her. From the over-stocked fireplace the flames had spread, first igniting the fabrics, then consuming the vast amount of woodwork. Within no time at all, her world had been razed by the inferno, and there wasn't a damn thing she could do about it.

The beasts inside - both natural and unnatural - continued to duel. Agnes could hear the growls and moans from where she stood in the plot. The wolf, even though his effort was valiant, was beginning to wane. Soon his fight would be over, the best outcome Agnes could hope for was that he had distracted the monster long enough for her home to become its funeral pyre.

Choked up on fumes and tears - *with eyes stinging from both* - Agnes turned away for the last time. She knew now that she would never return, no matter what the outcome, she would not *see* her home reduced to charcoal bones and ash. That was one satisfaction she would permanently deny the beast of ruin.

...

Any other season, the journey to the truck was an easy-going, downhill stroll. Now that the snow had arrived and swarmed over everything, it was not so much. Agnes couldn't use the footpath as the heavy-set banks on either side were flooding it with their run-off, creating a shallow stream of treacherously slippery mud and slush. It would be nigh on impossible to hike on it without taking *(what would likely be for Agnes)* a devastating fall. Instead, she had to run a course parallel with it through thigh-high drifts and ankle-snapping roots.

The collar of her jacket blocked out a good deal of the cold, but what she really wished she had was a hat; especially when ducking under the low branches that snatched at her and tried to get at her, already raw, scalp. She had come far enough now to be out of sight of the cabin. All that was visible from here was a black tower of soot and smoke and a warm glow. She hoped and prayed that the monster continued to burn for all eternity.

It was amazing how easily a blanket of white made it for her to become turned around, on more than one occasion she had to back-track to find the path. Every direction looked the same, and without landmarks to guide her she was in real danger of wandering into the frozen wilds and becoming hopelessly lost. She had put her faith in the gradient of the slope to provide her with a rough navigation but, due to the unpredictable layout of the snowbanks, even this proved unreliable.

A shadow cast darkly up ahead through the dense pines. Its shape stood out distinctly in contrast to the vertical trees. She allowed herself a sigh of relief. She had, miraculously, found the truck. The sigh changed pitch to become a groan, then a wail of exasperation. However she got down off the mountain, it sure as hell wasn't going to be in the comfort of the 4x4.

...

The beast *(or more precisely, the twisted beings controlling it)* had been one step ahead of her. While she had been carelessly soaking in the tub, the monster had been ensuring that, in the unlikely event she escaped its clutches; she would not be leaving the highlands in the truck's warm cab. There *was* no cab. There was barely anything salvageable left. The truck that Wilson had used for decades, essentially providing them with the outside resources they needed to maintain their chosen lifestyle, had been obliterated. A junkyard crusher couldn't have done a better job.

The wheels had been ripped off along with parts of their axles. The whole thing had been flipped on its side. Glass and torn metal lay half buried in the snow. The smell of fuel lingered in the air and offended the nostrils. Agnes could see that even the engine had been thoroughly mangled. To add insult to injury, the creature had torn down branches *(and in some cases, entire trees)* and blocked off the access road so that, not only could she not get out, but any chance of outside help getting *in* was also impossible.

Agnes was at a loss. What was she meant to do now? She definitely couldn't go home - seeing as it didn't exist anymore. Even if she did return, there was a small possibility that she wouldn't be alone. If, by some cruel twist of fate, the beast had somehow survived, then she would be as good as offering herself up to it on a silver platter. She could try and hike her way down, but with the weather conditions as they were and her lack of rations, clothing and survival gear she would be dead in a couple of hours. Then there was her health. A younger person would struggle to make the journey, never mind an old hen with more complaints than a hospital waiting room.

Finding a slightly sheltered spot beside the wreckage, Agnes sat down and contemplated the various ways death would come find her.

CHAPTER 49

S he must have nodded off. Either that or she had taken a mighty long blink. The sky above had somehow managed to get even darker; it appeared so low that Agnes reached out in the wild belief that she might be able to touch it. The cold was intense, but at least the wind was calm. She couldn't believe that, after all the crap she had gone through, her fate was to freeze to death beside this old hunk of junk. '*What a steaming pile of bullshit,*' she thought, miserably.

The snowflakes were gathering in their numbers over her knees and shoulders, soon she would be buried; invisible. Maybe in the thaw some new hikers would come along and find her still sitting with her back to the truck. She would probably become a local legend, another mystery of the mountain's lore. They could call her the Ice Maiden. They would see the destruction of her vehicle and the cremated remains of her home and scratch their heads and wonder '*What the fuck happened here?*' Even if they didn't find the charred corpse of a deranged monster in her bathroom, the puzzle would still baffle even the greatest minds. Who knows, maybe someone would make her story into a documentary? Now, wouldn't that stink of irony?

...

Agnes had taken one of her turns, apparently. Like waking from a dream, she suddenly found herself surrounded by some of the forest's eldest residents. Their boughs were misshapen and were covered in large cyst-like burls; their bark split in deep lacerations from hundreds of years of being exposed to the elements.

Her mouth moved rapidly and she was conscious to the fact that she was yammering incessantly as she slowly came back to reality. She had no memory of leaving the wreckage, nor did she have the faintest idea of which direction she had chosen to wander. She may have been granted permission to return to a state of *compos mentis*, but her coherence only served to highlight the fact that her untimely space-out had probably doomed her.

She kept trudging onwards, but only because it was way too cold to stand still. There was no telling how long she had been 'gone' - nor did she have a clue how far she had travelled. This would likely have been the time when she would have thrown in the towel and gave up; stuck two fingers to the skies and cried out *'Sod it, you win!'* had it not been for a random encounter with a familiar sight.

They twinkled like rubies against their matte grey surroundings. *Ilex Verticillata*, the berries of the holly plant. Not on her usual foraging list due to their toxicity but, accompanied with a cluster of their leaves, they made excellent decorations for the festive period. Agnes knew of only one location where they grew and, if she was where she hoped, then there as a small chance she had just found herself a safe haven. With a renewed spring in her step, she clamored through the grove until she was rewarded with a view that, at any other time, would have made her uneasy. Today, it looked like a palace.

CHAPTER 50

It had been abandoned long before Agnes and Wilson had even debuted on the mountain. Back then, it had only just started its journey towards dereliction; now, it was little more than a rotten shell on fragile stilts. To the young couple, the neglected ranger station was an exciting find, and one that they returned to often to further explore. In those early years they had been full of whimsy and the perishing structure had provided a certain allure; it suggested the possibility of adventure with a sly wink and a glint in its eye. Over time, it had lost its enchantment. The mask had slipped; the pair came to realize that what had maybe once been a place of magic was really nothing more than an empty lookout tower covered in bird shit. It was also extremely dangerous and falling apart. The view had been nice though.

It had been a very long time since Agnes had last set eyes on it. It had not fared well against the ravages of time. Climbing plants had whipped up from the forest floor and strangled its supports with their vines; the wood had become worn and bleached by the decades of summer sun so that it looked like the bones of some long-dead giant.

Agnes moved close enough to see that the staircase that ran up and around three of its sides looked, for the most part, to be structurally sound. Some of the planks that made up the steps were missing *(a section around halfway up had completely rotted away)*, but Agnes felt confident that if she tread lightly she could make it up to the sheltered box room up top. Her faith in the decaying stairs did not stretch to the handrail, which had been the first part to succumb to rot and woodlice and was lying below, buried in the snow except for a few beams that extended upwards like strange, rectangular saplings. The boards creaked and cracked under her subtle weight, they felt soft and sponge-like; Agnes was beginning to have doubts about their sturdiness.

Unlike her aversion to confined spaces, Agnes had never really had any major issues with heights, until now that was. The tower stood perched on an outcrop of rock that *(in clear weather)*, provided magnificent views across the range. The drop that she was currently crossing over was high enough for her to look down upon the tallest trees. She thought back to when a younger, more reckless, version of herself had often stood on the overhanging rocks of The Edge and reckoned she must've had a headful of loose screws. The hardest part was hauling herself up the gap left by the missing flight of stairs; a single spar of wood still stuck out from the main framework that gave her the leverage she needed, but if it was to break…

Thankfully, the stations floor and the deck that ran around it seemed, not only intact, but surprisingly well preserved. To get to the entrance *(the door had fallen from its hinges long ago)* she had to walk round to the other side. One side of the walk had significantly less snow piling up on it, so she chose it. In the middle of the viewing deck she paused to look out over the distant mountains; she caught herself just as she was about to lean on the handrail, remembering its fallen comrade.

The view would have been spectacular, had it not been obscured by the whiteout that billowed across the hillsides and treetops like the train of an enormous wedding dress. This frozen, unforgiving tundra was not the final impression she wanted to leave with, but it did make it easier to say goodbye.

Agnes skirted around a patch on the flooring where the wood looked much darker and sodden, not trusting it to hold her weight, and swept in through the open doorway. Inside, the raised shack was bleaker than bleak. The glass panes in the encircling windows had been shattered long ago and their gaping wounds allowed the snow to occasionally flurry in when a change in the wind's direction occurred. A 'U' shape of unit tops curled around three of the walls where rangers would have worked and studied. Agnes could tell she would find nothing of use, but she checked the cupboards anyway. All she found was a cluster of gnarly-looking mushrooms and a mouse skeleton.

She got her hopes up when she spied a distinct sheen of blue nylon shoved down the side of one of the counters, but it turned out to be a discarded sleeping bag that was not only drenched through, but smelled as if it had been soiled. Moodily, she held it aloft at arm's reach and carried it outside. There had to be a story as to how it had got here, but Agnes wasn't sure she wanted to hear it. She tossed it over the railing and watched as it disappeared into the furor below. She hated it; it was like it had been sent to tease her. She was done with being mocked.

Nestled into a corner that kept her clear of most of the worst of the wind and cold, she huddled up and tried to sleep. Come morning she would have some difficult decisions to make. She could only hope the answers resided in her dreams.

CHAPTER 51

Something had roused her enough that she was fully awake and alert. Sleep had been beyond her grasp, the setting had been too creepy and cold for her to let her defenses down. The entire structure moved with the stronger gusts of wind which made the creaking boards sound like someone was trying to sneak up on her. She had managed to rest a little though, and eventually she would probably have zonked out due to exhaustion. Whatever it was that had triggered her reflexes had done so on a subconscious level. She had tried to ignore it and resume her quest for sleep, but the 'feeling' wasn't going to go away until she had satisfied it that all was fine.

Out-with the confines of the rickety tower, Agnes was surprised by how chilly it was. It might not have been pretty, but without this moldy old pile of timber, she would most certainly have expired by now.

About an hour ago, maybe two at a push, her guts had gone into spasm again; the evidence of which sat steaming in a crimson puddle in the opposite corner from her nest. She could understand the shame the boy, Simon, had no doubt felt. Now, there was only blood, and lots of it. The smell of copper lingered in the air and she wished she had braved the cold and taken care of it outside on the lookout deck.

The storm had calmed from a blizzard to a moderate, but constant, snowfall. A fat, gloomy, yellow moon sat on the snow-capped mountains far on the horizon. Agnes thought it looked like a giant, observing eye.

The white of the ground made the darkness of the conifers look as thick as crude oil. She peered into their congregation for any signs of trouble, anything that didn't 'fit'. The elder forest, from where she had sprung forth, looked like the twisted woods of an old European fairy tale. There was no witch's house made of sweet treats in there though, only her own burnt homestead, and even then that was a long way off.

Agnes stepped back a little so that she was enveloped in the shadow of the eaves; she felt eyes upon her and, whether real or imagined, the sensation made her anxious.

There was another scent wafting around her head that was mixing with the odor of her own embarrassing mess. Without turning her back on the deep, dark woods, Agnes stepped slowly backwards into her haven and retrieved her rifle.

...

Agnes let the flakes settle on the parts of her that were exposed. She kept everything below her waist tucked away inside, while her upper body lay flat out of the doorway. The rifle's barrel aimed at the tree line.

It (*they*) were here. The beast, ironically, may have had the patience of a saint, but Agnes had grown wise to its predatory tactics. It was there alright, she could *smell* it. The monster had already stank to high heaven, but now it had an additional aroma: flame-grilled rotten meat.

All she needed was one clean shot. The preacher – he was the key. Kill the head and the body would follow. Well, so she hoped.

She knew its plan and hated the fact it was working. It wanted her paranoid, questioning herself. She was meant to lose faith in her instincts, think she was going crazy. Maybe she was, after all, how long had she been lying here freezing her ass off with nothing but a mysterious scent to go on?

No…

This stalemate wasn't going to swing in her favor. It was time to take the lead and (*surprising no one more than herself*), Agnes wasn't afraid.

'Show yourself!' she shouted out to the great wide open. She stood in front of the railing with the rifle lowered. 'Come on, you overgrown pork chop!' At first nothing so much as stirred, but Agnes knew how the monster felt about defiance. A few more insults and she would make it expose itself. It could not control its actions; it was governed by its hate. 'Hey, you hear me, you ugly son of a bitch? A reddening glow pulsed weakly amongst the gnarled trees. 'What's the matter, chicken-shit? You pissed off 'cause I killed your piglet?' Burning embers, beating in time with the monster's various blistered hearts, throbbed as its rage seethed below the surface of its charred skin. 'What are you waiting for, an invitation? Face me, you bastard!'

There he was, right where her eyes had been focused. The many limbs and odd anatomical shapes that protruded from its core allowed it to blend in with the ancient trees around it. Had she not coaxed it out, she would probably never have spotted it until it was too late.

It was puffing out smoke from its sores as the collective souls inside it heaved with anger. Agnes had started something now, something she couldn't have stopped even if she had wanted to. Venting it all out at her enemy felt good. For the first time since they had started this war, Agnes felt powerful.

The beast sensed it too. Gone was the confident prowess of an alpha predator; it crept along the tree line, sticking to the shadows cautiously.

'You trying to hide down there? I can see you, you twisted fuck! Agnes only had one magazine of five shots in her coat, plus the remaining two in the Springfield's loading chamber. She flipped the switch from single shot to repeater. The temptation to pop a few rounds into the creature was too good to resist. As long as she loaded up the magazine quickly then she was sure she would be ready for it before it could get to her.

'Michelle...' she uttered as she pulled the trigger. The crack of gunshot was deafening on the quiet mountain. The monster hollered in pain as one of its members took the hit. 'Simon...' Another thunderous snap and again the beast recoiled as one of its numbers caught a bullet. Each impact sent a flurry of ash and embers scattering into the air.

Agnes fumbled furiously with the bullets, her fingers tight with the cold. There was no need to worry, she had cleaned the gun well, the magazine slid in easily, like a knife through butter. Rifle raised, she drew another bead on the beast but held back from firing; her previous double tap had provoked the reaction she had wanted.

The monster bawled in outrage. The fire inside it had been thoroughly stoked. The figures flexed, ready to attack; *(except for two that hung limply from its body like revolting growths).*

'Vengeance!'

'Kill...her!'

Agnes saw the leader, the figurehead of the cursed vessel, snarl at her. *'Make...it...slow'* he growled.

The charge came, and it was more frightful than Agnes could ever have envisioned. The mass of woven bodies moved as one, but without order. They rolled and scurried with a movement that defied logic. Any part of the monster that came into contact with the ground was used to propel it forward. Clawed hands raked at the snow, gouging deep enough to score the soil below. Elbow joints, faces, it did not matter. Agnes saw necks snap and arms flail limply, the monster would sacrifice whatever was required, as long as it got to *her*.

It crossed the open faster than Agnes would have thought possible. The tracks it left in its wake were a complex tangle of crisscrosses and sweeps. It reached the foot of her tower and didn't stop. The beast didn't even consider using the stairs, instead, opting to scale the timber frame right up towards her.

Hand over fist, it climbed. Those who were out of reach of the wood turned their attention to clawing the air, stretching themselves in the hope of being the first to draw Agnes' blood. She had wanted to lure it close enough to deliver a kill shot, now that it was happening; Agnes was beginning to have second thoughts.

Five scorched hands snatched the rail in front of her and she began back-stepping. The beast pulled itself up; the cult's master materialized from behind as the creature rolled its weight. His arms outstretched, rising like an unholy effigy.

'*Nowhere…to…run…*' the ringleader chuckled, menacingly.

'Who's running?' Agnes bit back. 'I'm still here, ain't I? So come get me. Finish it!'

The monster launched itself at her. She fell back; the handrail cracked but stopped her from going over into the darkness below. It straddled itself between the roof and the observation deck like a giant spider. Instead of venom, it dripped blood as dark and thick as tar.

Its next strike happened so fast that Agnes had no time to think. It was primal instinct alone that guided her hand. The creature leapt at her with the main cultist at its forefront, this was the shot she needed. She swept the rifle up in an arc and took aim. The sound of splintering wood cried out from below.

'To hell with you!' she screamed as she tugged hard with her trigger finger. The bullet shot out but the preacher had anticipated such a move and had torn free one of his fallen brethren to use as a shield. The bastard managed to swing the lifeless corpse in front of him just in the nick of time.

Agnes could not believe it. She had been foiled again. A numbness brought on by defeat washed over her as she, the beast, and the broken fragments of the tower toppled over the edge. Her stomach lurched with the falling feeling as she hopelessly watched the sky retreat away from her. The monster was screeching as pieces of debris rained down around it. Agnes hoped she had done enough. She closed her eyes and waited for the black.

CHAPTER 52

The serene peace of the mountainside had been thrown into chaos. Agnes *had* seen the black, but only for a brief spell when she had collided with the ground. If it hadn't been for the branches that slowed her fall and the deep snow that cushioned her impact, then it might have been a different story.

She knew she wasn't dead by the amount of pain she was in. She couldn't lift her arm, and when she cleared her head enough to look, she saw why. This time she *had* broken her wrist. Badly.

Large sections of the tower lay in jagged chunks around her, along with the various branches and pine needles that they had ripped from the trees on their way down. It was a miracle she had not been crushed. She looked around but couldn't find the gun; Old Bess had been lost in the pandemonium of the descent. A thought dropped into her mind like a lead weight and she hurriedly scrambled to her feet, ignoring the new collection of aches that seemed determined to drag her down. If *she* had survived the fall then…

Then where was '*It*'?

She couldn't see it. It had definitely taken the tumble with her, she was sure of that. She did a sweep of the ground but couldn't find any trace of the monster. Groggy from the bump on her noggin, she looked up the rocky Cliffside in confusion.

Bingo.

No wonder she hadn't been able to locate the beast. It hadn't made the full trip. Agnes smiled in satisfaction; it really '*did*' blend in with the trees. Especially the one it had been impaled on. She started laughing. Even to her own ears she sounded crazy, but she couldn't stop.

'How'd you like that, huh? Damn, I hope that hurt, I hope that hurt like a bitch! End of the line, asshole!'

The manic smile was wiped from her face. The creature stirred. 'No…nonononono…' What did she have to do? What was it going to take?

Many of its 'appendages' had perished in its brutal plummet; those that remained busied themselves with trying to free the beast from its pike – all except for one. The leader was staring at her, and he looked pissed.

At some point in its long and drawn out rebirth, she had become its obsession; its white whale. It could have ignored her, even when she had involuntarily got herself involved with its sinister business, it could have simply moved on. To what and where, Agnes had no clue, and didn't want to. The only thing that mattered was that she had, through a series of horrifying events, allowed herself to become the sole reason for the monster's existence.

She could never outrun the beast; it would always come for her. She had been marked, and no matter how far she travelled; how many borders she crossed, it would always follow. *She* was its reason for being, and this feud would only end when one of them bested the other. Permanently.

The tree that had put a halt to the monster's descent had taken its share of damage too. Of its 50 plus feet, Agnes guessed that the top 15-20 had been shaved of branches. The creature had taken the lion's share of the impact though, and the 'residents' of the boar's husk were struggling to come to their senses, their actions slow and disorientated. Agnes had no doubt that it would only be a matter of time before it freed itself of its *Vlad Tepes* style punishment and resumed the chase. She had a window, not much, but enough to get a head start.

She picked up a broken spar from the tower's wreckage and used her scarf to form a make-shift splint. Her wrist hurt like a bitch but it didn't matter, it would only be for a little while. Agnes took to her heels, running once again, but this time, without the intention of making an escape.

...

For all the curses of old age, Agnes had always been grateful that her eyes *(although a little rheumy)* had remained in reasonable working order. They had served her well, and been a godsend, especially after Wilson's death when she had come to rely on herself to survive. It seemed only fitting that, after bashing her head, they too would join the long list of body parts that had gone kaput. She was seeing more than double which, when fleeing downhill through densely packed woodland, complicated the situation ten-fold. Trees, branches, and all sorts of pointy shadows loomed and spun in her vision. They raked her cheeks and careened into her, making her pirouette like a dancer at a masquerade ball. At no point did she allow them to slow her down though. She couldn't afford to. Judging by the sounds crashing up the path behind her, the beast was not only free of its vertical prison, but hastily racing after its prey.

Agnes ducked and dived as best she could. When she tumbled and fell she used the momentum to carry her forward. She only had a rough estimation of her location, but it wasn't important; her intended destination was unmissable. When the trees stopped rearing up through her tears she knew she had arrived and that her slalom through the forest was over.

The monster was almost upon her, which was a good thing. For what she had to do next had to happen fast, otherwise she could never go through with it. In all the madness of the night, she had forgotten about the one last ace up her sleeve – except it wasn't a playing card, and instead of her coat, it was in her boot. All 12 inches of it.

CHAPTER 53

Agnes took her position on the same rock she had done so when her body was young and her hair not so void of color. The drop-off – *The Edge*. As if to bring awareness to the significance of her chosen spot, the wind sent forth a protesting gust up the face of the cliff that tried to toss her clear of the imminent danger. Even the forces of nature weren't keen on her outrageous plan. It was too late, there was no other way, she had made up her mind.

Downslope towards her, the trees parted, forced aside by malevolence incarnate. Agnes watched as the tops swayed violently in a straight line in front of her. The monster had no interest in weaving a cautious path.

The beast burst into the clearing as a mass of broken bodies, some of which - accepting their fate, were in the throes of dying. The leader, whose eyes burned with a volatile combination of hate and madness, seemed to have lost all interest in his cohorts. As pawns, they had served their purpose, now they were collateral damage. Dead weight; literally. The king and queen were in checkmate.

He *(it)* paused at the edge of the forest and took in the sight of the frail old woman poised on a rock at the end of the world. A throaty cackle came from somewhere inside him as he sneered and held the dead boar's head as though it were his steed, and not just another part of himself.

'*End... of... the... line...*' it spoke, deliberately throwing her own phrase back at her. '*You... have... failed...*' Agnes didn't embrace its will for conversation. The exchanging of words could serve no purpose with this monstrosity; except to hurl some final insults. The only reason it had held back its attack was for its own vanity; it wanted to see her face when it told her of its triumph. It wanted her to know who had won.

'*All... for... nothing...*' it purred, pacing like a lion before the kill. '*You... are...weak... You... are...*'

Agnes spat at it, '*You* talk too much.'

Infuriated, the beast let go of its senses. The venomous hatred that had been driving it consumed all of its rational thoughts and it charged at her with everything it had left to give.

'*You... will... DIE!!!*'

The thing so grotesque that it should never have existed even in the wildest of nightmares leapt at her. Agnes squatted down and pulled the knife from her boot.

'So... will... YOU!' she screamed into the leader's leathery face. She thrust the blade upwards, plunging its steel under his jaw until she came to the hilt. The creature shrieked as it realized it had been led to its own demise. The old woman of the woods and the abomination tumbled over the drop-off together, locked in an embrace of death. Agnes looked to the moon as she fell and gave it a wink.

'*Hope you enjoyed the show, big boy.*'

With one final act of defiance, Agnes twisted the blade. The leader's head turned horizontally with a sickening slurping sound. Against all odds, in the face of every challenge that could be thrown her way, she had won. The beast was dead and, as the wind whistled in celebration of her accomplishment around her, so was she.

EPILOGUE

Agnes didn't need to open her eyes to know that the world around her had changed. She was no longer cold, and instead of packed snow, she felt herself lying on a cozy, springy bed of moss. It felt pleasant under her fingertips, comforting.

She blinked as her eyes adjusted to the new light conditions. Overhead, the sun shone brightly through a haze, shards of its vibrant light danced through the canopy like dawn through tilted shades.

She felt no urgency to move, for the first time in a long time she felt no pressure, no obligations, and no rush. Her chest rose and fell, calm and controlled, relaxed. Bemused, she became aware that here was no pain for her to acknowledge. None. Even her wrist felt whole and functioning. Dare she say…fine?

Using her elbows as leverage, she raised herself and looked around. Wherever she was it wasn't at the foot of the drop-off. No cliff face scarred with sharp rocks and scree could be seen in any direction; just beautiful woodland of emerald greens and gold. The summer birds had returned, they filled the previously quiet forest with their wonderful songs and melodies.

Behind a curtain of green drapery, Agnes spied the cautionary movements of a deer herd going about their business. Just out of reach, and able to disappear in the time it takes one to blink; such is the way of their kind.

Agnes walked slowly, not because of pain or fear, not anymore, but out of awe. It was as though she were observing the woods for the first time. It was like she was seeing through new eyes. The world around her presented itself in a clarity that she could not help but pause and wonder at its marvels.

She parted a veil of hanging willow and stepped out into a heartwarmingly familiar setting. What had last been the sight of ash and fire was now born anew. The little log cabin, even the waterwheel and its crystal clear pond, were now picturesque; a backdrop to the world's most exceptional oil painting. The garden was in full bloom, more than it had ever been before, flowers of every color grew in tremendous bunches and climbed in their droves up the walls.

As she neared the only home she had ever known, she realized she was not alone. A figure sat with his back to her on an exquisitely decorated bench. She could not find her voice so ran towards him with a flutter in her chest. Butterflies darted in play around her, drawing out her laughter as they flitted by.

The figure, without turning to face her, patted the seat beside him which she sat in gleefully. He smiled at her and she took his face in her hands as tears of joy ran down her own. For now, there were no words necessary. For now, all that mattered was that she was home. Truly home. And this home, under a dream-like sky, would last forever.

ABOUT THE AUTHOR

Derek Allan Robb was born in Dundee, Scotland in 1985.
Frail and Brittle Bones is his debut novel (and about time too!)

Printed in Great Britain
by Amazon

39404667R10169